Wheels of Love

Amy Leah Magaw

Dedication

To The Lord Jesus Christ, for Your Salvation, and for Your many blessings on me. I am unworthy of the opportunities that You afford me daily.

To My Dear Husband, Brian, I can hardly believe all that you have done for me. I love you with all my heart.

Acknowledgements

Special Thanks:

To Mrs. Frances Simpson, and her daughters, Mrs. Cindy Owen, and Mrs. Gwen Hathcock for sharing their fond memories with a loved one,

To Mrs. Sheri Easter for sharing her insight about 'Life on the Road for Jesus' with a sister in Christ whom she had never met,

To Mrs. Jan Barker for 'The Second Look',

To My Brother, Gary Berry, Jr., and his lovely wife, Lacey Strong Berry, my "Super Models",

To Mr. Elliott Thomas of Thomas tours for use of his bus for our photo shoot,

And

To my children, Del & Summer, for helping with the housework while I was writing!
I love you!

For Sneak Peeks, To Order, Or To See More Products, including VBS Materials, Visit our Website:

www.vcpbooks.com

"And Jacob served seven years for Rachel; and they seemed unto him but a few days, for the love he had to her."

Genesis 29:20

Chapter One

The crowd stood to their feet cheering, and shouting 'Hallelujah's as Mandie held the final note of the concert's finale. As she ended the song, she leaned forward taking her bow. A smile adorned Mandie's face as the applause and praises for God warmed her heart and gratified her spirit. She loved this. Serving the Lord through performing Southern Gospel music was a dream that Mandie and her family, the McCormick's, had realized now for the past two years. Standing there on that stage, face glistening with perspiration from the stage lights, Mandie new that this was right where God wanted her to be. And yet, there was still something missing. The curtain closed and as quickly as the smile swept across her face, it faded. Mandie quickly detached the cord from her microphone and began to wrap the wire.

Mrs. McCormick immediately noticed her change in demeanor. "Mandie! What are you doing? You know we always come back to tear down the equipment! We have autograph session right now in the lobby!"

"I'm sorry, Moma. I'm just not feeling up to signing autographs tonight. Y'all can do that without me," she snapped.

"Now, Mandie," her mother whispered as she sidled up to her daughter. Margie McCormick always played the peacemaker of the family-and she knew how to play it well, as she had played it often on the road the past two years. Between her headstrong daughter and jokester son, Shane, she had learned how to effectively diffuse attitudes off the cuff. "You know that wouldn't be right to the fans. I'll bet that some people drove hours to get here, just hoping to get your autograph or speak to you. We'll never know until we get to Heaven just how we've touched someone's life-for the better or for the worse. I don't know about you, but I know that that one day I'd like to see that I changed someone's life in a good way, wouldn't you?"

Mandie knew that her mother was right. She was pouting-plain and simple. "I know Moma. It was a good show. I really did enjoy the songs myself-and I could tell

1

that folks were really gettin' blessed. It does make me feel really good to be a part of something special like this-but..."

"There's always a 'but'! And with you it's always a big 'butt'!" teased Shane as he walked by with a load of microphone cords in his hand heading off of the stage towards the lobby to begin signing his autographs. Shane NEVER missed autograph session.

"Shut-up, Shane. I wasn't talkin' to you," shouted Mandie. Her mother touched her arm and directed her attention back to their conversation. "Anyways, you have Dad to share in your blessings and good times. I don't have anybody," she continued as the emptiness began to creep back into her heart. "I'm twenty years old. We've been on the road for a little over two years now, and the last date that I had was before we left home! And he was a total dud! I know that we are in the perfect will of God doing this, Moma. I know that in my heart, but I'm lonely and worse than that I'm confused! I want to keep doing this, but I want a husband and a family too! I'm not sure how all that fits into this life and ministry in which we have the privilege of serving. I love this, and it was all well and fine at first, and it really still is, it's just...different. Does that make any sense at all?" pleaded an exasperated Mandie.

"Of course it does. It's only right for you to want those things. You have met several good looking fellows on the road, from good churches and family too, from what I gather. And I know that it has been hard to date on the road..." replied Mrs. McCormick, only to be interrupted.

"Hard? Email has been the only mode of communication with anyone! I've really only kept up with a few of them. I'm more like a novelty than a girl to them. I just can't see how I'll ever meet anyone to have a serious relationship with," Mandie lamented.

"Well, if you want a sweetheart, that's no problem," said Grandpa George as he snuck in the middle of the ladies' huddle and stole a quick kiss on the cheek from his granddaughter. "I love you, sweetie." That brought an automatic smile to Mandie's face. There was no one in the world like Grandpa! Mandie was so glad when her Dad announced two years ago that Grandpa would be going on the road with them serving as their tour bus driver. He had retired from a long career as an investment banker and was tired of 'spending his life in a box' as he so eloquently described it. Life was 'passing him by', and he wasn't 'going back in the box again, until it was just his empty shell of a body going in a pine box to be planted,' he claimed! He retired from his firm, and began driving the school bus for his home church's Christian school. Grandma Sally had passed away many years before, so Grandpa had nothing at home to look forward to. He really needed a change of scenery. IIis Commercial Driver's License made him the perfect candidate to drive the bus for the family-the family that he desperately needed. He not only drove the bus for the family, but he served as the 'unofficial' road crew chief, delegating and helping with set-up and tear-down duties and keeping the family in line. "I hate to break up this pow-wow, girls, but there are fans waiting out there for you; Shane's already out there, and if we leave him out there alone any longer, soaking up all the fandom, we won't be able to get his head in the bus!" Grandpa said with a chuckle.

"Thanks, Grandpa. We're coming," Margie replied, nodding for her dad to go on to the lobby. She turned to Mandie once more as they both began walking down the stairs leading off of the stage. "We'll do what we always do. We'll pray about it." The girls continued walking on towards the lobby to join Shane for the autograph meet and greet. "God knows the desires of your heart, dear. We'll pray that He will have His will done in the situation, and we'll believe that He will take care of it. Okay?"

"Okay, Moma. I will definitely start praying specifically about this again. Until then, I'll keep focusing on the highs, and not the lows!" Mandie replied.

"That's my girl!" her mother said as Mandie opened the door to the lobby, meeting a barrage of camera flashes and cheering fans.

Derek strode up the walkway to the recruiters' office. He had been looking forward to this for weeks now. The Army seemed to be the right choice as he prayerfully sought the Lord in the plans for his life. His cowboy boots clopped up the sidewalk as he made his way towards the door. As his hand touched the door's lever, he stopped in his tracks. He sensed the Lord speaking to his heart immediately. *'No; don't go in'*, he seemed to hear as he pulled the lever. "Lord, is that You speaking to me, or is it me just getting cold feet?" Derek thought out loud. He pulled on the lever again-and the same heaviness gripped his heart. Derek looked over to the side and noticed a bench sandwiched in between two bushes. He thought it best at this point that he take a seat.

As he sat down, he silently prayed and examined the plans that he thought were in the perfect will of God. After the death of his father, and the loss of the family farm, Derek and his mother had moved in with his Uncle Joe, his mother's brother. Derek had prepared to spend his life on the road, traveling across America with his own independent truck driving business. Immediately after high school he enrolled in the Johnsonville School of Driving and earned his CDL. He couldn't wait to leave the farm and Tennessee; but then tragedy struck and his father was crushed by a combine in the fields; literally cut down in his prime. The sudden disaster left Derek and his mother Sophia in financial peril, and the farm had to be sold to cover his father's debts. But when that was still not enough, Derek, without reservation, supplied his startup capital, which was also his life's savings, to satisfy the financial obligations.

The move to Uncle Joe's was a miracle from God. His bachelor uncle whole-heartedly opened his home to them. When he and his mom were settled there, Derek felt again the urge that he should travel the country. After much prayer and contemplation, he had decided that the Army was the way to go. Now, he sat on this bench, heavy-hearted and unsure of which way to go. He knew when the Lord spoke to him, and he knew that this was one of those moments; but he still felt the undying urge to enter the building. *'Lord, I thought that this issue was settled. I had perfect peace about this,'* Derek wrestled in his heart and mind.

Derek stood to his feet and turned to the door once more. Again, he placed his hand to the lever, and again, the heaviness engulfed his heart. "Okay, Lord. You win. I'll wait on you," Derek conceded as he turned and walked back to his truck.

"Wait on the LORD:
be of good courage, and
he shall strengthen
thine heart: wait, I
say, on the LORD."

Psalm 27:14

Chapter Two

"Zip....zip...zip...zip," muttered Shane.

"Stop that! What are you doing, Shane?" screamed Mandie as she threw her pillow at her annoying brother.

"I'm just admiring America, as we cross the miles, again, as the yellow lines go by...zip...zip...zip," answered Shane, as if he were depressed. "I don't understand what all the hype is about cross-country travel. It all looks the same to me."

"You are so...oh...I don't know what you are!" she replied in thorough disgust. "There are many interesting places that we've seen since we've been on the road that we probably would never have gotten to see if we had not been traveling like this!"

"Psh!" said Shane as he whipped back his head in dismissal. "I'm just glad that we are heading back home to Campbell's Grove."

"Hey, Angel" came a call from the downstairs driver's compartment.

"Yeah, Grandpa?" Mandie answered.

"Can you please bring me the Tums?" asked Grandpa George.

"Sure, I'm on it," Mandie called down the front stairwell. She made her way down the stairs to the galley. She quickly rummaged through the cabinets where she found the bottle of chalky tablets and made her way down the main aisle, past Shane's and her bunk to the driver's compartment at the front of the bus. Mandie unscrewed the cap and handed the tablets to her Grandpa. "Are you feeling okay?"

"Yeah, Sweetheart. I think I'm just having some indigestion. Those chili dogs we had for lunch are coming back to haunt me." Grandpa George replied as he rubbed his chest.

"Okay. Let me know if you need anything else, okay?"

"Will do, honey," he said with a smile, as he turned his attention back to the road.

Mandie climbed back upstairs to the upper front lounge where she and Shane loved to watch the road. The lounge doubled as their dining room, as the small galley was right there in between the front lounge and her parents' bedroom, which was complete with a small bathroom on the upper level of the semi-decker bus. She and Shane slept on the lower level, just behind the driver's cove, in the two long sides of the bus. When the family originally purchased the used tour bus it contained berths for twelve people in "slots" so small that one couldn't even roll over! Mr. McCormick, Grandpa and Shane, gutted those berths and created two nice, private spaces for the brother and sister to sleep and a small bathroom for them to reluctantly share. While they had the bus "under construction," they also converted a hearty portion of the bus' luggage compartment into Grandpa's sleeping quarters that was now accessible by a short stairwell that led from the lower level where Mandie and Shane slept to the newly converted "luggage to bedroom area."

As she sat down on the booth cushion back in the upper front lounge, she picked up her mini-keyboard and began to fiddle with a melody. As she began to press the keys, she heard the most awful sound. The bus was crossing the grooves on the shoulder of the interstate. As she sprang up to see the cause, the bus swerved severely, throwing her back down into the booth.

Mandie struggled to gain her footing, and felt the swift breeze of her Dad, Brian, rushing past her towards the stairwell at the front of the bus. Then Shane blew by. As she was finally able to stand, Mandie made her way towards the stairs to the driver's compartment where, looking down, she witnessed the horrific scene. Grandpa George was slumped over in the driver's seat, and the bus was veering off of the road. All seemed to move in slow motion as Shane reached from behind Grandpa to take the wheel as Mandie's dad, Brian, pulled and tugged, finally pulling Grandpa from the seat. At that moment, Shane cleared the railing behind the driver's cove, and began slowing the bus to a stop.

"Mandie! Don't just stand there! Where's the phone?" screamed her mother, who had rushed from her bedroom compartment at the back of the upper level, and up to Mandie, grabbing her by the shoulders. "Call 911!" she commanded. As if in a trance, Mandie slowly turned her head to the side in a dumb-founded stare. "Mandie! Wake up! Hand me your cell phone!" said Margie as she dug into Mandie's pockets retrieving the phone.

Only minutes later sirens blared as the Interstate Response team wheeled to a screeching halt beside the bus. The paramedics hurriedly boarded the bus with the crash kits and began rolling up Grandpa's sleeves and unbuttoning his shirt to begin checking his vital signs. "Sir, Sir! Can you hear me, sir?" one asked as the other spoke with Brian asking Grandpa's name and a quick recount of the events that had just occurred.

As the crew worked to gather their information, Mandie could not move. She stood there in utter disbelief and silence as she watched with a heavy heart. Her legs and arms felt as if they weighed ten tons each. *'I had only just handed Grandpa the Tums! It was only indigestion!'* The words raced through her heart and mind as she stared at the scene that lay before her- which was surreal. *'Grandpa, wake up! Wake-up!'* she screamed in her mind, but her lips would not move. She squinted as the bus became darker and darker until...

"Mandie!" Margie cried as she ran to catch her collapsing daughter.

Sophia sat at the kitchen table, clipping coupons when she heard the clopping of cowboy boots coming towards the back door. She knew that Derek had come back from the recruiters' office. With those boots, Derek couldn't sneak up on anybody! The sudden death of her husband had been hard, but her Lord had helped her-and was still helping her daily. When Derek had shared with her his decision to join the Army, she thought that she would have a hard time coping-but she reckoned that if that was where God wanted her only child, then that was the safest place in the world for him to be. Her thoughts were interrupted with the opening of the back door.

"Hat, honey." Sophia nodded, reminding her son.

"Sorry, Mama," Derek politely replied as he removed his white Stetson.

"Well, son, how did it go?" she asked.

"I couldn't do it, Mama. I didn't even go in the building." Derek answered. Sophia sat in silence and with no expression. She was afraid that this would happen. Since the death of her husband, Sophia sensed the protector in her son. She was afraid that that protector in him would not want to leave her side.

"Son, I just don't quite know what to say. I thought that you had everything decided! I thought that this was what God wanted for you!" she began.

"So did I, Mama. So did I." Derek said as he sat down at the kitchen table across from his mother. "I went down to the recruiter's office. I was determined. I had peace in my heart about it all-until I placed my hand on that door pull. It was then that I knew the Lord was telling me not to do it. Mama, I sat there on the garden bench outside and wrestled with the Lord about it. I had to make sure it wasn't just me, but I'm telling you, Ma, it wasn't the right thing to do."

"Well, what changed from this morning, son?" she asked carefully.

"I don't know. I really don't know," he answered as he hung his head in contemplation.

"It wouldn't have anything to do with being my caretaker, would it?" Derek just looked up at his mother in disgruntlement. "I know how you've been looking over my shoulder these past few months, and I know how you've been worrying about leaving me here..."

"No, Ma..." he interrupted.

"No, now, you just let me finish," Sophia rebutted. "I know that you feel that you have to take care of me, but I'll let you know one thing. There's only One Person who has ever taken care of me, and that is Jesus! Oh, sure, he may have used your Dad to accomplish some of that while he was here on this side, but it was always Jesus watching out for us. He tells us in the book of Matthew to consider those lilies.

They don't work for anything, and yet he dresses them in the finest clothes they can have. And those sparrows always have plenty of worms to eat! He doesn't forget about them, and how much more important are we to Him than sparrows?" she reminded. Derek sat and listened intently. "Now, we moved here to Campbell's Grove and Uncle Joe's so that he could help. Your uncle is just another one of God's instruments. Jesus will keep on taking care of me whether you're here or not. Now, you just get back out there and go do what God wants you to do!" Sophia ordered.

"Ma, I wish I could, but the Lord won't let me. I know that you'll be alright. I really do. But, I've got to have that peace, and right now, I just don't have it." Derek pleaded.

Sophia looked into her son's eyes and saw his sincerity. He was telling the truth. Something was unsettled in him, and now she could see it. "Alright, son. We'll keep on praying. Maybe God just wanted to test you; you know, like Abraham, just to see if you were willing. Maybe he has something better for you."

"I hope so, Ma. But I can definitely tell you that it's not the Army. I don't know what it is; but what I do know is that it won't be long. I've been sensing an urgency of change that I really can't explain. I thought that it was just the excitement of enlisting, but now, I don't know what it's about. But, I truly believe that we'll find out soon enough." Derek explained as he walked over and kissed his mother on the temple.

Sophia grabbed his hand in hers and kissed it. "That's good enough for me, son. I love you."

"I love you, too, Ma," said Derek as he turned and walked up the stairs.

As she watched him go, Sophia prayed, *'Lord, please take care of my boy. Please show him Your will. He wants to serve You so bad. Thank You for giving me such a wonderful son; and thank You for Your Son, Jesus, my Best Friend. I love You, Lord, Amen.'*

"Rest in the LORD, and wait patiently for him:"

Psalm 37:7a

Chapter Three

The lights shone brightly as Grandpa struggled to open his eyes while lying in the hospital bed. As he regained his consciousness he began to look around at the faces of those standing in a circle about his bed. "My Lord..." he muttered.

"What Grandpa? What is it?" asked Mandie as she neared her grandpa's face carefully.

"I've died and gone to heaven. I'm surrounded by Angels!" he answered with a smile.

"Oh, Grandpa!" scolded Mandie as she backed away from the bed. She replaced the icepack to the knot on her head that she had gained when she fainted on the bus. Margie straightened the covers back up over her dad.

"How are you feeling, Dad?" asked Margie.

"Like I had a heart attack," he replied.

"Well, now, looks like you hit the nail right on the head," started a voice coming in the door from behind the grateful family. "I'm Dr. Calhoun; I'm new here to Campbell's Grove-the bottom cardiologist on the totem pole, but I've had plenty of experience over the years. I'm glad to see that you're awake now. I've been going over your test results and I've gotta tell you, this was a close call, Mr. Sanders. You've gotta start taking it easy," the doctor said as he strode up to the bedside, taking a careful look at the patient's chart. "Tell me, Mr. Sanders, what do you do for a living?"

"Well, I'm the bus driver for my lovely family here. These here are the McCormick's. Surely you've heard of them?" Grandpa bragged.

"Yes, well, I thought that I'd recognized your faces, from the CD's. My wife is a big fan. She'd be tickled if she knew that your grandpa here was my patient."

"Well, now," Brian began as he reached out for a handshake with the doctor, "I'm Brian McCormick-the head of this here family. It's nice to meet you." The doctor nodded in agreement. "I believe that I've got some CD's in the bus that we'd be glad to autograph." Shane go down to the bus and get some CD's for the good doctor," his dad instructed.

"Sure thing, pop," said Shane as he bounded out of the door and down towards the bus.

"That sounds great. I really appreciate it. Listen, Dad, could we talk outside for a moment?" asked Dr. Calhoun.

"Sure. Let's just step outside here," said Brian as he opened the door for the doctor and stepped into the hall. Shane breezed by them both right back into Grandpa's room with the CD's and Sharpies. *'He must have sprinted to the bus...'* thought Brian to himself. *'There ain't nothin' that boy won't do so that he can give an autograph!'*

Once the two men were assured of confidentiality, the doctor continued, and Brian turned back his attention. "Mr. McCormick, this heart attack has really set him back. The test results that I'm seeing here are not good. Mr. Sanders really needs to get some rest. And what's worse here, is that he mentioned that he drives the bus for you and your family, is that right?" he asked.

"Yes, but..." began Brian.

"Well, this episode and these test results will disqualify him from driving the bus. There's no way that he will be able to pass the Department of Transportation physical that is required to keep his Commercial Driver's License. He will not be able to go back on the road with you. He needs to be in a more stable situation," explained the doctor.

"You don't mean like a nursing home, do you?" asked Brian.

"No; nothing like that. He just needs to be in a more relaxed and stress free environment. He needs to stay home. I'll order a home health nurse to come by and check his blood pressures three times weekly, and we'll keep close tabs on him. I hate that this happened on the road, but I'm so glad that you all were on the way home. We'll do our best to prevent this from happening again."

"Wow. I can't believe this. I'll have to break the news to him. I have a feeling that he'll be crushed. But we would never do anything to jeopardize Grandpa's health; of course-please set everything up and please let me know what I need to do on my end," Brian began as he reached for his handkerchief.

"I will have my nurse take care of the paperwork. She'll contact you with the particulars, but right now, I think you'll have the hardest job of all," Dr. Calhoun explained as he motioned toward Grandpa's room, which was still filled with the rest of the family.

"Thank you, Doctor." said Brian somberly as he shook the doctor's hand again and headed back into the room muttering under his breath, "Well, here it goes."

"Hey, guys. I'm glad that you're all having a great time with Grandpa, but can I please have a couple of minutes with him alone?" he asked.

"Sure, honey; but is everything okay?" asked Margie.

"Oh, yes, yes. Everything's fine. Just gimme a few minutes, okay?" Brian asked again.

"Sure thing, Dad." Mandie replied as she grabbed her purse. "I was getting a little thirsty anyways. Come on Shane," Mandie said as she walked out with Shane and Margie trailing behind.

Brian walked up beside the bed and took a seat on the edge beside Grandpa. "Grandpa, we need to talk," he began.

"Am I dying? I'm ready to go, you know. I've known the Lord ever since I was a teenager. Just tell me plain." Grandpa started.

"No, Grandpa. You're going to be fine. The doctor wants to have a home health nurse come by and take weekly blood pressure readings, and check on you, but..." Brian began.

"Now, here's my 'big butt', as Shane would say..." said Grandpa with a chuckle.

"Well, Grandpa, here's the thing. The doctor says that with the damage done from the heart attack and the current test results, there's no way that you'll be able to pass your DOT physical. It won't be possible for you to drive the bus anymore. You're gonna have to move back home," explained a heavy hearted Brian.

"Oh. Is that all?" said Grandpa, as he began laughing, quite heartily. So heartily, in fact, that Brian began to wonder if Grandpa had lost his mind in the heart attack as well.

"I've been praying about coming off of the road for a while now, Brian, but I didn't want to let the Lord or the family down. Boy, I guess the Lord really has a way of making up your mind for you sometimes, doesn't He?" said Grandpa as he wiped the laughing tears from his eyes. "I love watching you and the family serving the Lord this way, but the truth is: I'm tired; and I've been tired for a while. I think that home is exactly where I need to be," he conceded.

"Well, I thought that you'd be a little more upset about it. But I'm glad that you're not. We are surely going to miss you-a lot..." said Brian as he grabbed Grandpa's hand and squeezed it, "...a lot."

Suddenly the sound of the 'Amazing Grace' ring tone on Brian's phone began to sound. Mr. McCormick checked the caller ID, which showed his pastor, Pastor Creighton from the Lighthouse of Campbell's Grove.

"Hello, Preacher! How are you?" Brian began as he motioned to Grandpa that he was stepping into the hall to take the call. Grandpa motioned for him to go on.

"I'm glad to hear that Grandpa George is going to be alright. I've just heard from Margie. We've had the prayer chain going here at the church," said the pastor.

"We really do appreciate it. It's going to be a long road ahead, but we really do think that he will be fine. But now, we have another issue at hand. The heart attack made it impossible for Grandpa to go back on the road with us." Brian explained.

"Well, my advice is to take some time off of the road to help Grandpa get settled and pray about it," Pastor Creighton offered.

"I agree. I've always said that when you don't know what to do just sit still and wait." Brian replied.

"That sounds like good advice to me. I'll be praying about this issue too. I'll also say that it will be good having you and your family back in the services."

"We will be looking forward to it sir." Brian replied as he flipped his phone shut and began his descent to the hospital cafeteria to join his family.

Brian stepped out of the elevator and rounded the corner to the cafeteria to find his family seated and practically devouring their food. Margie and Shane had grabbed themselves a sub from the deli shop, but Mandie sat alone in the corner.

"Mandie, what's wrong? Aren't you hungry? We're all famished," asked her Dad.

"I'm so thankful that Grandpa is going to be okay. I just feel like it's all my fault," she confessed.

"Now, how do you figure that?" Brian asked as he sat down beside his daughter.

"I had just given him the Tums. He said he had indigestion. I should've paid attention. I should have seen that it was more than just heartburn!" she continued.

"Now, Mandie; there's no way that you could have known that Grandpa was experiencing a heart attack! Goodness gracious, girl! You did all you could!"

"Yeah, and I almost got us all killed! If Shane hadn't jumped behind the wheel and stopped the bus, who knows where we'd all be!" she lamented.

"Well, I'll tell you where we'd be-in Heaven, that's where! Look, the Lord knows what He's doing. He knew that Grandpa would have that heart attack, and he put that Interstate Response Ambulance right nearby when Grandpa needed it. Mandie, God is in control and He has a reason for everything that He does. Just because you got a little light headed..."

"Dad, I passed out, I didn't just get light headed. Some help I was," she said with a heavy heart.

"Don't be so down on yourself. Pray about it. The Lord will show you the Truth."

"I know. I will. It just helps to have someone to talk things over with-someone to confide in."

Brian sensed that Mandie was opening up a whole other subject. "Yes, your Moma mentioned that she was praying for the Lord to send you a special someone. She asked me to be praying as well. And I have been, you know."

"Aw, Mom! I can't believe that she told you those things! Isn't anything sacred between a mother and daughter?" she complained in her embarrassment.

"Well, as you will learn later on, there are some things that wives and husbands just don't keep from each other; especially when it concerns their children.   Don't worry, honey. I'll never use it against you. I'm just praying, for you, and I love you very much. I know that God will send you the right man-someone who loves Him and wants to serve Him; and someone who loves you with all of his heart."

"Do you really think so, Dad?" she asked with hope in her eyes.

"I know He will. I'm not giving you up to anyone else but a man like that!" said Brian with a laugh.

Chapter Four

It seemed like Sunday morning came all too quickly, and Derek, Sophie and Uncle Joe were running late to Sunday school. They managed to make it in the front door to the church to find everyone all abuzz. The tardy family found their way to their seats and got settled for the opening prayers and scripture reading. The minutes trickled down to ten a.m., but everyone was still crowded around a group of people towards the front of the church.

Uncle Joe leaned up to speak to the gentleman sitting on the pew in front of him. "Good morning, Brother Berry."

"Good morning, Brother Sanders. How are you this morning?"

"I'm just fine. This here's my sister, Sophie, and my nephew, Derek Jensen," said Joe as he presented his family to his fellow brother in the Lord.

"It's nice to meet you," Brother Berry said as he turned his attentions back to the mob at the front of the church.

"What's going on up there?" asked Uncle Joe.

"Oh! The McCormick's are back. Grandpa George had a heart attack," explained Brother Berry. Seeing the concern on Uncle Joe's face, he continued. "He'll be okay, but he won't be able to go back on the road, though. They're getting him all set up here at the old homestead out on highway six."

"Oh! Well, we'll definitely be praying for them. They'll have some decisions to make," replied Uncle Joe. He leaned back to take his Bible and turn to the Psalms.

Derek leaned over to his uncle and whispered, "When you say The McCormick's, did you mean, The McCormick's?"

"I'm not sure that I'm following you Derek," replied Uncle Joe.

"I mean the singing McCormick's? Southern Gospel family?" continued Derek.

"Those would be the ones. They're members here," he answered.

Derek sat back in awe. He had every CD that the McCormick's had made, and never once did he bother to read the fine print that listed the Lighthouse of Campbell's Grove to be their home church! This was such a small town, and a small church for that matter! He never expected the McCormick's church to be this one! The song leader stepped to the pulpit and began to call the service to order. Slowly, the people began to find their seats, and then he saw her- Mandie McCormick. There wasn't a song that she sang that he didn't love. He was one of her biggest fans.

As the congregation stood to sing the opening hymn, Derek thought to himself, *'I wonder if all they need is a driver?'* Derek wasn't the only one that had that thought, as he caught his mother looking at him. He looked back at her, then leaned over and whispered, "Oh, no you don't. I can see your wheels just a-turnin'. I don't know if this is the answer!"

"Well, there's no harm in letting Pastor Creighton know that you have a CDL," Sophia whispered back.

"Yeah, Ma, but I only have a class B, which is good for hauling and trucking. I don't have a passenger endorsement."

"Well, I think that I'll let the pastor know about it, just the same," whispered a determined Sophia.

With the conclusion of the opening hymn, and the morning scripture reading, the song leader dismissed the congregation to their respective Sunday school classes. Uncle Joe mentioned to Derek that he would find his Sunday school class for the college students in the second room on the left of the Sunday School Wing.

As Derek made his way down the hall towards the classroom, he found himself walking alongside Shane McCormick, who was headed in the same direction. Upon entering the classroom, the two young men sat down in chairs next to each other. Shane promptly extended his hand to Derek. "Hey there! I'm Shane McCormick."

"It's really nice to meet you. I'm Derek Jensen."

"I don't remember seeing you here the last time we were home. Are you new in town?" Shane asked.

"Yes. My Mama and I just moved here from Tennessee. We're staying with my Uncle-Joe Sanders."

"Oh! Brother Sanders! He's a nice guy."

"Thanks. I must say, you're really down to earth for a celebrity," Derek said.

"Celebrity? Well, okay. We're just normal people. But I appreciate the compliment." Shane replied as Brother Berry stood at the front of the class to begin his lesson.

Derek leaned over and whispered, "How about your sister? Isn't she coming?"

"Naw. She's just hanging out with my parents today. I guess she thinks that she's too old for Sunday school." Shane replied as both men directed their attentions to the teacher and the lesson.

After a wonderful Sunday school lesson on Mephibosheth and how his story is a beautiful picture of God's Salvation for man, Brother Berry dismissed the class to the sanctuary for the morning worship service. The two young men walked into the church, and Shane motioned for Derek to come up front with him. "Come on up here, Derek. There's someone that I want you to meet."

Derek's palms became sweaty as he followed Shane up to the row where Mandie was seated with her family. Shane slid into the row in front of his family and gestured for Derek to fall in line. "Mom, Dad, this is Derek Jensen. He's new to the church here; he's brother Sanders' nephew. "

Derek reached out his hand to Mr. McCormick which he readily accepted. "It's an honor, sir." Derek said. Derek then nodded to Mrs. McCormick, "Ma'am"

"And this is just my sister, Mandie," said Shane as he gestured to her sitting on the pew.

Mandie looked up at Derek. He was a handsome, strong-looking, dark haired young man, who looked very mature, all except for the hint of remaining childhood freckles dusted across the bridge of his nose and tops of his cheeks. The blue oxford shirt he was wearing brought out his clear blue eyes. She smiled at him, in politeness. "Mr. Jensen," she replied. "How are you this morning?"

Derek looked at Mandie with the goofiest grin that she had ever seen. "Ma'am," he nodded as he acknowledged the introduction. It was evident. He was star struck. *She is so nice, and so beautiful in person,*' he thought to himself. He knew that he'd better get it together or he'd be drooling and blubbering incoherent sentences soon. There she was: the great Mandie McCormick-and she was speaking to him!

"Derek, where are your parents? I'd like to meet them as well," Mrs. Margie inquired.

"Well, my mother is back there with Uncle Joe, but my daddy died a year ago, hence the reason that we've moved here -to be close to family," he replied.

Pastor Creighton then stepped forward to call the service to order with a special request. "It's a blessing to have the McCormick family home with us for a little while. I wonder if I could get y'all to come up here and start the service off with a song."

"I guess that's us," said Shane as he and his family rose to make their way to the platform.

Derek turned and made his way back to his seat beside his mother, Sophia. As he sat down he heard the McCormick's begin to tune up their instruments, with Shane on the bass and Mr. McCormick on the acoustic guitar. Mrs. McCormick placed the strap of her mandolin around her back, and Mr. Brian McCormick began to strum out the introduction.

Derek sat in wonder as Mandie picked up her microphone and began to sing. Her voice was angelic and even though he looked at a platform containing four people, he only saw one.

After the family finished their song, the service continued. Pastor Creighton preached a wonderful message on modern day idols in the lives of Christians. He explained how Christians sometimes place things they love in the place of the Saviour. Those things could be people, jobs, family, and even spouses; but the bottom line was that anything that Christians allow to take the pre-eminence over the Saviour would be an idol.

Derek thought about his ogling behavior towards Mandie only a few minutes earlier. He wondered if that bordered idol worship. He made up his mind that he would be careful how highly he regarded someone; even someone as beautiful as Mandie.

After the conclusion of the service, Shane made his way towards the back door where Derek was also waiting to leave the building. He came towards him. "It was very nice meeting, you Derek."

"Likewise. I really enjoyed the songs. They were a real blessing," he answered.

"So, we'll be seeing you around?" Shane asked.

"Definitely," Derek replied as she shook Shane's hand and walked towards his Uncle Joe's Jeep.

"A man that hath friends must shew himself friendly: and there is a friend that sticketh closer than a brother."

Proverbs 18:24

Chapter Five

Brian McCormick spent the morning cleaning out the shed in the back of the family homestead and talking with the Lord. With the bed of his old Ford pick-up truck backed into the opened barn door, he continuously stacked and heaped on broken and mis-matched pieces of junk and other "treasures". It had only been a week since the McCormick family had returned to Sunset, and Brian still wasn't exactly sure where to take his family from there. He knew that he couldn't just sit around the house and do nothing, so he decided that he would get busy around the grounds. There was always something to be worked on, and he decided that the shed was as good as place as any to start working. Through his strenuous hefting of boxes and crates, he didn't hear his wife's approach, and nearly jumped out of his skin at her words.

"Honey, the phone's for you-it's Pastor Creighton." said Margie as she handed her husband the cordless handset with a chuckle.

Brian took a deep breath to slow his heart rate, after the scare that his wife had given him. After a dramatic pause, he was finally able to answer. "Hello, Pastor. How are you today?"

"I'm doing well, quite well, Brother McCormick. I hope that Grandpa's doing well today." he remarked.

"Yes, sir, he's settling in pretty good. I've been out here in the shed cleaning out things. I know Grandpa too well, and if there's any work left out here to be done, he'd be out here tending to it as soon as the bus cleared the end of the lane!" answered Brian.

"You know, you're right?" answered Pastor Creighton with a chuckle. "Well, brother, I know that you've been praying about the situation with your family being on the road. I've come upon some information which might be of interest to you. There's a new young man and his mother who have recently moved here and joined the church. Her husband has passed away, and the mother and son have moved here to be close to family..." he began.

"Yes, you mean Derek Jensen. I met him last week at the Sunday service. He and Shane seemed to hit it off really well," Brian interjected.

"Yes; he is a very congenial young man, and I have recently learned that he is in possession of a commercial driver's license. Now, I'm not sure about the details of it, but, I do know that he's been praying about what direction to take with his life in terms of employment. Perhaps this is something that may be in God's plan for you, perhaps not, but I thought that you should know either way."

"Well, now. That is interesting. It could be an answer to our prayers." replied Mr. McCormick.

"Maybe you could pray more about it-maybe give him a call so that you can both pray about it together," suggested Pastor Creighton.

"That sounds like a wonderful idea. I will pray about it, and then if the Lord leads, I'll give him a call. Thank you for letting me know about him. I really appreciate it."

"You're more than welcome; and I'll still be praying for you about this. You have a good rest of the day." he concluded.

"You too, Pastor. Goodbye," said Brian as he pressed the end button on the cordless handset.

Margie had never moved from the spot where she had handed over the phone to her husband. "Well, what was all of that about?" she asked in an almost desperate tone.

"It seems that God has been working behind the scenes in a great many lives for a while in regards to our situation," Brian responded as he stared at the back of the truck bed which was now lipping full of junk.

"What on earth do you mean? What did the pastor say? And what does it all have to do with that young man, Derek Jensen?" she asked.

"Just let me pray about it for a couple of days. Just gimme a little time. I don't want to move too fast and make a mistake," he answered earnestly, as he closed the tailgate, and leaned on it for a moment. "I'll let you know something as soon as I know what to do. Let's keep a lid on everything for just now-even the Pastor's call, okay? Just pray for me, alright, Hon?"

Margie stood there solemnly, dying to know the other side of the conversation that she had not been privy to. Knowing her husband, and his sincere desire to serve the Lord in His Perfect Will, Margie knew that the confidentiality of the situation was indeed warranted. "Alright. I trust you. I won't say anything to the kids, or anyone else."

"Thank you," Brian said as he placed his hand on his wife's shoulder. "I love you. I'm not trying to keep things from you..."

"Oh, I know. I understand. I will be praying for you, love..." she said as she embraced her husband and trusted in his guidance, as she knew that it came from the Lord.

"Well, let me run on and take these pieces down to the landfill," he said as they made their way arm in arm toward the cab of the truck.

"I'll go in and start some lunch and have it ready by the time you get back. Sound good?" Margie offered.

"Sounds great," he replied, as he turned back and stared at the shed's open gate; and then with a hearty laugh he concluded, "We'll eat lunch, and then I'll come back and do this all over again!"

🚌 🚌 🚌 🚌 🚌

"Derek! Derek!" called Sophia out of the back door. Derek looked up from the lawn mower that he was pouring gas into.

"Ma'am?" he called as he looked towards the house.

"You have a telephone call," his mother replied.

Derek capped the gas tank on the mower and walked up the hill to the house and answered the kitchen phone. "Hello, this is Derek."

"Derek, this is Mr. Brian McCormick. How are you today?"

"Oh, I'm doing fine sir, and you?" Derek responded.

"Just fine. Well, the reason that I'm calling today is that I would like to talk to you about a potential business arrangement. Last week, Pastor Rhodes gave me a call with some information. He let me know that you are a licensed truck driver."

"Yes, sir. I have a Commercial Driver's License, a class B," Derek answered.

"Well, I probably don't have to tell you, but we need a good man to drive our bus while we're on tour. I've been praying about this for over a week now, and I feel like you're the man for the job. I won't expect an answer today, I imagine that you'd like to pray over it," Brian offered.

"Well, sir, I have been praying over my future for months now, and the truth is, the thought of being your driver did enter my mind when I first learned that you and your family were back at home. I decided that I would let the Lord handle it, and if it was to be, then you would call me. So, I accept your offer, sir, and I am very grateful." Derek answered as he felt the peace that he had longed for. He knew that this was right, for a change. "There's only one problem, though, sir. I don't have a passenger endorsement. I'm only licensed to haul things."

"Well, these laws change so much, but right now, because there's only five of us, you're not required to carry that passenger endorsement. If that changes, well, we'll cross that bridge when we come to it. But, right now, you're more than qualified." answered Mr. McCormick.

"That's great, sir. I was a little concerned about that."

"Why don't you drop by our house tomorrow and we'll get you started on learning our bus!" replied Mr. McCormick as he bid Derek a good afternoon.

"That sounds wonderful, Sir. You have a great day, and I'll look forward to seeing you on tomorrow," said Derek as he hung up the kitchen phone. He took a moment of silent prayer, thanking God for the distinctive peace that He had given him. Then, he turned to the more immediate matter at hand. "You can come out now from around that corner, Ma," Derek teased.

Sophia sheepishly walked into the kitchen from her hiding place in the hallway. She looked up at her son with a smile and retorted, "Now, I don't know what you mean!"

"You knew who that was. You just had to tell the Pastor, didn't you?" Derek said.

"Well, now, facts are facts. And there's nothing wrong with people knowing the facts? Is there?"

"No, Ma'am." Derek answered with a laugh. This is all working out the way that it should Ma. Don't worry. I'll be outta your hair soon!" he teased as his Mama slapped him on the arm. "You're looking at the new bus driver for the McCormick's!"

"Oh! Praise the Lord!" Sophia shouted as she hugged her son with a renewed excitement. Finally, he would embark on a new chapter of his life, without her; but moving in the right direction. Sophia's joy could hardly be contained. No longer would Derek be there taking care of her, but for once, he would be taking care of himself. Sophia's thoughts flooded her mind. *'And then, perhaps, he could find someone else closer by that needs taking care of...'*

"*Faithful is he that calleth you, who also will do it.*"

I Thessalonians 5:24

"Pass the orange juice please," Mandie asked as she scooped some scrambled eggs onto her breakfast plate.

"Sure thing," Shane replied as he handed her the carton. As Mandie herself poured a small glass, her Dad walked quickly into the kitchen and slid into his seat.

"What'll it be this morning, Hon?" asked Margie.

"Just a quick bowl of cereal for me this morning; He'll be here soon," Brian answered.

"Who'll be here soon?" asked Shane.

"Our new bus driver," his mother said as she poured Brian a cup of coffee.

"That's great. I didn't even know that you found someone! What's his name?" inquired Mandie.

"It's that new young man at church-Derek Jensen," replied her dad.

"Awesome! I didn't know he could drive! Finally! Someone I can relate too! I'll finally be able to tolerate road trips!" exclaimed Shane.

"And that will keep you from annoying me-you can annoy him instead!" answered Mandie.

Brian smiled at the display of sibling love. "Well, I'm glad that you all are on board, because he's coming by this morning to take the bus for a spin. We'll be going on the road again next week."

"Wow! That fast?!" replied Mandie. "It was so good to be in my own room again. We stay on the road so much, my room feels like a hotel and my bunk on the bus feels like my room! But I'm not complaining...I've never been happier."

"Well, that's a change!" said Margie as she finally sat down to her own breakfast. "What happened?"

"Well," began Mandie as she leaned in to her mother's ear. "I received an e-mail from 'an old friend' last night."

"Really!" remarked Margie as her curiosity was beginning to peak. "Do tell? Who from?" she said sarcastically.

"From Mitchell Collins, from Brother Bledsoe's church in Augusta, Georgia-you remember him, don't you?"

"Yes, I do. He was the dashing young man who thought an awful lot of himself in his fancy suits and shoes," answered Mandie's mom.

"Now, Moma-don't be judging. You can't judge someone by their outward appearance. Even the Bible says that "man looketh on the outward appearance, but the LORD looketh on the heart."

"Well-it wasn't just the clothes that he wore. It was how he carried himself. He had a very proud aura about him. And the Bible also says, 'For every tree is known by his own fruit.' He was handsome, but there was just something about him." explained Margie.

"He was always very nice to me. He said that he was sorry to hear about Grandpa, and that he hopes that we would be able to keep our concert on Jekyll Island at the end of the month. He said that he was planning on driving over from Augusta and spending some time with me. I'm really looking forward to it." said Mandie with a cheery enthusiasm.

"I could be wrong. I hope that I'm wrong. I'm glad to see that you're happy for a change!" said Margie with a supportive smile.

"Thanks, Moma. I'll help you clear away the dishes." offered Mandie as she rose from her chair and began picking up plates and mugs. Shane had already slipped off after inhaling his breakfast.

"But I'm not even done yet!" objected Margie.

"Thanks, dear. The coffee and cereal was great." said Brian as he rose from his chair and kissed his wife on the cheek.

"Don't worry, Moma. Take all the time you need-you deserve it." Mandie replied as she patted her mother on the shoulder. She began to fill the sink with hot water, and dispensed the dish liquid. While she swished her hand around in the basin to speedily activate the bubbles, the doorbell rang. Margie was sipping her coffee, and began to rise to answer it.

"No, no, no," Mandie responded quickly, "Keep your seat. I'll get it."

Mandie quickly grabbed the dish towel and headed for the door. "Hang on! I'm coming!" she shouted as she jogged to the front door. She opened the door to find a tall young man dressed in a red t-shirt, jeans, and a huge white Stetson standing on the McCormick family welcome mat.

"Yes, can I help you?" she asked.

"Good Morning, Miss Mandie. Is your Daddy at home?" he asked.

"Yes, I think that he's out back. He's expecting someone." she replied. "I'll go get him."

"Yeah, he's expecting me! It's me-Derek Jensen, from church? Don't you remember me?" Derek asked with a laugh.

Mandie squinted and took a closer look. "Oh, my! I'm so sorry! I didn't recognize you...under that...hat." Mandie began as she tried to back out of the embarrassing situation. "Like I said, he's around back. Would you like me to take you to him?"

"Um, that's alright Miss Mandie," Derek replied, sensing her predicament, "I think I can find my way. Thank you, though."

"You're welcome." Mandie said curtly as she quickly closed the door. As she turned around she came face to face with her mom, and she stopped dead in her tracks. Her mom stood there, smiling.

"What?" inquired Mandie as she continued to watch Margie just standing there smiling; and then it hit her. "Oh, no. Oh, no you don't. You think that God has sent that boy here for me, don't you?"

Mandie had hit the nail on the head. "Well, he is handsome, and we know that he comes from good family. This could be your answered prayer from the Lord! Just think-God could have orchestrated everything behind the scenes and brought him to you 'for such a time as this!'"

"If you would have hacked behind that last syllable, I'd be convinced that you were preachin' like Pastor Creighton.

"Now, you know better than that! But I can't help but see that he is a possibility-right under your nose."

"Absolutely not! He's a hick! Did you see that big ole' hat? And you should have heard him clomping away in those boots! It's repulsive! No way, Moma! He is not the one for me. I can't handle Stetsons and cowboy boots. I want a normal guy! And don't be trying to play the match maker either. I know how you work!"

Margie began to laugh. "No dear, I wouldn't think of it!"

Derek walked around the side of the house and found Mr. Brian McCormick cleaning out the luggage compartment of the family's tour bus. Hearing Derek's boots clicking in stride, he glanced up to greet him. "Well, hello there! I'm glad you could make it."

"It's good to see you, too, sir," Derek began, "Again, I just want to thank you for this opportunity. Not only will I be working, but I'll be taking part in your ministry for the Lord. I'm really looking forward to it."

"Well, I'm glad to have you on board." said Brian as he extended his hand to Derek for a hearty handshake. "Well, now, whattya say we take this old girl out for a spin?"

"That sounds good, sir." Derek answered as he followed Brian to the doors of the bus. Derek slipped right into the captain's chair and got the layout of the controls of the dash. After locating everything he needed, he cranked up the bus, and got ready to take off. Suddenly, he put the bus back in park. "I just wanna check with you sir; did you run through the pre-trip inspection?"

Brian smiled, and felt totally at peace with his decision to hire Derek to drive the bus. He knew that was putting his family into very capable hands. "Not the entire routine, like the test at the DMV, but I checked out all of the important things-tires, fluids, lights, brakes; you know, stuff like that."

"And the air tanks for the brakes, they were good?" Derek asked.

"Yes; everything looked fine." Brian confirmed.

"Well, if you're not insulted, sir, I'd like to go down the official checklist, if you don't mind. I don't take this responsibility lightly." said Derek. "I surely don't want anything bad to happen while y'all are on my watch!"

"Well, now, that makes me feel really good about choosing you for the job! We're good to go on the road for right now though," answered Mr. McCormick.

"Alrighty then. Here we go!" replied Derek as he placed the gear in 'drive' and began to take off towards the driveway.

He made it out of the driveway without taking out the mailbox, so in all Mr. McCormick was encouraged. He decided to see if Derek could 'chew bubble gum and walk at the same time.' "So Derek, not only does this position require driving the bus, but we also need you to help with setting up the sound equipment. Do you think that you can handle that?"

Without taking his eyes from the road, Derek was able to answer Mr. McCormick over his shoulder. "Yes sir. That will be fine. I can lift and lug, but you'll have to teach me about settings and hooking up wires and all, 'cuz I don't know anything 'bout that."

"Oh, that won't be a problem. Our system is very easy to learn. Shane'll have you trained in no time! Take a left up here."

"That sounds great, sir. I'd like that," Derek continued over his shoulder. "I'd love to do more to help. Is there anything else that you'll be requiring of me, sir?"

"Yeah, sleep."

Derek looked puzzled at Mr. McCormick.

"I'd like for you to do a bit of driving at night. Sometimes we tear down immediately after a show, if we're only there for one evening, and then I like to get on down the road to the next stop. I'd like for you to be well rested so that we can make some time on the interstates while the traffic is not so bad." explained Mr. McCormick. "Now, turn right up here at the hardware store."

"Alright. I was hoping to be able to catch some of the shows, too, though. Would that be possible at all?" Derek asked.

"Oh, yes. In fact, there may be times that there is no one qualified to monitor the levels on the sound board, and you may have to watch the controls during the show."

"Wonderful!"

"Well, now that all that's settled, I'll just let you know that the pay will be fair, and we'll cover your meals and any hotel expenses. While you're on the job, you're our responsibility."

"Sir! That's so much! I don't expect you to pay for my meals! Even folks who go to an office job everyday take a lunch break and pay for their own lunch?!" Derek objected.

"No, now, it's always been that way, even with Grandpa driving," insisted Mr. McCormick.

"But, sir, he was family!"

"Well, now, you're joining our family, so to speak; instead of adopted, we'll just call you adapted! How 'bout that?!" Mr. McCormick answered with a hearty chuckle. "Now, if you don't mind, take another right up here at the Piggly Wiggly."

"Alrighty, sir. Now, when will we be leaving for the next show?" Derek asked.

"I've gotta make some more calls, but I think that the next show on the itinerary that I hadn't cancelled yet is in Manning, South Carolina, at the Weldon Auditorium. It's still newly renovated, and I would feel really bad about letting that one go. That show is next week. From there, we will go down to the Jekyll Island Convention Center for a Tri-County show there; then we go to Atlanta for two big auditorium shows there, and then off to Dollywood, in Sevierville, Tennessee for the Southern Gospel Harvest Festival. Take another right up here, and you'll see our driveway up ahead."

"Alrighty, then. You know, I had planned on joining the Army to see the world-but I'm glad that I chose the Lord's Army instead!" Derek said with a laugh as he turned the corner, swinging that bus around like it was a Pinto. He had no problem handling the vehicle, and it was obvious to

Mr. Brian that Derek would be a good fit for the Lord's Ministry and their family-in more ways than one!

"He that is slow to anger is better than the mighty; and he that ruleth his spirit than he that taketh a city."

Proverbs 16:32

Chapter Seven

Derek stood on the McCormick's welcome mat with his huge green duffle bag stuffed to the gills. His mom had picked it up from the Army Surplus store to remind him that he was still in the Army-just the Lord's Army- as Derek had put it to Mr. McCormick. He rang the doorbell, and blew out a nervous sigh, "Whew. Here we go."

He heard heavy slow steps coming to the front door to answer him. The door flung open to find a sleepy-eyed, bed-headed Mandie who was still in her Spongebob Capri Pajamas. "It's too early for this," she muttered.

"Now, we gotta rise and shine, Miss Mandie. We gotta get ready to get on down to South Carolina and get ready for that show!" replied a very spry and energetic Derek.

"Ugh!" she answered, as she handed him the bus keys from the hooks beside the front door. It seemed to be the easiest way to that 'morning person' out of her face.

"Well, thank you, Miss Mandie. I guess I'll be makin' my way over to the bus to start getting it ready," Derek said as he tipped his hat and began to make his way towards the bus. Mandie rolled her eyes and closed the door, returning to her room to get ready for the trip.

As Derek opened the doors to the bus, Mr. McCormick came out of the back door of the house and met him there. "Good Morning, Derek," he called.

"Good morning, sir," he responded.

"Are you ready?" Brian asked.

"As ready as I'll ever be!" Derek answered as he tipped his white Stetson backwards on his head.

"Well, Shane-who was right behind me-will be out here in a minute to start loading the sound equipment." Derek nodded. "You can go ahead below and make yourself at home in your new 'room on the road.' You'll hear Shane when he's out-I promise!" Mr. McCormick continued.

"Thank you, sir." said Derek as he boarded the bus and walked down the narrow aisle to the small stairwell that led to his new 'home'. He looked around at the small room, and noticed the futon that pulled out to his new bed. He had some small built-in shelves, with a few drawers underneath. There was a small "pantry-style" narrow closet, with a short closet rod, only about six inches long; but hanging on that rod were special "space-saver" collapsible hangers to maximize the closet's accommodation. In front of the bed, there was a small alcove where there was a small built-in flat screen television which was bolted to the wall for safety. Derek threw his duffle onto the futon and took another good look around. The quarters were small to be sure, but to Derek this adventure had only just begun, and he wasn't about to become discouraged.

Just then, Derek heard a chipper voice sounding down the stairwell. "Yo, Newbie!" shouted Shane. "Are you ready to load that equipment?"

"Sure. Let's get going," Derek answered eagerly.

"Newbie...you are about to get broke in!" Shane teased as they wound their way up the stairs, and back through the small galley to the bus doors.

As they stormed through the bus doors, Shane almost knocked Mandie down. She had made her way from the house to the bus, with her eyes barely open, dragging two bags alongside her as if they weighed ten tons.

"Watch out!" shouted Shane as he blew by her on his way to the garage where the sound equipment was stored. He never even looked back.

"Excuse me, Miss Mandie," Derek said as he stepped aside, waving his arm to present the way clear for Mandie to climb aboard the bus. And he couldn't help but smile. Every time that he saw her, whether she was congenial or not, he couldn't help but smile.

"Umm...thank you, I think..." Mandie muttered as she trudged onto the bus. She lunged forward dramatically towards the first step of the bus, and losing her balance, slammed into the door frame.

"Whoa, careful there, Ma'am," said Derek, as he reached forward to steady her on her feet. Her bags, which acted as anchors, seemed to be pulling her right on down. "Be careful there..."

"Come 'on, Derek. She can take care of herself," Shane yelled, in total disregard for his sister.

"Yeah...I can take care of myself," Mandie muttered as she pulled away from Derek, regaining her footing. She pulled herself onto the bus with a counterfeit confidence that could be spotted a mile away.

"Well, alright then," Derek replied as he turned towards Shane and the garage to start loading the huge speakers-and then cases of wires-and then cases of microphones-and then the sound board! Derek wiped the sweat from his brown and looked towards the bus, remembering his previous encounter, and thought to himself, *'Whew! I really am gettin' broke in today...'* and as he saw Mandie through the bus windows he realized, *'in more ways than one.'*

🚌 🚌 🚌 🚌 🚌

After loading the bus to the gills, Derek finally pulled the bus onto the road. It was an uneventful, 'three-hour-tour' down Interstate 95 to the small town of Manning, South Carolina. As they exited, Derek pulled into the Travel Center Truck Stop while Mr. McCormick consulted his map. They realized that they needed to travel on down to Highway 301 via Highway 261, which they had turned on from the exit ramp. Derek pulled the big bus back on to the highway, and made his way to the Weldon Auditorium. He parked in the back of the building that was the old town High School Auditorium that had been newly renovated to be used as the town's civic center.

"We'll take a small break and then we'll unload the equipment," announced Mr. McCormick as the group broke to find what they would need from the bus for the show. The ladies knew that getting ready in the Auditorium's dressing rooms would be much easier that fighting over the two small bathrooms in the bus. So with garment bags in arms and makeup kits in tow, Mandie and Mrs. McCormick trudged out of the bus, weary from the early morning travel, but ready to make themselves 'at home' for the next six to seven hours.

Mr. McCormick went inside the office and met the Auditorium's director. They spent the next few minutes confirming show times and synchronizing watches, while Shane and Derek began unloading the sound equipment. Mr. McCormick met them at the back stage door.

"Hey guys, this is Don Kellum. He's the sound manager here." The young men offered their 'hello's' as Mr. McCormick continued. "We'll be setting up under his supervision, and he will show us how to tie into the building's sound controls."

"I hope that you don't mind that I'll be running the board during the concert. I know what our board can do, and what resonates the best in here," explained Mr. Kellum.

"Oh, no sir, we don't mind at all," answered Mr. McCormick, "This is our new bus driver, who will also be serving as our part-time sound man. He really hasn't learned all about the acoustics yet. In fact, Derek..." began Brian as he directed his attention towards him, "it would be a good idea if you could nap during the first rehearsal, and then sit in on the dress rehearsal, and take some notes."

"Yes, sir. That will be fine; just let me and Shane finish this set up, and I'll hit the hay," he agreed.

🚌 🚌 🚌 🚌 🚌

The equipment was set. The McCormick's had settled themselves into their dressing rooms and were ready for the first rehearsal; and Derek was exhausted! He shuffled his way down the back stairwell to his sleeping quarters. He pulled out the futon and opened his duffle bag. In the top laid the quilt that covered his bed at home-his mom had packed it, thankfully. Before spreading it out over his new 'bed', he lifted it up and buried his face in it-it smelled like home!

Realizing what a 'sap' he must have looked like, Derek spread the quilt over the mattress, and then sat down to kick off his boots. With that done, he looked for a place to lay his Stetson. He looked at the little shelves that were built in above the drawers, but they weren't deep enough to accommodate the hat. Laying it on the floor was definitely not an option. Derek thought, *'Note to self: install hook for hanging hat.'* Being the fellow of ingenuity that he was, he gathered his boots together side-by-side, and used them as a post on which to rest his Stetson. It was then off with the shirt and jeans-no time for pajama pants. His eyelids were crashing fast. He crawled into the futon, surrounding himself with the softness and comforting scents of home, and tried to forget the early start to his day that had disappointed him so-Mandie's crassness. She had not spoken to him the whole day, other that assuring him, in her dreamlike state that *'she could take care of herself.'*

Thoughts raced through his tired mind as he tried to rest. *'Maybe she just needs to get used to me. Maybe she doesn't like me at all. Maybe she is uncomfortable around me. Maybe she doesn't care either way;'* Derek then took a look at the bright side of things, like he always did-well almost always-and he remembered that he needed to set the alarm clock on his cell phone so that he could be up and ready by the dress rehearsal. *'Maybe-no; surely-no, definitely that will go better than this morning;'* he decided as he finally closed his eyes in blissful hibernation.

🚌 🚌 🚌 🚌 🚌

"Derek...," the sweet tender voice whispered in his ear. "Derek...," the angelic sound echoed again in his ear. "Derek, sweetheart, it's time to get up-you'll miss me at dress rehearsal," the voice seemed to say as a soft, smooth, silky hand caressed his face. *'It sounds like, no, it can't be...Mandie's voice,'* thought Derek.

"Honey, please...don't keep me waiting..." the voice pleaded.

"Mandie...," Derek called as he rolled over to see the sweetest, most beautiful face of his beloved Mandie, hovering over him with a smile bigger than Texas. "Mandie?" Derek asked again as he reached out to touch her face. As his hand almost reached her chin, the face morphed into the angriest, ugliest, Army drill sergeant that Derek had ever seen!

"No, this ain't no Mandie, and you'd better be gittin' your hind end outta bed, soldier. This ain't no bed and breakfast we're runnin' here! This is the Army, Mama's boy-you're in the Army now!" the sergeant growled as a stunned and confused Derek jumped up out of bed. "Now drop down and gimme 150 pushups for being a lazy grunt," the sergeant ordered.

"Sir, yes, Sir...Sir, yes, Sir... Sir, yes, Sir..." Derek shouted as he struggled to do the pushups. Up and down, up and down, as the drill sergeant began his horrible, cackling laughter that thundered in Derek's ears.

"I can't hear ya, boy! Louder!" cried the sergeant.

"Sir, yes, Sir...Sir, yes, sir..." Derek continued to moan in agony as his muscles began to ache. Then the rain began to fall. "Sir, yes, Sir..." he continued. All of a sudden, the drill sergeant leaned down, flipped Derek over and grabbed his shoulders. He began shaking him while hollering, "Wake up, boy! Wake up!"

"Sir, yes, Sir...Sir, yes, Sir..." Derek continued to mumble and groan as Shane continued to shake him.

"Derek, wake up, man! You must be having the most horrible dream! Wake up!" Shane yelled as he continued to wring the water from the dish cloth that he had retrieved from the galley when he heard Derek talking and struggling in his sleep. The droplets fells over his face, disguised as raindrops in Derek's nightmare. "Come on, man! Wake up!" Shane continued.

As the water droplets hit Derek's face, the drill sergeant seemed to melt away in the rain, as Derek's arms ached from 'push-ups' that he had been doing. "Huh!" Derek mustered as he sat straight up in the futon, with the water draining down his face. "What's happening?" he muttered.

"Well, it's about time!" shouted Shane. "Man, you must have been having a terrible dream! You were talking in your sleep, and tossin' and turnin'!" Shane explained.

Derek shook his head to clear it. "Whoa. I'm up, I'm up," he answered as he began to rub his biceps. He then

44

realized that the aching pain in his arms from loading, and unloading, and setting up all of the sounds equipment had manifested itself in his feverish pushup dream! And Mandie, well, he already knew where that came from. "Sorry man, I'm up now. I'll be out in just a minute."

"Alright. We'll be in our final dress rehearsal in about twenty minutes. Don't be late! We're runnin' on a tight schedule tonight." Shane warned as he left the downstairs compartment, and raced back through the bus, desperately making his way towards the auditorium.

"Okay. I'll be there Shane," Derek yelled as he began looking around for his clothes. After finally locating his T-shirt and jeans, Derek grabbed his Stetson and boots, and raced up the stairwell towards the front of the bus, stepping into his Dingo's as he ran. At that very moment, an oblivious Mandie was also coming up the front steps from the bus doors. Just as the two young people entered the hallway corridor past the galley, they collided, just in front of Mandie's bunk. "Oh, my goodness, Miss Mandie! I'm so sorry!"

"Why in the world can't you watch where you're going?" shouted Mandie, more out of embarrassment than anger. "Oh, I know why! It's that stupid big hat of yours! That's why you can't see anything!"

Derek settled his Stetson, which had fallen off during their little accident, back on his head. "Well, it seems this was all my fault. I'm really sorry. I was just on my way to the auditorium to meet with the sound director about the show tonight. I should've been paying more attention to where I was goin'," Derek said sheepishly.

"Well, how 'bout don't be messin' up the sound tonight tryin' to prove yourself on your first day on the job. We don't want to put on a bad show," she fussed trying her best to be as mean as possible.

It was evident that Mandie cared nothing for him. Her rude and uncaring façade confused Derek. Surely someone that sang for the Lord with such conviction-such emotion-such passion-couldn't be this mean. *'Melt that heart with kindness, boy!'* shouted a tiny Drill sergeant angel with camouflage wings from the general direction of Derek's right shoulder.   Derek snapped his head back into the present conversation, unsure of the trick that his mind was playing on him.   "Well, now, I don't think I'm actually runnin' anything tonight, so don't you worry your pretty little head about it, Ma'am. I think everything will turn out just fine. Don't be nervous; I'll be prayin' for ya," Derek replied. "Now, if you'll excuse me, I need to be goin'," he said as he tipped his hat to her, squeezing by her and making his way out of the bus doors.

Mandie walked a few steps further to her bunk, where she had left her favorite hairbrush earlier. It was then that she heard her mother's steps coming from the upper level master bunk. "Mandie McCormick! I want you to know that what you said to him was just down right rude!"

"Well, Moma, he ran right into me! That clumsy hick! He's always in a hurry-just stampeding his way around in those boots.   He could've really hurt me," Mandie retaliated.

"Well, even yet, Mandie, he did apologize, and then went out his way to be extra nice to you. You have to be kind! What kind of Christian life are you living when you're so rude to someone? I've got a good mind not to let you sing tonight until you're in a better way, girl!" her mother admonished.

Mandie knew that her mother was right. She was really going out of her way to make sure that Derek knew that he was not on her 'favorite persons' list. "Moma, I guess I'm sorry,"

"You guess?"

"Yes, I am sorry that I was so mean. I just...I just..."

"Yes? You just what?" her mother prodded.

"I just don't want to encourage him. I don't want him to get the wrong idea. He is not the one for me. I am not going out with that geeky cow poke!" she said in defense mode.

"Mandie, just being nice and civil to someone is not making them think that you want to date them! Give the boy more credit than that! Even after you chewed him up and spit him out, he still spoke to you in civility and Christian love. He even told you that he'd be praying for you. Um, hm. I'd be careful if I were you. We'll keep a fire extinguisher nearby tonight."

"Why is that, Moma? I know that I'm saved! I'm not in danger in Hell's fire for being mean?!" Mandie snorted.

"Of course not, but we might have to put out the flames," said Mrs. McCormick.

"What flames?" hollered and exasperated Mandie.

"...the ones that'll be startin' form the coals that boy's heapin' on your head with his prayers!" answered Margie with her left eye cocked sideways like the wise old owl just reeking of motherly wisdom. "You own him an apology. He is not the enemy. The last time I checked, we were all on the same team-and it's the winning side, at that!"

"I don't want to make an enemy. I just don't want to lead him on, Moma. It's bad enough that he'll be with us twenty-four, seven," said Mandie as she tried to make excuses for herself.

"Let me just ask you a couple of things: has the boy asked you to go somewhere with him? Has he told you that you're pretty? Has he done anything, other than be polite to you, to make you think that he's even interested in you?"

"Well, no, not really, but..." Mandie tried to defend herself once more.

"Well, somebody must think that they are pretty high and mighty to have every man or boy them come into contact with just pining over them. He might not even like you! He might just be being polite because it's the right thing to do, you know-being a gentleman and all."

"Well, I just know how you work, Moma, and I can already see those wheels a turnin'," said Mandie as she tried to turn the subject around.

"And what wheels might those be?" her mother asked with the epitome of sarcasm.

"The Wheels of Conspiracy! You've got us married with two kids already in your mind, I just know it!" complained Mandie.

"No, I haven't, and you know what? I think that you see the world revolving around you-but the last time I checked, this planet revolves around both of its suns; the s-u-n, and the S-o-n. Now, you take some time to cool off, and talk to the Lord before the show tonight. Just see if you can put things in better perspective," Margie said as she walked past Mandie and out of the front doors of the bus.

Chapter Eight

Mandie sat at the lighted vanity table in her dressing room, applying the finishing touches to her makeup before the dress rehearsal. As she painted on the last bit of lip gloss, she noticed her phone light up out of the corner of her eye. She had mail! *'I wonder if it's from...It is! It's Mitch! Hurry! Hurry!'* she thought to herself as she scrolled down her smart phone and logged into her Facebook account to read the message. *'Now, that's a real man. Suave, debonair', handsome, and refined! He's so much better than that ole' country bumpkin!'* she thought to herself. *'He's a real Prince Charming!'*

Her heart pounded as she finally clicked on the message link and began to read:

> *Hello, Bu T Ful! On D way 2 JKL*
> *rite now. Can't w8t 2 C U. Its bn 2*
> *long. Sing gud 4 me 2nite.*
> *C U soon.   Mitch*

"Aw! He called me beautiful!" Mandie swooned out loud. She saved the email to the special folder she created entitled, 'Prospects'. Just as the cartoon heart bubbles began to float above her head, they all popped with the brisk knocking at the door. Mandie rolled her eyes, and shouted, "Come in!"

Shane poked his head in the door. "Come on, Miss Vain. Your mug ain't gettin' no better no matter how long you sit in front of that mirror. We're going on stage for dress right now," teased Shane as he hurried Mandie along.

"Ok, Ok." said Mandie, as she stood up, and plugged her cell phone into the outlet on the vanity top to charge. *'We don't want to miss any messages, now do we?!'* she playfully thought as she walked to the door. She opened the dressing room door, and peered out, looking both ways, as if she were crossing the street. Down the backstage hall to her right, she saw Derek, complete with Stetson and earphone

49

headset, coming from her Mom and Dad's dressing room, and walking her way towards to the stage. She purposely stood still in order to avoid any more 'collisions'.

As Derek approached her door way, he noticed that she stood there in waiting. He immediately stopped himself, and gestured for her to go ahead of him. "Ladies first..." he insisted.

"Thank you," Mandie replied sheepishly. This time, she acted as a should lady when she was with him. She knew what she had to do. She couldn't be totally right with the Lord until she apologized and asked Derek's forgiveness, too.

"Look, Derek. I'm sorry about earlier. I was very rude to you." She watched Derek become, surprisingly, shy, and look down at the ground. "I was just...well I ..." she continued, stumbling over her words, as she realized that she couldn't tell him the true reason that she was so mean to him. "I was...well, I was just wrong. I apologize. Can you please forgive me?" she begged.

Derek's head snapped up in disbelief. "Oh, now, it's nothin' Miss Mandie. It's just your nerves, I'm sure. I don't know how you do it- getting' up there on that stage and singing in front of all those folks like that."

"Well, I can't very well do that-sing for the Lord- without His help. And I know that He can't help me with sin in my life-and I treated you badly. So I do apologize; I've asked the Lord to forgive me; and I hope you will, too."

"I sure do. And please don't worry yourself about that. I didn't hardly think anything about it. Now, I believe they're waiting for you on stage, and Mr. Kellum's waitin' for me up in the sound booth. Ma'am." He concluded as he tipped his hat, and walked past her on his way to the sound booth.

Just as soon as he walked past her, she rolled her eyes. *'Ugh! That stupid hat!'* she thought. She was sorry for being so rude; but she knew that she couldn't continue to be mean and still be right with the Lord. Her mother was right- she was always right.

Mandie took her place alongside her family on the stage as Derek and Mr. Kellum began to 'run the show' from start to finish according to the playbill. Derek was ready to go, sitting on a stool next to Mr. Kellum with a clipboard, taking notes as they quickly ran through the first verse and chorus of every song on the schedule. Derek learned about setting the sound levels, and changes in the lighting that would highlight the singers and bring out the best in the overall performance. The whole practice was very smooth, but, yet, Derek really didn't have time to enjoy it, as he was constantly writing notes, and learning how to be a 'sound man' so that he could further help the McCormick's in their ministry.

After the dress rehearsal, Derek took a few minutes to hang out with Shane in his dressing room before he would have to once again climb the stairs to the sound booth, and begin setting the levels on the lighting.

"So, how has your first day been so far, Newbie?" Shane asked as he sat down in his chair. He propped his feet up on the vanity, and laid himself back with his arms crossed behind his head. He grinned, as he knew that even though this farm boy was used to hard work, this had been a new kind of work, and he probably wasn't prepared for all of what the job entailed.

"Well, it's been alright, so far. The speakers are a little bit heavier than the bales of hay at the farm back in Tennessee, but, I can handle it." Derek replied as he also, kicked back in his chair to rest his eyes for just a moment.

"How've you been getting along with Mandie?" asked Shane, with a sly look on his face.

"You mean, Man-Die? Oh, we're getting along just swell!" said Derek with a laugh. "No thanks, man."

"What do you mean?" asked Shane as he tried to open up a can of worms. "Most guys usually drool over Mandie the moment that they see her! From what I noticed at church the first time that you met her, I thought that you'd be no different," Shane admitted.

"Well, I've gotta tell ya...did you say drool?" said Derek, as it hit him that his starstruck condition had been obvious.

Shane only laughed and nodded.

"I did not drool!" Derek retorted.

"Whatever. You were saying?" begged Shane as he kept the conversation going.

"Well, she's made it very clear, no matter how gentleman-like I am to her, that she's not interested in me. She did apologize a little while ago, but, I can just tell, I'm not her most favorite person!"

"Well, I can tell you, from experience, that you're not missing out on much. She's your typical annoying big sister-and that's all. She really needs to be put in her place. In fact, keeping up the Prince Charming gig will probably just make it worse. Just ignore her."

"Now, I'm sure that that will be impossible to do; and besides, your point-of-view is a little messed up. I might try to take a few hints from you, if you think that it would help ease the tension. I always wanted a sibling to tease a little, but it was always just me. I always thought that she was...I just...well, she is some kinda different from what I imagined." Derek confessed.

"Hey. Now exactly what have you been imagining about my sister?" Shane asked with a humorous but yet serious look on his face.

"Nothing! I just thought that she'd be a little more friendly-that's all."

"Yeah, she can be pretty self-centered sometimes. She thinks it's all about her, all the time-pretty high and mighty if you ask me. And starting tomorrow, she'll be down-right intolerable." Shane teased.

"Why? What's happening tomorrow?" Derek asked.

"Oh, that jerk, Mitchell Collins is driving over from Augusta to 'spend some time' with our beloved Mandie. I overheard her telling Mama something like that."

"Is he one of her 'droolies', as you put it?"

"No, not so much. He's an idiot with more money than brains. He thinks he's the best thing since instant oatmeal. Actually now that you step back and think about it, he and Mandie are probably the match of the century. They both think very highly of themselves.

"Well, she is a beautiful lady, and a very talented singer. You can tell that she really puts her heart into what she's doing," defended Derek.

"I see..." replied Shane, slowly and deliberately as he let Derek's words really sink in, "...and how exactly do you know all that?" Shane asked seriously.

"I can just tell..." answered Derek, as he glanced down at his watch. "Oh, man!" he yelled as he tried to jump up, almost tipping over in his chair, "We've gotta get going. I've gotta get to the sound booth, and you've gotta get ready to get on stage," rambled Derek as he began to get nervous.

"Whoa, there, Cowboy. Everything's gonna be fine. We're the ones on stage, and you're not even running the booth tonight! Calm down!"

"I know, but I don't want to miss anything. I may have to run the next show, and I want to make sure that I've got it all down right."

"Well, The Alamo wasn't built in a day!" teased Shane.

"Huh?!" asked Derek in confusion.

"Never mind. I'm sure that you're gonna do fine," said Shane as just shook his head at his failed attempt to assure Derek with his version of the old saying. "Go ahead, Cowboy. Get going."

"You got it," Derek answered as he swept up his Stetson that had fallen from his head earlier-and with that he ran out of the door.

🚌 🚌 🚌 🚌 🚌

Mr. Kellum had already begun rolling some background music by other Southern Gospel recording artists to set the mood for those early birds who began arriving to get a good seat. Derek climbed up into the sound booth, and took his place next to the director with his clipboard in hand. Everything was rolling right on time. Derek couldn't believe how the clock ticked away! It was already five minutes until show time. It was time to cue up the spotlight.

As the Master of Ceremonies was about to take to the stage, the backstage director communicated with Mr. Kellum up in the sound booth. He asked the backstage director to have the host to speak into his lapel microphone to insure that it was working properly. Only Mr. Kellum could hear the feed at this time. It was in perfect condition, so Mr. Kellum 'flipped the switch' and gave the go ahead to start the show. He nodded to Derek to go ahead and cue the spotlight light when the host stepped onto the stage. Derek prayed a silent prayer in his heart for the Lord to calm his nerves. He surely did not want to be the cause of calamity in the McCormick's concert! The audience had already filled every seat in the house and he knew that there could definitely be someone there that did not know the Lord Jesus as their Saviour in the crowd. He prayed that God would bless the family as they sang, and that someone there in that auditorium would accept Jesus as their Saviour while hearing the Gospel message through song.

Then he saw him. The host began his walk onto the stage, and Derek was able to shine the spotlight in just the right place to highlight it all. The audience began their applause as the host walked to center stage. "Good Evening, folks! It's so good to see all of you out tonight. Who's ready for some good Southern Gospel Music?" he asked.

The crowd went wild with applause and shouts of praise.

Mandie and her family were on stage in place behind the red velvet curtain. They stood silently-waiting and listening to the host's welcome. The nerves crept up Mandie's spine, and then calmed as she prayed for help from the Lord. Their first number featured her singing lead, and her family singing backup while playing their instruments. Her father, Brian, stood armed with his Acoustic guitar, with Shane ready with his Bass Guitar. Mrs. Margie was all set to begin the introduction with her Mandolin.

"Well, without further delay, Weldon Auditorium gives you, 'The McCormicks'," announced the host as he stepped out of the way. The backstage director began to electronically raise the red velvet curtain. Derek kept the spotlight steady in the center of the stage, as he knew that Mandie would be standing there for the opening number.

At the first movement of the curtain, Mrs. McCormick began picking her introduction on the Mandolin.

By the time that the curtain had risen fully, Mandie had begun to gingerly sing into the microphone. The levels were all perfect, and the sound filled the auditorium with sweet musical praise to the Lord.

Derek was in awe at how Mandie stood with such poise and confidence. He was to hold the spotlight there for her; and thankfully so, as he had fallen into his starstruck state once more. Her voice, and her beauty sent him sailing amongst the stars. *'What a beautiful creature standing before me,'* he thought; and the sounds that she offered up to the heavens lingered in his heart like a sweet mist that saturated that deserted space.

Forgotten were the harsh words spoken to him; even the apology now escaped his memory, because there she stood, in her radiance. He had become her captive. Even though she stood in front of an audience of over five hundred, she might as well have been standing there singing just for him.

"Sing unto him a new song; play skilfully with a loud noise."

Psalm 33:3

Chapter Nine

The show was a great blessing! As the family exited the stage they made their way to the lobby for autograph session. Derek seized the opportunity to go ahead and begin tearing down the sound equipment, with Mr. Kellum's help. Shane arrived shortly thereafter, and began to help Derek load the trunks and cases onto the bus. It would prove to be a long night for Derek, as Mr. McCormick wanted to go ahead and get on the road. The family was heading for a three day show at the Jekyll Island Convention Center, just off the coast of Georgia in the Golden Isles.

Derek finally climbed into the captain's chair and got ready to fire up the bus, after his pre-trip inspection. Shane bounded up the stairs and patted Derek on the back. "I'm gonna catch a quick nap, brother, and then I'll ride shotgun with you on your first night-drive!"

"That sounds great. I'll be waitin' on ya!" he replied as he went to crank up the bus; but just then Mr. and Mrs. McCormick finally made their way to the bus. Mr. McCormick stepped aboard first, with his own luggage piled high. He headed straight for their upstairs bedroom suite. Mrs. McCormick wearily stepped up next. Derek could tell that she was exhausted. She could barely lift her makeup kit and garment bag. "Oh, Mrs. McCormick, Ma'am! Let me help you there," offered Derek as he climbed out of the captain's chair and grabbed her garment bag.

"Oh, thank you, Derek," answered Mrs. McCormick, "You can call me Mrs. Margie, if you want to."

"Thank you, Mrs. Margie," Derek replied as he also took the makeup case out of her hand. "I really appreciate that. By the way, it was a great show tonight. It really blessed my heart."

"Thank you so much, Derek. It's so good to have you with us. I know that it's hard work, and the schedule is very different, but it really is a wonderful way to serve the Lord," she continued.

Just then Mr. McCormick returned from their upstairs bedroom where he had dropped his garment and toiletry bags. "Here, Derek. I can take that now," said Mr.

57

Brian as he relieved him of the luggage. "Good job up there with the lights tonight. Did you learn a lot about the sound board from Mr. Kellum?"

"Yes, sir. I took some very good notes, and I think that if I stick to the list I made, then I'll be alright."

"That sounds good. Are you feeling okay to start your first night drive? Do you think that you'll make it? It's about three and a half hours drive, and it's already Midnight?"

"Yes, sir. I'll be fine, and Shane said he'd come visit with me in a little while."

"Very good; Well, we're turning in," said Mr. McCormick as he shook Derek's hand and headed towards the upstairs with Mrs. Margie.

Derek walked back to the captain's chair. He was just about to sit down and prepare for the trip, when he heard a commotion. He turned and looked through the bus doors. Mandie was last to show up at the bus doors for boarding. She also struggled underneath the load of her garment bag and makeup kit.

Derek took a glance her way as she began to trudge up the steps. "I would ask you if you needed my help, but I already know that you don't, so just let me know when you get all set up back there, and I'll get this bus rollin'."

As if she were insulted, Mandie let out a "Humph," and continued to struggle to the top of the stairs. "Well, I'll be soooo glad when we get there! We'll get to sleep in real beds, Shane will have you to keep him out of my hair, and oh, yes, Mitch will already be at the hotel, and we'll have all week to spend with each other."

"Oh, is that so?" said Derek, as he slowly got out of his captain's chair, and walked towards Mandie.

"Yes, that's so..." Mandie said continuing her rambling as Derek walked towards her slowly, taking the luggage out of her hands as she chanted on, "... and you and Shane had better not embarrass me. I can see that he's already been training you to follow in his footsteps," she said as she wagged her finger in his face, which had been freed by Derek taking her luggage from her and backing her down the hallway to her bunk.

"Well, thank you, Mandie..." Derek began.

"Well, what happened to the 'Miss'?" she asked.

"Well, it's the end of the first day, you're chewing me out again, and I thought we might be a little bit past that!" he replied as he gently set her bags down on her bunk.

Shane took that opportunity to jump in. "So, you're saying that you're missing that cowboy charm already?"

"Oh, that's what I'm hearing!" Derek chimed in agreement with a 'brotherhood nod' towards Shane. "And by the way..." he continued as he panned his arm out over her bunk, "thank you, *Miss Mandie*, for allowing me to help you with your bags!"

"Ugh!" Mandie yelled as she stomped her foot. She realized she had been played. "You're a real goober, you know that!"

"Hey! I was just respecting your independence," Derek said with a smile.

Mandie turned around and looked at Derek with eyes like daggers. "And I was nice to you!"

"Well, I wasn't mean! I just did you a favor, that's all." he returned.

"Yeah, right! Good night, Mr. Rude."

Derek tipped his hat to her as she snatched the divider closed with another, "Humph!"

Derek smile at Shane, who was getting ready to turn in, and then headed back to his new command post, smiling from ear to ear. He buckled up, and mumbled to himself, "I-95's a callin'; and this is gonna be fun..." as he pulled the bus out of the parking lot and onto the highway.

🚌 🚌 🚌 🚌 🚌

After about an hour, the dark wee morning hours began to catch up with Derek as he struggled to remain focused. He breathed a sigh of relief when the bus passed the 'Welcome to Georgia' sign as they crossed the Savannah River Bridge. The road was long, and there wasn't much traffic about; a few big rigs, and a few cars. Just when Derek thought that he may have just closed his eyes, he felt a hand on his shoulder. "Hey! No sleepin' on the job!" Shane teased as he pulled up the small galley stepstool.

"You are just in time, brother. I'm really gonna have to get used to this night driving. This is wearin' me out!' Derek replied as he tried to shake it off.

"Well, how'd you come about getting a CDL? Haven't you been driving long?"

"I had planned on starting my own Truck Driving business-you know-own my own rig; maybe even run some cross-country loads. I wanted to see the country, and establish myself."

"Then your Dad passed away, and you didn't want to leave your mom?"

"Yeah. My Mama can make it along without me, but, I had to help her, and well, with no start-up capital, it's hard to purchase a big rig. We had to sell the farm, and I helped Mom pay off some more bills; but, the Lord allowed us to be able to live with Uncle Joe."

"That must have been really hard; giving up your dream, like that."

"No, it really wasn't. It's always been my dream to be able to take care of my parents. It was just hard not being able to take care of both of them. I've just always wanted to serve the Lord, raise a family for Him, and honor my parents. I can do that in just about anywhere that the Lord puts me!"

"That's a blessing-it really is." Shane replied.

Derek took this opportunity to turn the tables on Shane, so that he didn't dig any deeper. It still hurt too much. "Speaking of giving up things, what about you? Don't you miss high school?"

"Sometimes. I didn't have very many friends at high school, mostly friendly acquaintances. We all kind of hung out in a group. I tell you what I really do miss-the football games, and my most favorite part..."

Derek joined in and answered with him in unison, "the CHEERLEADERS."

"Yeah. I used to go and hang out with some of the other students there. I had a few of the guys come to church activities with me, but none of them ever came back. I think

60

about them sometimes, and I wonder...I wonder if any of them will stumble into hell because of me; because of something that I did or said, or something that I didn't do or say. Sometimes I'm glad that I'm on the road."

"Shane, you can't hide from life. You are right. People do watch us-every word and every action. And I know, only too well, that life is short. The Bible says that life is but a vapor. We need to tell as many people as we can about the Lord before it's too late. That's why I'm really glad to be on your team. This is a wonderful ministry," Derek confessed.

"And we are really happy to have you. I never had a brother." Shane stopped himself before he went totally soft, and he automatically entered into sarcastic mode, *"And Mandie just doesn't understand me..."*

Derek just laughed and shook his head. "So, *brother*, are you gonna be plucking those strings forever?" Derek inquired.

"I'm finishing up classes by correspondence with the high school, and I'll walk with them in June, and after that I'm not sure. I know that we're all doing exactly what we need to be doing right now. I just take one day at a time."

"That sounds like the best advice I've heard in a while-I won't forget it," Derek replied with deep resolution.

"Well, on a lighter note, what's the deal with your Cowboy hat and boots?" Shane asked with a smile.

"What do you mean?"

"NOBODY wears that stuff anymore!"

"Well, this is what I wore when I worked on the farm. It's part of who I am-and I like it. I really don't care what other people think. I noticed that Mandie doesn't like it!"

"You could tell, huh?!"

"She's not very subtle, that's for sure!"

The young men continued their male bonding session until Derek finally saw their exit. After leaving the interstate, Derek drove a bit down the highway until finding his turn onto the causeway leading onto Jekyll Island. Immediately, he drove past the two stately white gatehouses that stood as ghostly guardians of the island. "Whoa! Shane, what is this place that we're going to?" he asked as he snapped his head back around to get another look.

"We came here last year for a show. This is Jekyll Island. This place has a lot of history! At one time, it was the personal playground of a handful of Young American Aristocrats.-the 'New Money' of Young America. We'll get to take some of the tours, and probably go by the Horton House," Shane answered nonchalantly.

"What's so special about some house?"

"Well, it's not really a house-it's what's left of it. Some ruins."

"Awesome. That'll really be something to see!"

"If we really get to see any of it-remember Mr. Wonderful's already here waiting to ruin our 'fun-time'," Shane lamented. "There's our hotel."

Derek pulled the bus into the parking lot and breathed a sigh of relief. Shane was about to pop up and run out of the doors to stretch, when Derek grabbed his arm. "Well, I say, let's make him our 'fun-time'."

Shane nodded in impish agreement, "Yeah..."

Chapter Ten

The crew checked into the hotel after arriving on the island around three-thirty a.m. Most of the family had rested on the three and a half hour drive from Manning, and had no trouble going back to sleep. Derek was definitely no exception to that rule. When Shane unlocked the door to their room, he barely had time to remove the key card from the lock before Derek stumbled past him and collapsed onto the bed, without even pulling the spread back.

The next morning was Sunday, and the family never scheduled concerts for Sunday. If a church that they visited asked them to sing, they would, but they never sold tickets for a concert on that day-it was the Lord's Day. Mr. McCormick had rented a van when scheduling the concert on Jekyll Island, so that they would not have to drive the bus everywhere during their stay. When the family met for the continental breakfast they all synchronized their watches to meet in the lobby to 'saddle up' for church.

At nine-fifteen, Shane and Derek entered the lobby, as planned, and made their way to the two high back chairs centered by the fireplace. On their way, they encountered someone sitting in that same corner. "Oh, boy!" Shane said under his breath, but not so quiet that Derek couldn't hear. "There he is..." and he finished with a snicker, "what does he think this is, Miami Vice?"

Derek looked ahead to see a dark haired young man dressed in an aqua tee shirt, cream-colored sports coat with matching chinos, and loafers with no socks. He had to consciously control his laughter, as he remembered the game plan that he and Shane had agreed upon the night before. *'He is making this way to easy,'* Derek thought to himself.

The young man finally looked up from the USA Today he was reading, and recognized Shane. "Shane McCormick," he said as he stood up and extended his hand to Shane.

"Mitch Collins, how are you?" Shane answered.

"I'm doing well, and thank you for asking," he replied, and then he stood there waiting for Shane to

63

introduce him. When Shane failed to do so, Mitch cleared his throat.

"Oh, um, sorry, Mitch, this is Derek Jensen, our new bus driver. Derek, *this* is Mitch Collins, Mandie's friend."

Derek extended his hand to Mitch, which he took. Derek was not impressed. It was the weakest, most clammy grip that Derek had ever encountered. He simply smiled and gave his best nod, since he was resting his Stetson for church.

"Well, I actually like to think of myself as a friend of the family, Shane," Mitch said in rebuttal.

"Sure, yeah, I'm sorry, Mitch," Shane rebounded as he turned his attention to Derek, "I stand corrected."

As soon as the words left Shane's lips, Mitch's attention was immediately diverted to the brunette beauty that graced the lobby with her presence. Mandie entered the room. She was dressed in her white eyelet sundress with spaghetti straps and a contrasting white satin sash at the waist. She carried a white bolero shrug, which she held limply in her hands. Her aura radiated warmth and confidence-not pride, but a solid, contented sense of self. She wasn't the thinnest girl in the room, and she was okay with that. There was not an eye in the room that didn't turn her way. Mitch approached her with arms extended, and she walked into his embrace. Shane looked to Derek in repulsion, and found that Derek was still enthralled in the depths of her beauty.

"Hey, brother, you did remember your handkerchief, didn't you?" Shane asked. And then he asked again. "Derek? Derek!" It was useless. Derek didn't hear a word that Shane was saying to him. Shane reached in his pocket and pulled out his handkerchief. He turned the tip end of it up and dabbed the corner of Derek's mouth.

As soon as the cloth touched his face, he immediately snapped out of his trance. "What in the world are you doing?" he asked with a scowl, pushing Shane's hand away.

"Wiping your chin, Droolie," he answered with the most understood 'I-told-you-so' look that was ever given.

At that moment, Mr. & Mrs. McCormick made their way into the lobby. "Alrighty, troops. Let's load up," Mr.

McCormick announced as he turned immediately towards the doors, and led the group straight out to the fifteen passenger rental van.

Derek walked around to the driver's side, unaware that Mr. McCormick had headed in that same direction. As they met at the door, Derek looked towards Brian. "The keys, sir?" he humbly asked.

"You drive the bus, son. I'll drive the van," he answered with a smile.

Derek hung his head, in complete and genuine gratitude. He was still 'saddle sore' from the day before. He said in his most sincere voice, "God bless you, sir. Thank you," as he headed around the van to load up. He walked up to the door to find Mandie and Mitch sitting on the front row seat together.

"Do you need a hand there, friend?" Mitch asked.

"No thanks," he replied, remembering the previous encounter with Mitch's hand. "I can manage," he said as he bounded up into the vehicle. He headed straight to the back seat where Shane had already made his place. There were two rows of seats between them and the couple, and Shane leaned over to discuss the plan of action.

"So, what do you think? Spit balls, bits of paper in his hair? I'm waiting for orders, sir!"

"How old are you?"

"Okay, maybe not spit balls, but really I am waiting for instructions."

"Shane, we're on the way to church! Let's just get through the day, alright?" Derek said as he settled back for the ride.

"You're not wimping out on me, are you brother?" Shane asked.

Derek turned his head and just looked at him as if to say, *what do you think?*

"No, I didn't think so."

Mr. McCormick started up the van, and began to drive off of the island, past the two large white gatehouses. Derek watched them in a peculiar fashion. He seemed to want to stay turned around to see them as they began their ascent up the bridge. "Why are we leaving?" he asked.

"The church that we're going to is on the next island over-St. Simon's Island." Shane answered.

"Well, how many islands are there around here?" Derek further inquired.

Mitch decided to jump into their conversation. "Actually, I believe that there are five small islands that make up the chain called 'The Golden Isles'. That would be Jekyll Island, St. Simon's Island, Little St. Simon's, Sea Island, and Cumberland Island."

"You know, I did not realize that," Mandie answered, as if she was impressed. "We came here last year, and I don't remember hearing that, not even once!"

"Well, thank you for that interesting tidbit, Mitch," Derek answered, as he continued to look out of the window as they crossed the bridge. "That's so much water..." he said as his voice trailed off.

"Derek, have you never seen the ocean?" Mrs. Margie asked.

"No, Ma'am, I sure haven't"

"Oh, my goodness gracious! We will make sure to get you down to the beach before we leave."

"Thank you, ma'am. That would be real nice," he answered as he seemed to breathe a sigh of relief when the van came back down to the highway.

"And where are you from, Eric?" Mitch asked.

"Tennessee," he responded, but only faintly, as he couldn't take his eyes off of the ocean.

"Well this is only the intra-coastal waterway, and I believe that some call this portion of it St. Simon's Sound, but I could be wrong," Mitch proceeded to tell. "I just can't believe that you've never seen the ocean!"

"Well, I've fished in some pretty big lakes, and some ice cold mountain streams, but I never have gotten around to the coast; should be quite an experience; and by the way, the name's Derek," he responded as he kept his attentions focused outside.

"Oh, right you are. Sorry," apologized Mitch, desperately trying to be the 'man of the hour'.

Shane watched on with perplexity. He was quite unsure of what was rumbling through Derek's mind. *'Surely, he's not afraid of water? Last night he talked all about fly fishing, and cat fishing at night. And surely he's not afraid of heights? He lived in the mountains, for crying out loud!'* Whatever the issue, Shane had come to know Derek well enough to know that something was on his mind, and he didn't think that it was Mandie. No, that was a different look altogether. Something was amiss, and Shane knew that this would be something he dared not ask about.

Both Derek and Shane remained quiet for the rest of the drive, while Mitch's incessant chatter filled the cab of the van. Finally, the van pulled into the parking lot. They were all so glad when they read the sign, *Island Shores Community Church, Pastor Daniel Wagner.*

The family entered the church greeted by Pastor Wagner and a barrage of warm-hearted, welcoming fellow Christians. The Pastor began the service and asked the family if they wouldn't mind singing maybe one or two songs, which they happily agreed to do. Without the full instrument set up, Mandie took her place at the piano.

Derek had never heard her play in person. Her fingers gracefully flowed over the keys in what sounded like a flawless introduction to "Glory to His Name", sang only as the McCormick Family could. *'All I can do is drive a bus! How blessed is this family to be so gifted, with every voice lifted together to the Lord in harmony. Thank you, Lord, for letting me be a part of it,'* he silently prayed in his heart.

After several hearty 'Amens', the family took their seats. Mandie and Mitch sat two rows in front of Shane and Derek, and Mr. & Mrs. McCormick were sitting on the row in front of them. Pastor Wagner began his message by asking the congregation to turn in their Bibles the book of John, chapter one, verses fourteen through sixteen. He centered on one verse, number fourteen: *"And the Word was made flesh, and dwelt among us, (and we beheld his glory, the glory as of the only begotten of the Father,) full of grace and truth."*

He began to preach on the most perfect subject of all time, Jesus Christ. He explained how we know from verse one, that God the Father was in the beginning, and the Word was with him. "Then later we read, in verse fourteen, that the

Word was made flesh and dwelt among us. "This, my friends, is the man, Christ Jesus. Jesus is the Word. God sent His Son, the Word, to earth for us to be a perfect example of everything that we need to know to live in this life. Yes, friends, what God had to say, he said in the man, Jesus Christ."

Only moments after the words of Pastor Wagner faded away, Mandie began scrambling in her purse. Her movements immediately caught Derek's eye. She finally found her treasure-a pen and her notebook. She began scribbling words frantically. By this time, Shane noticed that Derek had noticed; only Shane had seen this behavior before. He leaned over and whispered, "Can't you see 'em turnin'?"

Derek whispered in return, "What's turnin'?"

"The Wheels!"

"What wheels?"

"The Wheels of Inspiration," Shane explained. "She's heard something in the sermon and God's given her a song. She's writing it down before she forgets it. She does that a lot. She wrote three songs on our last album."

Derek sat back in admiration for this beautiful creature. His thoughts overtook him. *I know that I have to keep this in perspective. The Bible says, "Thou shalt have no other gods before me." This I know. Lord, it just sure is good to sit back and appreciate Your handiwork. She sure is something.*

Pastor Wagner preached on like a wild man-praising the Lord and yet challenging the congregation. After the last 'Amen', Derek couldn't resist finishing the conversation of earlier. "Hey, Shane, you know that thing..." he began as he casually nodded his head in Mandie's general direction, "...that we were talking about earlier? You know, the Wheels?"

"Yeah..."

"Well, what happens next?"

"Why are you so interested?"

"Just humor me. I find it intriguing," he replied.

"Hum. Intriguing! I see! Well, Mr. Intrigued, if you must know, she'll be up half the night in the bus on her keyboard working out the melody; and then she'll turn in to the hotel room for some much needed beauty sleep."

"Beauty sleep? She could afford to stay up all night, if she wanted to."

🚌 🚌 🚌 🚌 🚌

After the evening service, Shane and Derek walked from the hotel over to the island's Dairy Queen for a Blizzard, but not before Derek had reclaimed his Stetson. He felt absolutely lost without it. After two cheeseburgers, fries, a Blizzard, and about an hour of failed flirting attempts with the waitress, Shane decided that it was time for him to turn in. They left the Dairy Queen and began their walk back down the paved bike trails bound for the hotel.

"Shane, you are a mess! I'll bet when you left home, there were girls just crying pools of tears!"

"No, now, I wouldn't say all that!"

"You mean you don't have a girl waiting back home for ya?"

"No. I mean to be free. As you can see, you never know who you're gonna meet on the road. I gotta keep my options open!"

"You know you probably won't see her again-ever!"

"Now, that's not so! We were here last year!"

"Yeah, but was she here? What's the turnover rate at the local Dairy Queen? I'd dare say that it's pretty high!"

"Brother! I didn't ask her to marry me, I just flirted around a little bit! It probably made her day!" said Shane as he stuck out his bird chest!

"There ain't no help for you!" Derek said as he shook his head.

As they approached the parking lot, they heard familiar voices coming in from the hotel terrace. "Shh. I think that's Mandie and Mitch. Stop here," whispered Shane.

Derek stopped in his tracks and the two young men looked on.

"Mandie, do you really have to do that now?" Mitch asked in a whining tone.

"Yes, Mitch. I'm sorry-but look! If you give me tonight alone, then I know that I can be all done by tomorrow and I can totally concentrate on you the rest of the week."

"Well, that's just the thing, Mandie, I can't stay all week like I'd wanted to. Something came up, and I've got to get back to Augusta on the day after tomorrow."

Mandie's countenance fell. She had been looking forward to spending time with Mitch all week. She had even boldly announced it to Derek and Shane! Now, not only was she going to miss her much desired time with Mitch, but she was also going to have to eat crow; but she knew, the longer she delayed with her mission, the less effective it would be.

"I'm sorry, Mitch. I've gotta do this. The Lord comes first."

"I know, Mandie. You're making the right decision. That's what I love aboutcha," Mitch said as he opened his arms for a hug. Mandie stepped right in, and felt a light kiss on the cheek, which made her blush. "Don't stay up too late now, you gotta get your beauty sleep!" he said, as he turned and walked into the hotel.

Mandie giggled on the inside as she turned and began to walk towards the bus, as it occurred to her, *'did he say that's what he loved about me?'* She pondered this some more as she opened the doors with her key, and walked in and up to the upstairs lounge where she kept her keyboard. She took out her notebook from earlier, and began to fiddle around with the keyboard. Just as she started penciling chords above her words, she heard the doors open to the bus. Startled, she called, "Who's there?"

"Hey, Man-Die! It's just us!" called Derek up the stairs, as he followed Shane up.

"Man, you weren't supposed to say anything! We were supposed to *'scare her'* OOOOOOOO!!!!!" moaned Shane as he came at Mandie with ghostly arms grabbing at her hair.

"So, where's ole' Mitchell Crockett? Wasn't that his name? Isn't he Sonny's cousin?!" Derek asked with a laugh.

Shane could hardly contain himself! "Yeah, Mandie, maybe that's why he knows all about these islands 'cuz he's been runnin' all over these waters chasing bad guys with the Miami Vice!"

"Y'all get out here! There was nothing wrong with what he was wearing! It was charming!" Mandie blurted out in defense. She was already getting riled up.

"He sounded so pitiful telling you goodnight!" Shane said as he agitated her even more.

"I know! I thought that he was gonna cry hard and get the Tubbs-Oh, I mean snubs!" Derek said as both young men fell out with laughter!

"That was a good one!" Shane mentioned to get out between the howls of laughter.

"Alright! That's it! I've had just about enough of you two! Y'all git on outta here! I'm working on something important!" ordered Mandie.

"Yeah, we know; whew;" breathed Shane as he tried to catch his breath. "We saw you this morning in church. You got another song, didn't ya?"

"Yes, if you must know. And by the way, I'll have you know that I don't appreciate y'all's eavesdropping on my private conversations."

By this time, Derek had found his composure. "Aw, come'on Mandie. You know we're just pickin'! Now, come on' Shane, let's get outta here. She does have important work to do."

"Oh! Derek! We were just gettin' started!" complained Shane as he moped on towards the stairs.

'Now, see here, we're goin' on, I promise. I'll even lock the door on my way out, so no one will bother you. And no kidding around-I was really impressed when I saw the way that the Lord was using you today, by your singing and by your songwriting. That was really something."

"Well, thank you, I think. Look, I guess y'all heard I've only got one day left with Mitch on tomorrow-would you two please leave us alone?"

"NOOOO!" Shane yelled as he exited the bus doors. Mandie watched him walk across the parking lot to the hotel lobby doors.

She turned her attention back to Derek, who stood there at the top of the stairwell, with his hat in hand.

"OOOOH! I wish you'd talk some sense into him! Can't you promise me that you'll make him behave?" she begged.

"No, now I can't promise that; but I can promise you one thing..."

"What's that?" she asked in exasperation.

"You don't need any beauty sleep. Good night," and with that he walked down the stairs and off of the bus, locking the door behind him, just like he promised. And he always meant what he promised.

Chapter Eleven

The sun rose all too quickly for Mandie. The late night at the keyboard had definitely taken its toll. As she drug her carcass out of bed, she went straight to the mirror. She had to inspect the damage. Her eyes yielded a slightly darker shade, but nothing a little concealer couldn't fix. She had to be perfect today, as this would be her last full day with Mitch. Mitch-*'just a little slice of Heaven sent here just for me...'* she thought to herself. Those thoughts were interrupted with her chiming signal of a text message from her cell.

Nearly running to the nightstand, she quickly plopped herself onto the bed and began to read:

Gud mrnin bu T ful. Watz d plnz 4 2dA?

Mandie began to text frantically filling Mitch in with the plans of the day. The plans before the night's concert included breakfast in the Lobby, sight-seeing in the morning, lunch at the Driftwood Bistro, and dress rehearsal in the afternoon. She could hardly wait for Mitch to reply. She clung to his every word.

The chimes nearly gave her a heart attack, as she had never set the phone down.

Gr8t! C ya N 1 hr N D Lby.

'One hour?' Mandie thought to herself as she began to become frantic. She scurried to the bathroom and began to run the shower. The primping process had begun.

🚌 🚌 🚌 🚌 🚌

Exactly forty-five minutes later, Mandie made her entrance into the hotel lobby, where the Hot Buffet Style Breakfast was being served. She stood at the opening of the room, poised, as she searched for Mitch. In the midst of her scan, she spied Shane and Derek, eating at a small table for two, and laughing to beat the band, already. *'Surely those two will behave today, Lord,'* she thought to herself as she made her way to their table. "Good morning, boys," Mandie said as she greeted them.

"Mornin',"muttered Shane as he stuffed his mouth with a forkful of omelet.

"Good morning, Mandie," Derek answered as he stood, and began to pull her chair out for her. "Won't you join us?" he offered.

"Oh, thank you, no. I am meeting Mitch for breakfast this morning. You haven't seen him, have you?" she asked.

"Uh-uh," Shane managed to get out as he also grabbed at a glazed doughnut.

Derek began to look around the room. He spied *'Mr. Wonderful'* at a table for two in the corner next to the pool exit. "Oh, there's Mr. Crockett-waiting for you in the corner over there. He looks sort of covert. Do you think he's on a stake-out?" Derek asked with a smile.

Mandie's countenance fell. She had sincerely hoped that the Miami Vice jokes would be old today. "Please, Derek, Shane," she began as she looked towards her brother with a very humble plea, "Please leave me alone today. He's leaving tomorrow. I only have this once chance."

"Chance? Chance for what?" asked Shane with his usual confused look.

Derek was just as confused, but he felt from the desperate tone in her request, that the issue was of a private nature.

"Just, please, Shane, please. Leave us alone today," she begged as she turned and put on her best smile and walked towards Mitch's table. As she neared the breakfast nook, Mitch also rose from his seat and made her comfortable.

"Good morning, beautiful! You look like a million bucks!" he offered with his usual flattering tone. "Can I bring you something to drink? Coffee?"

"Just a glass of cranberry juice and one of those omelets. Shane had one on his plate, briefly, I might add, and it looked pretty good."

74

Mitch laughed. "One omelet coming right up!" Mitch replied as he stood and began walking towards the buffet. He turned around and caught Mandie's attention as he was still walking, "Did I tell you how beautiful you look this morning?" he said loud enough for others to hear.

Mandie blushed. She was used to attention; plenty of attention-just not this kind. It made her feel strange. *Is this what it's like to have that special someone? Maybe I'm just not used to it,'* she thought to herself as she set her purse in the seat of the chair next to her. Her thoughts were interrupted with Mitch's return. He set the table for her and she began to eat and listen to Mitch regale her with stories of the events in Augusta. She remembered most of the names that he mentioned. It was so hard to remember everyone that she met while on tour. She remembered one name, though, Diane Livingston. She was a member of Mitch's church, and was the daughter of one of the local physicians. She was a very quiet, not snobby, but genuine type of person. Mandie had enjoyed her time spent with her. "Oh! It's funny that you mention Diane. How is she?" Mandie asked.

"Oh, she's doing fine, I guess. She and Murray Robinson are going out again. It's been such an on-again, off-again relationship, you know." Mitch explained.

"No, I don't know. But I do know that she's an awfully sweet girl; I hope that she's happy and doing well. Please tell her that I said 'hello' when you get back," Mandie asked.

"I will. I know that she'll be glad to hear from you," he promised.

Mandie thanked Mitch for the breakfast and returned to her room for some final primping and then she met the rest of the family at the van for their sight-seeing. The first stop was the Horton House Ruins. The Tabby House of Jekyll Island stood on the Intracoastal side of the island, and had done so since about 1736.

As the family walked towards the shell of a house, Mandie was absolutely entranced. The walls were so beautiful. It was obvious where restoration crews had patched erosion and deterioration, but as a whole, the house that was built with 'tabby', a mixture of sand, lime, oyster shell and water, had stood the test of time. Mandie entered through the front door, and stood in what must have been the family room, or parlor, in that day. She looked straight up and noticed how the second floor, which had long since decayed away, had been built on the ledge of the ground floor walls. She marveled at the engineering skills of the colonial day.

"It's really something, isn't it?" Mitch asked as he sidled up to Mandie. His voice broke her concentration.

"Yep. It really is something," answered Shane, loudly, as he busted right in on their conversation. "These big ole' slabs of rock sure are 'purty'," he continued in a false, exaggerated southern drawl.

"Shane, don't you have somewhere to go?" Mandie suggested nicely, "...and where is your bosom buddy?" she asked as she turned around and spotted Derek just entering through the front door. "Oh, good, there you are. Don't you and Shane have some fishing to do, or something?" she asked as she stretched her eyes in emphasis, pleading them to 'go away'.

"Well, I don't know, see, the thing is, I love fishing and all, but you really don't get to see stuff like this every day. I think I'll just hang around here for a while, Mandie, but thanks for the suggestion. We might try to slip a little fishing in before we leave," Derek responded slowly, just to irritate her-and Mitch. From the look on Mitch's face, it was working.

"Y'all see'em turnin'?" asked Shane as he yelled out over the group.

"See what turning?" asked Mitch, as he looked up over all of the ruins.

"Her wheels of imagination. She's looking up there tryin' to imagine those rafters, and those rooms; yeah, her wheels are definitely turnin'!" Shane teased.

"Well, I can't see 'em turnin', but they must be workin' real hard, 'cause I can smell the smoke coming out of her ears from way over here!" said Derek as he joined in the taunt.

Mandie rolled her eyes in disgust, and began to walk out into what used to be the gardens on the grounds. Mitch followed behind, but not before throwing a dirty look in the general direction of Derek and Shane, who were laughing and exchanging fist bumps!

Mr. & Mrs. McCormick decided that they wanted to drive on up to the other historic buildings on the island. They had passed a rental shack for some little red golf carts and felt like that would be a great idea. Once they'd talked it over, they decided that they'd take Shane and Derek with them on the van to the rental shack and rent three carts for the day: one for them, one for Shane and Derek, and one for Mandie and Mitch. Shane was absolutely wild about the idea and was more than willing to jump into the van.

Mandie seized the opportunity to spend a few moments alone with Mitch as the van drove out of the parking lot. "I wonder how many ladies in their glamorous gowns made their way down this same path back in the day?" Mandie said as she continued to stroll down around the large oaks that dripped with Spanish moss.

"I'm not sure. I just know that there is one glamorous lady walking these grounds right now," Mitch answered.

Mandie blushed. "Oh, Mitch, really."

"I mean it, Mandie. You're beautiful. You know..." he began as he stopped and took hold of Mandie's hand, "...we've been talkin' for a while now, and well I've..."

Mandie's heart began to flutter as she wondered where Mitch was going. She hoped that it was in the right direction. She really liked Mitch-he was handsome, he treated her well every time they were together, and to tell the truth, she thought that they made a wonderful couple. She almost became so lost in her anticipation that she lost track of listening!

"I've been thinking, and we've been talking for a while now and..." he continued, looking at the ground, "well I just want to keep on talking to you. Every day; every week; every month;" he said as he began to move in closer. "Well, I guess what I'm trying to say is that I want us to be...I just want to know, that you're my girl."

"That I'm your girl?" Mandie asked in disbelief.

"Well, I really like you Mandie, and I think you like me too, and I just want to, you know, make it official," he said as he looked up and caught Mandie's eyes which were shining like stars in the cobalt blue night.

"Official?" she repeated as he moved in brushed his lips against hers in a soft henpeck.

"You know, sealed with a kiss?" he whispered as he kissed her again, only this time, he lingered.

Mandie reached her arms around his neck and steadied herself. Just as she thought that it couldn't get any better, she jumped out of his arms when the voice of Derek startled her.

"Uh-Um," he muttered, clearing his throat, to alert the couple to his presence.

"I'm sorry, Mandie;" Derek said sheepishly as he handed the key to the little red cart to her. "Here's the key to y'all's cart. I left it parked in the little lot on the other side of the road. Your Dad just said to be at the convention center at 2:30 for the first rehearsal."

Mitch reached over and took the key from Derek's hand. "I think we can manage that," Mitch replied in a voice of unnecessary authority.

Not backing down from the bull that was attempting to mark his territory, Derek simply replied, "See that you do," and turned back walking towards Shane who was waiting for him in the little red cart. Before jumping into the passenger side, he turned again to the now fuming Mitch and yelled with his best smile, "Watch out for that Man-Die! She's ruthless!"

Mandie was appalled! *'Man-Die,'* she thought to herself, *'just what does he mean by that? Well, if he wants to play that game, then he'll really get it!'*

After a lazy morning of strolling down the historic lanes of the island, Mandie and Mitch did meet with her family at the Driftwood Bistro for lunch as planned. They enjoyed the local fare with different variations of shrimp delicacies and then Mandie and Mitch slipped off again to the Sea Turtle Center.

There they learned about the life of the sea turtle and even visited the Sea Turtle Rehabilitation center, where injured turtles are helped to rejoin life in the sea. Mandie seemed to float about in a trance with her hand resting softly in Mitch's. This was the best that she had felt in so long. It really felt good to 'belong' to someone.

Mitch had to remind her that they had somewhere that they had to be. He made sure to have Mandie at the Convention Center promptly at 2:30 for rehearsal, just as he said he would; but he parted ways with Mandie at the door. He knew that he would be leaving that night, and he wanted to take a quick nap in his car, since he had had to check out of the hotel. Of course, Mandie offered her dressing room to him, which he gladly accepted.

Since the family was staying two more nights, Derek was able to sit in on both rehearsals and that night's show. As he sat in the sound booth, Derek watched as Mandie taught her family the new song that the Lord had given her last night. He just couldn't get over the amazing talents that God had bestowed on this family, and especially on Mandie. *'It just seems such a waste-Mandie and that fella. There's just something about him that I don't like,'* he thought to himself. *'I'm glad that he won't be around that much, I hope.'*

That evening, as it was time for the family to take their place on the stage, Derek was leaving Shane's dressing room to take his place in the sound booth with the stage manager. He and Shane strolled towards the stage and met Mandie and Mitch as she was just about to go on stage.

"Knock 'em dead, gorgeous," Mitch said as she snuck in a little peck on the cheek, just for Derek's benefit. Mandie giggled and climbed the steps to the stage.

Shane rolled his eyes and retorted, "Ugh. Coodies!" as he scurried up the steps behind Mandie.

Derek and Mitch stood there looking on from the wings for a moment. "You know, you guys really think you're something," Mitch started.

"We do? Whatcha mean?" Derek asked, playing it off.

"You know what I mean-you and Shane-trying to bust us up this morning-trying to throw a wrench in my plans."

"Your plans?" Derek poked.

"Yeah, **MY** plans. Well, I had her all to myself all this afternoon," Mitch bragged.

Derek turned and looked square into Mitch's eyes before he turned to walk away, "And when you roll outta here tonight, I'll have her all to myself for the next two months."

It was on!

🚌 🚌 🚌 🚌 🚌

The McCormick's performed an awesome show that night, and the new song was delivered flawlessly. After the autograph session, the family retreated to the van to make their way back to the hotel for some 'well-deserved shut-eye' as Derek called it-all except for Mandie who had walked with Mitch to his car to bid him farewell.

Shane caught a glimpse of the two of them. He grabbed Derek by the arm. "This just won't do!" he said as he drug Derek with him up toward Mitch's car. He took out his handkerchief and began waving it in the air. "Goodbye, Mitchell; Goodbye!" Shane bellowed in a high girlish falsetto.

Derek caught on quickly. "Bon Voyage, Mitch! Don't forget to write!" he echoed.

Shane ran up to Mandie and grabbed his sister away. He began pulling her back towards the van.

"Text me when you get home, Mitch. I don't care how late it is!" Mandie yelled as Shane drug her along.

"I will," he replied as he reluctantly slipped into his car.

"We'll take good care of her while you're gone," Shane hollered.

Derek looked at Mitch, who was staring a hole through him from his car. If looks could kill, Derek would have been a 'goner'; but Derek simply smiled, tipped his Stetson to him, and climbed into the van.

Chapter Twelve

The family spent one more day of vacation by touring the St. Simon's Lighthouse on the next island over, and then delivered one more awesome show before leaving Jekyll Island bound for Atlanta, Georgia. The family would put on two shows there, and then on to the Southern Gospel Harvest Festival at Dollywood Amusement Park in Sevierville, Tennessee. Derek had mixed emotions about that leg of the trip. He longed to see the Great Smoky Mountains again, but then, he thought about the heartbreak that he would feel as he saw them in the rear view mirror one last time; but he had another week before he had to think about that.

Derek felt refreshed after a good night's sleep in the comfort of the hotel bed, and when the family checked out bright and early that morning, he was ready to go. They had about a five hour drive ahead of them, and Mr. Brian didn't want to stop this time.

The family spent their morning in the upper lounge area practicing through some new songs from the recording label's catalog of songs. The family would make a stop in Nashville to record their next album after 'Harvest Fest', if they could secure some studio time before their show in Louisville, Kentucky. To prepare, the family had to take advantage of every moment that they could to practice together.

Mandie was busy at the keyboard fingering out the melodies for the vocals, and the more that they practiced, the easier the harmonies came. In no time flat, Shane had the bass line worked out. This particular song, Mr. Brian decided, longed for the sound of a mandolin. Since Mrs. Margie's arthritis had flared up again, Shane passed the bass guitar to his mother, and picked up the instrument and began to pick. *'Mr. Brian sure knows his music,'* Derek thought to himself as he listened to the mandolin place the crowning touch on the musical number.

The family stopped practicing around 11:30 to get some lunch ready. As Mandie and Mrs. Margie walked down to the galley to prepare the food, the concerned mother took the opportunity to talk with her daughter. "So, Mandie, how was your little visit with Mitch this time?" she asked as she handed Mandie a loaf of bread to start making the sandwiches.

"Well, I thought that it went really well. He wanted to make sure that we would be an item."

"Are you an item?" Mrs. Margie asked.

"Yes, I'd definitely say that we are. He sent a text last night when he made it home with the sweetest 'goodnight' on it." Mandie replied with a smile. She was really in 'La-La-Land.'

"Oh, really?" her mother said with surprise.

"Yes. Moma, I think that the Lord has really answered my prayers with Mitch. I think he's the one."

"Now, Mandie, you've only spent a couple of days with him, and it was a solid six months since you had seen him before that. How can you be so sure?"

"I just know, Moma. The conversations that we have, and the e-mail letters and texts that are just heavenly! He's so refined! Only, you should have seen him when he was 'making it official'. He was stutterin' and stammerin'-just a lookin' for the right words to use. He was so cute!"

"Cute, huh?" Margie answered, almost in apathy. Mandie could tell that she wasn't thrilled about Mandie's choice.

"Moma, I know that you think I'm wrong here, but, please believe me. I haven't felt this way-well, ever! This is different than any other crush I've ever had. He's the one-I know it! He's just what I've been looking for."

"Well, then I'm happy to hear it; and I'm happy that you're happy! Really!" her mother answered with a more genuine smile. "Well, only you can know for sure, and I'll keep praying for you."

"Thank you, Moma!" said Mandie with a smile as she hugged her Mother long and tight.

"Very good. Now, how about running this sandwich and drink up to Derek for me?" Mrs. Margie asked.

"Moma! You just told me that you were happy for me, and now you're at it again! No more match making! He's already been in 'co-hoots' with Shane to embarrass me to death! I just know he has a crush on me! And you're gonna make it worse! You know what he called me? 'Man-Die'!"

Mrs. Margie laughed silently. "He really said that, huh?"

"And I can tell that he's got his sights set on me, too. Even Mitch picked up on it. I've gotta do all I can to discourage him; believe me, Moma. It's for his own good!" she continued in an effort to persuade her mother to see her side of the situation.

"Mandie..." she began.

"Ma'am?"

"It's just a sandwich. The boy has to eat too, doesn't he?" she said as she handed her the lunch.

"I reckon," Mandie said as she grabbed the paper plate and can of soda, stomping her way up to the aisle towards the captain's cove of the bus.

Derek heard her approach, as did the next two cars in front of them. "Well, hello there, Mandie."

"Hey. Here's a sandwich for lunch. And a drink," she said as she practically threw the plate in his lap.

"Now, just hang on a minute. Let me get situated here," Derek answered as he changed hands on the wheel to be able to pick up the sandwich.

"What's the matter, you can't handle eatin' a sandwich behind the wheel, Tex?" she said in her most harsh, sarcastic tone.

"Yes, missy, I can. I just have to take it slow. This ain't no joke, driving you and your family around."

"Oh, well excuse me. I thought that you thought that everything was a joke," she retorted.

"Well, I don't. I can take that drink now, please," he asked as she handed it to him, and he placed it in the cup holder that was built-in to the arm of the captain's chair.

"Is that all, sir?" she asked hatefully.

"No-how about some chips? Do we have any chips?" asked Derek with a smile.

"Ugh!" said Mandie as she turned around and stomped back to the galley, only to find her mother standing there, holding back her laughter and holding out an individual size bag of potato chips. Mandie snatched the chips from her mom. "You see? You see what I have to deal with? He's just like Shane. I thought that the Lord was merciful to us in only making one 'Shane', but now here comes another one…" she continued to rant as she marched back down the aisle to Derek.

Again, her arrival was no surprise. "Oh, there you are! Say, would you mind opening the bag for me?" he asked with a devilish smile.

"Oh, not at all!" she answered as she opened the bag and then, in her rage, with both hands she squeezed the bag on both sides, crushing every chip inside. The look of shock on Derek's face immediately brought a sense of satisfaction. And then, the horror of realizing what she had actually done, and the speed at which she had done it, brought remorse just as quickly. She stood there, holding the little bag, not quite as proud of herself as she was only a moment ago.

"Oh, Mandie," Derek began slowly. "Thank you   so much! That's just the way I like 'em. Now I can just turn it up and eat those suckers straight outta the bag! It's much easier like that when you're drivin'! How'd you know?" he said with that same teasing smile.

And then her rage returned. "Well, you're welcome, Tex. Now, eat up!" she said in her little voice as she turned to walk back down to the galley to fix her own sandwich.

"Oh, by the way, I'm from Tennessee, not Texas," he replied.

Finally, Mandie felt like she had the upper hand. *'He's sensitive about his home, is he?'* she thought to herself. "Yeah, I know, Tex," she said as she walked away.

Derek only smiled, inside and out. He knew that he irritated her. And if that was the only interaction that she wanted to have with him, then he'd take it; because even in all of her beauty, she could be so trifling. But that's what he loved about her. He loved…yes, he admitted it; he loved her.

🚌 🚌 🚌 🚌 🚌

After lunch, Mandie began clearing the table away quickly, so that the family could get back to practicing. Mrs. Margie intended to help, but suddenly felt poorly and needed to lie down. Mandie assured her mom that she could handle the little bit of dishes and clutter to be put away. So, Mrs. Margie went up to the Master Loft and took a little rest. Shane, of course, never stuck around for any kitchen chores, *'that was woman's work'* he thought. So Mandie began to fill the small sink with water and dish liquid to wash the few remaining pieces.

As she began putting the food packages away into the cabinets, she heard whistling. She was actually amazed that she could hear it over the roar of the road and the bus engine. She searched for the direction until she realized that the melody was coming from Derek. She wanted so badly to slip back into her rage, which had subsided over lunch, but she couldn't help but wonder where she'd heard that song before. It was one of those times, when she knew that she knew the song, but just couldn't put her finger on the title!

As she continued in the galley, so did the whistling until she couldn't stand it anymore. She really didn't want to talk to Derek, but the suspense was killing her. She made her way up to the captain's cove. "Whatcha whistlin', Tex? I know it ain't 'Dixie'?" she asked.

Derek sang the title of the song in his best singing voice. "Jesus Is The Sweetest Name I Know".

It all came back to her-every line and every word. She ran over them in her head as she listened to Derek continue to whistle.

"You know, people nowadays forget all about the good ole hymns, and songs of Zion-you know, songs right outta the hymn book. Some of the most powerful and uplifting songs can be found there, right in the back of most pews, and yet, folks today are opting for LCD screens, and 'karaoke-style' sing-a-longs." Derek reflected.

85

"Hmm; I never thought of it that way," Mandie muttered, as her mind was obviously somewhere else. Without a 'thank you', or even a 'goodbye' she just turned and walked back through to the galley; just as she was turning to take the stairwell to the upper lounge, Shane almost crashed into her. "Watch where you're going, goof!" she said as she grabbed Shane's arm.

"You watch out. I'm going to the galley for a snack," Shane rebounded.

"No, you're not," said Mandie as she grabbed Shane's guitar from his bunk.

"Huh?" remarked a confused Shane.

"Come on up here," she said as she grabbed him by the collar.

"But Mandie! I wanted a Fudge Round!" he complained as she drug him upstairs.

🚌 🚌 🚌 🚌 🚌

After about two more hours, Derek pulled the bus up to their destination. The little town stood on the outskirts of Atlanta, and thankfully, not downtown. Derek wasn't quite sure about having to take that big ole bus through downtown Atlanta! These two concerts were being sponsored by two small churches and were being held in the local high school auditorium that also served as the suburban community center.

Since the churches were younger, smaller works, Mr. McCormick gratefully declined their offer of hotel rooms for the family. So when the family arrived at the high school, Mr. McCormick led Derek through his first set up with the bus parked for overnight stay. Afterwards, he was so worn out from all of the driving, that he opted to catch a few 'z's as the family rehearsed in the auditorium.

Derek didn't realize that he was so tired! He almost missed the entire show! He managed to make his way into the back of the auditorium, and he stood behind the sound crew.

After the applause for the last number died down, Mr. McCormick made an announcement, as Mrs. McCormick stepped back. "Thank y'all so much, and thank y'all for coming out tonight. For our final song of the evening, we're gonna try a little something different. Good night and God Bless," he concluded as followed Mrs. McCormick and stepped into the wings. The stage went dark, and then there was but a single spotlight, on Mandie, with Shane sitting near on a stool in the shadows with his acoustic guitar.

The house became nearly silent as they waited. Then Shane began to roll out the broken chords to a lovely, and yet familiar melody, in a slow bluegrass rhythm. Then Mandie's sweet voice delicately began to sing, *"There have been names that I have loved to hear; but never has there been a name so dear..."* She continued on singing the rest of *Jesus Is The Sweetest Name I Know*, as the audience sat captivated at the lovely truth of the words and the blissful simplicity of the music.

A warm smile crept over Derek's face and heart. It felt good to know that he had had a part in the show-well sort of! But what warmed his heart more was to think that Mandie had actually paid him some attention. She had actually been interested in something that he had to say.

As Mandie held the last note softly, but firmly, the audience gave their final hearty round of applause and the curtain was drawn. Derek had resolved to speak to her about the song later on the bus, but he just couldn't wait. He made his way backstage and met Shane with a hearty hand shake. "Great pickin', brother. I never had imagined that song played and sung quite that way. That was really good."

"Oh, I had nothing to do with it. It was all her. I had to keep playing, and playing, and playing until she was satisfied that it was the way that she was hearing the music in her head, the ole' heifer! But it turned out alright!" he said with his usual smile.

Mandie looked over and saw Derek with Shane. With no other way off of the stage, she tried to breeze by them, to avoid what could possibly turn into an awkward moment-but no such luck. Derek caught her by the arm. "Oh, excuse me, Mandie?"

She stopped and tried not to roll her eyes. "Yes?"

"That song was amazing. I was just telling Shane how I'd never thought that that song could sound so nice in that style. Thanks for doing that for me."

There it was-the awkward moment that she had tried to avoid. She couldn't make eye contact with him, because she knew what she had to do. "I didn't do it for you-you had a good song, and it was a blessing to others; that's all. *I didn't do it for you,*" she finished as she quickly walked away leaving Derek there, looking at the ground, knowing exactly what she meant.

Chapter Thirteen

"Mandie? Mandie?" called Mrs. Margie down the stairwell for her sleepy head daughter.

"Ma'am?" she answered as she cracked her eyes open. Then she heard her mother's footsteps as she came downstairs. WHAM! The basket of laundry hitting the bus floor almost made Mandie jump out of her skin!

"Mandie, the coach here at the high school was on the sound crew last night, and he said that they'd be more than happy to let us use their washer and dryer in the locker room. Your Daddy and I need to go to that little supermarket that we passed up the way to pick up some odds and ends. Can you please take care of this for me so that we can get back in a hurry? We only need one sound check rehearsal before the show tonight, and I'd like to ride the MARTA up to the Coca-Cola Museum. I just love that place," she concluded with a smile.

"Eew! Yucky! We're washing our clothes in the same tubs as smelly jerseys and gym socks?"

"Girl, we use the local Laundromats! There ain't no tellin' what's been in there!" her Moma answered. "Besides, it's soap and water for crying out loud. It kills the germs! Now, hop up and get going. Maybe you and the boys can actually catch the train up for some fun today too!"

Mandie rolled her eyes. "No thanks. I'll stick with the dirty laundry. At least I'll have Mitch to keep me company.

"From the looks of it, with all of the late night texts, you are never gonna get enough sleep. You need to start observing a proper bedtime-just for your own health!" her Moma warned.

"Oh, Moma, really. I could just talk to him and write him all night long. I really don't think that it will be long, Moma. I'm so excited."

"Now, don't go gettin' your hopes up, Mandie. Remember, even though he's got you on that electronic leash, you're not around him all the time. I'm really not trying to be the voice of doom here, but I just don't want to see you get hurt, baby, that's all."

89

"I know, Moma, and I appreciate it. I know what I'm doing."

"Yeah, I know what you're doing too-and it's called Laundry, and get on outta bed and get to steppin'!" said Mrs. Margie with a laugh as she pulled the covers off of Mandie.

"Alright, alright. I'm up!" said Mandie with a laugh as she pulled herself up out of bed.

🚌 🚌 🚌 🚌 🚌

As Mandie walked into the locker room, she almost gagged at the smell-that famous smell of sweaty gym clothes. She carried the small basket of clothes topped with the bottle of detergent and a box of fabric softener sheets. She prepared the load, emptied the basket and sat down to send a lovely text to Mitch. She sat there, hoping for an immediate reply, but it didn't come. Then she realized it was time for the interview. Today was the day that Mitch interviewed at his Dad's accounting firm. They had stayed up half the night texting about it. Mandie just knew that he was getting that job so that they could get married and set up house and *maybe get a small dog? No, a fish...'* she thought. *'No, the perfect home-just Mitch and me. Oh, well. I'm glad I brought this new Colleen Coble to read while I waited.'*

Just as she finished Chapter Five of her new Christian Romance Novel, the washer finished its final spin. She marked her place, and hopped up to put those wet clothes in the dryer. *'I'm halfway there!'* she thought to herself as she was pleased with the morning that she had had-until she heard the sound. Oh, that sound! That unmistakable sound of cowboy boots, cloppin' down the hall towards the locker room filled her ears with dread! Mandie quickly looked around for another door that led out of there, but sadly, she found none.

When Derek walked in with his gunny sack full of dirty clothes, Mandie stood there like a fox that'd been 'treed'. She really didn't want to be so mean to him last night, but he had to know where he stood with her-absolutely no where. Mitch had warned her about him-how he would try and charm her with his whole cowboy routine-and Mandie had assured him, that there was no contest. She wanted nothing to do with horses, or farms, or boots, or mud, or anything else that had to do with that hick-of-a-man, Derek Jensen. She hated being cruel to him, but it really was the only way that he was going to get the picture.

"Good morning, Mandie," said Derek as he walked in and set his duffle on the table in front of the washer.

"Hey, Tex. What's up this morning?" she asked, as if nothing rude had transpired between them the night before.

"Really, are we doing the 'Tex' thing now?" asked a slightly tired and frustrated Derek.

"Well, you started it," she answered.

"Me?"

"Well, you and Shane. Y'all and y'all's pickin'. Don't dish it, if you can't take it!"

"Oh, I can take it. I'm just not in the mood right now. I'm not gonna bother you; I just wanna get my laundry done, and I'll be on my way," he explained, in a rather sullen tone.

Mandie hadn't ever seen him this way. She truly hoped that nothing was the matter, but on the other hand, she didn't want her genuine friendly concern to be misconstrued as an interest of love, so she treaded carefully. "Well, what's the matter with you today? Are you all outta jokes?"

"Nope. Got plenty of those; but what I don't have is laundry detergent-or a working knowledge of a washing machine-or a dryer," he replied, almost in embarrassment.

"Derek Jensen, O mighty warrior of the road, have you never done your own laundry?" taunted Mandie.

"No; my Moma always took care of matters in the house, not that it's specifically woman's work, mind you, but I never had the need to learn."

Mandie now realized that Derek was truly humbled and embarrassed about asking for help with this. She just couldn't keep kickin' him when he was asking her for help.

"Alright, it's easy. Here, I'll do it for you," she offered.

"Oh, no you don't. You ain't doin' me no favors. Just show me how to work the machine and I'll be just fine," he rebutted.

"Alright already. Just set the knob to the setting for how long you want the clothes to wash-5, 10 or 15 minutes-that is if you want the regular wash cycle-now it's different for permanent press or delicates. You don't have any of those, do ya?" she teased.

"Darlin', if you ain't noticed by now, there ain't nothin' 'bout me that's delicate," he answered in an effort to regain some face with her; but he realized his lie no sooner than it had come out of his mouth. His heart was so delicate that she had nearly broken it in two last night with her snide comments.

"I didn't think so. Now, are you just shootin' for one load, or do you want to separate?" she asked.

"What do you mean?"

"You know, make two separate loads, one dark and one light? That way your colors won't bleed onto your lighter clothes?"

"Well, I don't know. What do you think that I should do?" he asked in genuine interest.

"Well, it all depends on what you're washing. Let's see whatcha got," said Mandie as she tried to peek inside his bag.

"Uh-uh. No way. I'll just wash it all together and take my chances," said Derek as he pulled the strings on the duffle tighter.

Mandie became persistent. "Come on, Tex! Whatcha hidin' in that bag?" she teased with a smile. "...Superman pajamas?"

"No," insisted Derek as Mandie turned him around in circle trying to see what was in that bag. "It ain't fittin'" Derek yelled.

"Oh, are you Mammy, now? Is this, 'Gone With The Wind?' I'm just trying to help you! I wash Shane's stuff all the time!"

"Well, that's different. Shane's your brother, and I'm...well...I'm not. So, just, thank you for your help, but I'll just take care of it myself. You don't need to be seein' another grown man's underclothes, before you're married. It just ain't right. Now, thank you for your help in the matter, and I'll just come back later."

Derek's seriousness about the situation just came crashing down on Mandie like a flash flood and she couldn't help but burst out laughing. She hadn't had such a good laugh in a while.

Derek stood there, in all seriousness, and could not for the life of him figure out what Mandie found so funny. "Mandie, I'm dead serious."

In between breaths, she replied, "I know...I know! Whew!" and then she started up again. She had turned plain giddy with laughter.

"Well, at least I can write this day down as the very first time that I ever made you laugh, even though I can't find even one thing that's funny about this situation."

Mandie finally regained her composure. "It's you! It's your, 'Ma'am you're not lookin' at my drawers, no matter how nice you ask' bit. It's absolutely hilarious! But, I will respect your privacy, sir. I should only have about fifteen minutes left on that load in the dryer. I'm going back to the bus, and you just come and let me know when the buzzer sounds, okay?"

"Alrighty then. If you would leave, I'd greatly appreciate it," he answered in his still serious, solemn tone.

Mandie grabbed her book and staggered, out of the locker room, still giggling and laughing at the spectacle that Derek had caused-all over a little laundry! "See ya later!" she yelled back over her shoulder.

Derek watched as she left the room, and even poked his head out of the door to make sure she was gone before returning to the table with his gunny sack. Then he opened up his bag and dumped it all out on the table-all blue jeans from the piles that he had sorted out in his room.

Later on that afternoon, the whole family took the MARTA up to Atlanta for a quick trip. Everyone ate lunch in the food court at "Underground Atlanta", a full scale underground mall and entertainment strip. Right before Mandie left with her parents to take a quick tour of the Coca-Cola Museum, something special caught her eye at a nearby cart vendor. A magazine rack filled with the latest issues of *Southern Bridal* Magazine. She immediately ran over a purchased a copy.

As usual, this did not go unnoticed by Shane. He punched Derek's elbow. "Look at her, bro. Can't ya see 'em turnin'?"

"Which wheels are these?" asked Derek, jokingly.

"Don't be sassin' the Wheels, bro. The Wheels are mighty important. You can learn many things from the Wheels!" replied Shane, as he moved his hands around like a magician.

"Quit that! You're starting' to look like one of those carnies around here. Now, what wheels, do you see today, sir?" Derek asked.

"The Wheels of Dreams-you did see what she just bought, didn't you?" Shane asked.

"No; I'm trying not to watch her every move, but sometimes, it is hard not to watch her, though. She does command attention."

Shane rolled his eyes. "Ok, Droolie, she bought a wedding magazine-you know filled with big poufy dresses, and names of the country's best caterers, and florists, and..."

"Dude-you know way too much about that stuff," Derek replied with a scoffing laugh.

"Well, I'm trying to look out for her."

"She's too hard-headed. She's gonna have to learn everything the hard way. You know, I think the more time that she spends talkin' with Mitch, the meaner she is to me?" Derek answered.

"I haven't really noticed. Mandie's mean to everybody, I don't even know why you like her!" Shane remarked.

"I think she's purposely pushing me away. I know she can't really hate me that much."

"Well, tell me this: did she pass the laundry test?" Shane asked.

94

"No. She failed. She actually laughed me to scorn. I really thought that she'd just leave the premises when I entered the room."

"Well, that's a good sign that she has some heart left," replied Shane.

"I can't believe you put me up to that. What does 'The Laundry Test' even prove anyways? I can't believe that I actually listened to you. Any child can wash clothes, for Goodness' Sakes!" Derek lamented.

Shane sat silently, pondering that thought-wondering why he had no clue about how to wash clothes. "No matter. This is not good, bro. She failed the laundry test, and now she's buying Bridal magazines; they're getting serious. It sounds like she's getting' too bold. That's what the Laundry Test is about-she's ready to get married. Must I teach you everything? We gotta do something," insisted Shane.

"I'm not doing anything else. I'm staying out of it. Besides, what if they really are supposed to be together?" objected Derek.

"Do you really believe that?" asked Shane, as he sat there with the very first serious look that Derek had ever seen on his face.

"No. But it doesn't mean that I'm the one for her either. She hates me with every fiber of her being. I'm like a brother to her. I'll never be more than that."

"Gee, thanks! What a pal!"

Derek laughed as he realized his unintentional insult. "Sorry, bro."

"Hey, let me see your new cell phone that you got from that Wireless Store," demanded Shane as Derek passed him his new gadget. Derek's cell phone was just about worn out, and he had missed a couple of calls from his Moma, which didn't go over too well. Shane looked it over one good time, and then handed it back to Derek. "So, what all does it do?"

'So what all does it do?' echoed the phone as Derek held down the playback button. He had set it to make a sound recording before handing it to Shane.

"COOL! We could get into so much trouble with this!" said Shane with a devilish smile on his face.

"And that's why I have one, and you don't," answered Derek, as he locked the keypad and placed it in his belt clip holder. "You never know when a little device like this will come in handy."

Chapter Fourteen

The concert that evening went off without a hitch, and Mr. McCormick decided that a night drive to Sevierville was in everyone's best interest. Derek hadn't napped, but he was rested enough, he declared, that he could make the four hour drive in no time flat. So, with Shane offering to ride shotgun with "Mr. Clean-Jeans" as he so wittingly called him, the two young men set up camp for the nocturnal haul.

Mandie, on the other hand, was snuggled in tight, just waiting for her phone to light up with the text from her beloved. The phone sat on her pillow, within reach, as she sat up with her overhead reading lights on delving through the *Southern Bridal* Magazine.

She laid there with her notebook, writing down page numbers, noting the styles, and fabrics of each dress that she thought might be the right one for her. Her thoughts drifted from the dresses that she fawned over, to the interview that Mitch was to have today. *'I wonder how it went. I hope that he got the job. I know that it's just an entry level position, but everyone has to start somewhere; it'll be enough to support the two of us.'* As she flipped the page, another thought occurred to her. *'But, I sure will miss all this. There is something about going to sleep in one town and waking up in another!'*

She continued to flip the ears down on some pages, marking them, and to write the style numbers in her notebook. She recorded information about everything from the Bridal Gowns to the Lingerie, to the floral arrangements, to possible honeymoon destinations! The more that she read, the higher that she flew in the clouds of her dream. It took the beacon light of her cell phone to bring her back to reality.

"Hey, there, Gorgeous. I hope I'm not calling too late," greeted Mitch.

"Oh, no; it's not too late," Mandie answered lovingly. "How are you?"

"Oh, I'm doing okay-I'm just missing you tonight," he remarked. "I sure do wish that you all were rollin' back my way."

97

"Well, we'll be home for Christmas. Maybe you can come up sometime around then?"

"Is that an official invitation?"

"Of course! You know that I want you there."

"Well, I was hoping that you would ask. It's only a couple of weeks away."

"I know! I can't believe that it's November already. We are booked for the end of the Festival this year. Last year, we were booked almost at the beginning of October. I wonder if it will really be any colder. I packed my sweater just in case!"

"I'm sorry that I couldn't come up this year. I've just got a lot of things in the works down here, and it's kinda hard to leave."

Mandie wondered if Mitch was referring to her. She longed for it. "Speaking of things going on down there, how did your job interview go today?"

"Well, that's why I wanted to call you tonight, even though it's so late. I got the job!"

"Oh, Mitch that's wonderful! I just knew that you would!"

"You are talking to the newest scrub at the accounting firm of James & Bigelow-the job is in the mail room."

"Oh, Mitch, that's okay. It's a good start," she consoled. "Your boss will see how hard you work, and I'm sure that you'll be on the way up in no time!"

"I will with a lady like you on my arm. I can't believe that you are actually my girl. You really are something special."

"Mitch, stop! I'm the one that's blessed. You have no idea how long that I've needed someone special in my life. You've been the answer to my prayers! I go through every day just waiting to hear from you."

"Well, I know one thing. This conversation only stuff is for the birds. Where will you be staying?"

"We're staying at the Park Vista in Gatlinburg; Why? I thought that you couldn't get away to come up."

"I'm sending you something. I just upgraded my laptop, and the new one has a built-in webcam, I'm sending you my old one. Now, we can Skype!"

"Mitch! Really? Oh, that'd be wonderful!"

"Seeing your beautiful face right before I close my eyes at night is something that I really want to do, so, I'm mailing it out via overnight mail in the morning. You'll get it before you leave the hotel."

"Thanks. I can't wait to 'see' you!" she said excitedly.

"I know! Me too! What's you next stop after the Festival?" he asked.

"Well, we're actually making a big loop! We're going right on up through Kentucky into southern Ohio, and then circling back around through West Virginia, Virginia, and then back home to good ole' North Carolina for Christmas. Dad's getting pretty good at the promotions, and he hates to turn down any shows, especially since we've got a bus driver now. He hated having to cancel any shows," she explained.

"Speaking of the rogue, has he been bothering you?" Mitch asked sternly.

"No; in fact he wasn't himself at all yesterday. I said something, and I know that it hurt his feelings. I really shouldn't have been so cruel," Mandie reported with a heavy heart.

"No, now remember what I told you. He'll just keep trying unless you really show him how you feel. Let him know that there's no chance. There is no chance, right?"

"Of course not; you said you wanted to make it official, right? And you did! So, there's no chance whatsoever!" she reassured him.

"Well, that's good; because I'm in love with you Mandie McCormick, and I'm not gonna share you with anybody-do you understand? Nobody."

She could hardly believe it. The three words that she desperately wanted to hear! There they were! He loved her!

"Mandie? Are you still there?"

"Yes...I'm still here," she answered.

"Did you hear me? I said, 'I love you'!"

"Yes...I love you, too!" she said as she sighed and fell back onto her pillow.

🚌 🚌 🚌 🚌 🚌

Derek pulled the bus into the hotel parking lot a little after one o'clock in the morning, and the family all stumbled out to their rooms. Only a few hours later, Shane was bouncing off the walls, rearing to go to the amusement park. He just couldn't wait to ride the new 'Barnstormer' ride. Mr. McCormick quickly reminded him, that they were there to do the morning show, and then they could ride some things; but until then, he needed him to be focused.

Upon arriving at Dollywood, the family made their way to the Showstreet Palace Theater where they would be performing. The Kingdom Heirs had already left to go on tour, and so The McCormick's would get to use their stage this day. Derek made his way to the dressing room with Shane, as the theater's crew took care of everything.

The house was packed! Before taking the stage, the family met together in the wings to have prayer, which Derek always loved. The Lord really used this family for His Good, and he loved being a part of it. After Mr. Brian said the final 'Amen', he took a moment to reaffirm the lineup with the stage director. That was when Shane took the opportunity to take a peek from around the curtain-and that was when he saw her.

Derek had begun to walk away to his director's chair sitting in the wings, but was almost slung to the ground when Shane grabbed his arm. "Do you see what I see sitting in the front row?"

Derek peered around the curtain in the same direction that Shane had looked. "See who? That row of girls on this side?"

"Not the row of girls, but her..." he began as his voice began to trail off.

"Like I said-row of girls-you are gonna have to be more specific!" said Derek sarcastically.

"The bubbling blonde beauty right there in the middle! Don't you see her?" Shane said without even turning his head to look at Derek. He was really taken.

"Oh, man. You'd better get it together. You're about to go on stage, and right now, you're the Droolie!" Derek warned as he tried to slap him around.

"Stop! Don't wake me from this dream!" Shane sarcastically sang in his melodramatic tone!

"Come on, Casanova, grab your bass and get out there!" Derek said as he pushed Shane out on the stage behind Mandie.

Shane feebly walked to his stool where he always sat to play the bass for the family as they sang. Mandie started the concert off with one of the family favorites 'The Winning Side'. It was a great opener and the crowd was already shouting and praising the Lord for His Goodness.

During the next song, Shane gathered the courage to look at the beautiful girl on the front row. Much to his delight, he found himself eye to eye with the lovely young lady. She smiled, and he found himself smiling back-almost to the point of laughing, in astonishment. She seemed to be as taken with him as he was with her. 'Well, alright!' he thought to himself as he began to 'kick it up a notch'. He was gonna show this little lady just what he could do. He threw in a little extra run on the bass line here and there.

Then, the next song was Mandie's latest composition, and Shane had to switch to the mandolin. In between switching instruments, Shane flashed the girl another smile, and this time a raised eyebrow, with which to say, 'How about me! I'm playing the mandolin too!'

She returned the same expression as if to say, 'Well! I'm impressed!' The lady sitting next to her, whispered something in her ear, and they both giggled.

This simply threw fuel on Shane's fire. He knew that they were talking about him. As he took his 'shine' on the mandolin during the solo break, he really hammed it up. He picked all over that little instrument and the harder he picked, the further he leaned the stool back until...CRASH! It was too late. The family stopped in astonishment, and the crowd was in stitches! Derek ran on stage from his chair in the wings and helped Shane up. His face was as read as a beet-and he couldn't even look at the girl!

"Are you okay?" Derek asked quietly with a straight face.

Shane simply nodded. But then it happened. Even Shane couldn't stop himself from laughing!

When Mr. McCormick, saw that Shane was in fact alright, he tried to get the show back together. He took his microphone and said, "You know, the Bible says in Proverbs, 'Pride goeth before destruction, and ...and uh, how does that end, there, Shane..."

"...And a haughty spirit before a fall," Shane answered with a little laugh. "I'm sorry y'all! I guess I just got carried away!"

The audience started clapping to let Shane know that they still loved him! "Alright now, son, let's take it from the chorus!" Mr. McCormick said as he rallied the family back into song, and in turn back on track!

🚌 🚌 🚌 🚌 🚌

After the concert, and a firm scolding for Shane from Mr. McCormick about 'paying attention and not trying to impress girls', the family decided to grab a bite of lunch from 'Aunt Granny's Buffet'. The family, of course now dressed in their street clothes, blended right in with the crowd, and they were able to slip in unnoticed to the restaurant. The food was delicious, and soon the family was enjoying the day as if nothing had happened.

Shane had a 'hankerin' for some more fried chicken and macaroni and cheese, or so he said, so he made his way back to the buffet and began to help himself. The hair stood up on the back of his neck as he heard a sweet, soft voice speak behind him.

"Excuse me...Mr. McCormick?"

Shane turned around to see his lovely lady from the front row. "Oh! It's you!" he said with delight.

"Are you okay? I'm so sorry! I feel like it was entirely my fault, distracting you the way that I did. I'm really kinda embarrassed..." she said as she looked at the ground.

"No, no, no!" Shane said as he gently touched her arm to take her attention. "It was all my fault. If I hadn't been trying to show off for you, I wouldn't have fallen. God has a good way of humbling us, doesn't He? Or me, at least!"

The young lady laughed, which brought a much needed smile to Shane's face as well.

"And please, call me Shane. Mr. McCormick is my Daddy!"

"Okay," answered the girl as she began to become star struck like she was in the concert.

"And what can I call you?" Shane asked.

"Oh! I'm so sorry. I'm Gwen. Gwen Rhodes." She extended her hand to shake his, and he quickly swapped his plate to his left hand to oblige her.

"Well, Miss Gwen, won't you come and join me and my family for lunch?" Shane invited as he turned and grabbed another chicken breast as he continued his conversation. He nodded his head for Gwen to follow him around the buffet.

"I'd love to, but I don't know if my parents will let me! You see, they brought me here for my birthday. My brother got married last year, and now it's just me at home—and of course, them too," she said out of nervousness.

"And where is home?" Shane asked.

"Sunset, North Carolina," she answered shyly.

"No kidding! That's only a couple of hours away from my hometown of..."

"Campbell's Grove. Yeah I know. My brother just married a girl from your church-you might know her by her maiden name, Michelle Brolin?"

"No way! Mr. Stan's girl? That's so cool! We heard about the wedding, but we haven't been home in a while; in fact the last time that we were home, I don't remember seeing Michelle," Shane mentioned as he dipped some macaroni and cheese on his plate. "Won't you have some?" he offered.

Gwen looked confused at first, but then grabbed a plate, "Sure. It's my favorite. They were up at our church, visiting for the weekend. She mentioned that they were missing your family that Sunday."

"Would you mind if I met your parents? You probably would after this morning's incidents!" Shane said with a laugh.

Gwen smiled. "No, not at all. They're right over here."

Shane looked over at his table to find every pair of eyes, including his parents, gazing at him, in disbelief at how he was carrying on this conversation with the petite blonde. He rolled his eyes and mouthed the words, 'I'll be back' to them as he followed Gwen to her table. They all looked at each other as confused as can be.

Gwen led Shane to her parents' table. Her Dad looked up and saw them coming. He stood up to greet him. "How are you, young man?"

"Better, sir, thank you," answered Shane with a smile.

"I'm Pastor Rhodes, Gwendolyn's Dad."

"I prefer Gwen," she said aside to Shane.

"I'm Shane McCormick, sir."

"It's nice to meet you," said Pastor Rhodes.

"Pastor Rhodes. *Pastor*," marveled Shane as he looked at Gwen. 'You didn't say that you were the Pastor's daughter."

"Does that matter, son?" Pastor Rhodes asked remembering how Shane had been distracted in the concert-realizing now that it was more than likely because of his daughter sitting in the front row.

"Not at all, sir. I'm honored to meet you and your family."

"Daddy, Shane is from Campbell's Grove. He goes to the Lighthouse," explained Gwen.

"Pastor Creighton's church? Well, just what about that! Isn't that something? My son lives there now since he got a job transfer. He's working for Max's Automotive World. Pull up a chair, son," offered Pastor Rhodes.

"Thank you, sir," said Shane as he diligently obeyed.

Shane and Gwen sat there for the next twenty minutes talking about Campbell's Grove and remarking about how much you miss when you're on the road. Shane could have sat there and listened to stories of home all day, but the tales were cut short when his family approached. He was suddenly reminded of the rest of the day to be had.

After introductions were made, Pastor Rhodes and Mr. McCormick agreed to let the young people go do some riding, while they enjoyed Craftsman's valley, with their wives. As long as they could meet back together around six o'clock for supper, Gwen could go along with them, much to Shane's delight.

As the young people made their way from the restaurant, Shane couldn't help but notice how close they were to the 'Barnstormer', and he had just been aching to ride it, so the group made that their first stop. As the four made their way to the line, Mandie stood in a separate line from Derek. Since Derek knew that they had a while to wait, he took the opportunity to try and make sense of the madness. As she stood staring straightforward, he leaned over the bars separating them.

"Mandie, is it really true that you hate me so much, that you would face riding this terrifying thing all by yourself, just so you don't have to ride with me?" he asked.

"It's not so bad," she replied as she looked at the ground.

"Mandie, look at me," asked Derek. "I know what your boyfriend's been tellin' ya. I know he thinks that I'm trying to steal ya away, but, you've made it pretty clear from day one that you're not interested in me, so, let's just call a truce right here, and right now. I won't pick about Mitch anymore, and maybe you won't have to be so mean to me anymore. Maybe you'll even end this silliness and ride with me today. Shane's definitely preoccupied, and we'll both be pretty miserable if we don't do something," he reasoned.

"Well, I don't know..." she muttered, pouting, knowing that Derek was right. She hated it when he was right. And she really didn't hate him-she hated the fact that he had her dead to rights. He knew that she was purposely being rude to him to deter him. She hated the fact that he was onto her.

"Mandie...Come on-let's be friends-just for today! You might even find that you like being my friend!" Derek offered.

"Well, if you'll stop being so 'hokey' about it, I'll give it a shot," she answered reluctantly.

"Yee haw!" Derek yelled as he jumped over the bars into Mandie's line.

"That does it! Get back over the there, right now," she started.

"Oh, no Ma'am. You said you were gonna be my friend today," he said loudly, trying to embarrass her-and it was working.

"And you said that we were calling a truce!" she reminded him. "That means, no more embarrassing, loud, 'hick-like hollerin'! You got it?" she demanded.

"Well, yes, Ma'am," Derek said, holding his Stetson over his heart.

Mandie spent the rest of the afternoon as Derek's riding partner. Some of it she actually enjoyed. He wasn't all that bad. And she knew that her mother wasn't really trying to push them together-in fact, now that she actually thought about it, her mother hadn't mentioned anything to her about Derek since that very first day at their home. Perhaps she was being mean for no reason at all.

Even though Mitch was after her to deter him, there was no need. He knew that she belonged to Mitch, and that's all he needed to know. Mandie decided that today would indeed be a truce for her as well. She would be nice to Derek-as long as he didn't begin to pursue her.

The young people made their way all around the park. Around five-thirty, Derek informed Shane that they needed to start making their way back to the restaurant, the rally point for the parents. The closer that it got to six o'clock, the heavier Shane's heart became. He couldn't believe how one day-one look-could change everything. When they reached the restaurant, Shane really had to put his game face on. He and Gwen exchanged phone numbers and emails, and said their 'good-byes'.

As the McCormick's left the restaurant, Mandie decided that she wanted to take a stroll down Craftman's Valley to the Custom Glassworks, where the artisans practiced glass-blowing. So, the family walked along together, just a tad weary from the day. They stood there and watched the master perform his craft. Mr. Brian remarked, "Look how he has to heat it up so. The Lord allows us to go through trials, and temptations, so that he can mold us, and breathe His Spirit upon us, while we're soft to take it; and look at the beautiful result."

Mrs. Margie added, "And look at all the different colors. He brings so many different people into our lives, to bring out the best in us; to change our lives forever," she said as she looked at Shane.

"I sure made an idiot of myself today," Shane muttered.

"Well, you had a good come back; I saw a different side to you today, Shane," remarked Derek.

"For once, I think that I'd have to agree with Derek," said Mandie. "You were quite the gentleman today."

"Well, don't you go expecting it for you, Missy. Sisters don't get that royal treatment," teased Shane.

"Well, they should," said Mrs. Margie, as she walked by her husband towards the gift shop. A silent Shane followed his dad in the same direction.

Derek turned to Mandie, "So, you actually agreed with me today?"

Mandie smiled. "Don't let it go to your head!" she replied as she turned in kind, walking into the gift shop. She looked around for a special little knick-knack to mark the day; the day she saw her brother fall-in love.

"Pride goeth before destruction, and an haughty spirit before a fall."

Proverbs 16:18

Chapter Fifteen

The next morning, Mandie was up at the front desk, bright and early. "Excuse me, I'm expecting a package. My name is Mandie McCormick. Has anything come for me?" she asked eagerly.

The desk attendant checked her notes. "Yes. The night manager left a note saying that the box in the office came at the end of the day yesterday. I'll be right back with it."

"Thank you so much," she answered. As she stood waiting, she heard her name echoing from the breakfast area. It was her parents, having their morning coffee, and reading their Bibles together. Mandie waved, and motioned that she'd be over in just a moment. *'Oh, I hope this Skype thing works. I can't wait to see Mitch!'* she thought to herself as she watched her parents. She longed for the day when she'd be able to sit at her own kitchen table-across from her husband-and share the very same love that her parents shared.

"Here it is, Ma'am. Sorry about your wait," said the attendant as she handed over the small box. Mandie thanked her and walked over to her parents' table. "Mornin' y'all!"

"Mornin', angel. Whatcha got in the box?" Mrs. Margie asked.

"It's a webcam from Mitch. He sent it here so that we could 'Skype' each other," she answered.

"What in the world does that mean?" asked Mr. Brian.

"It's like chatting online, but you can see who you are talking to!" Mandie replied.

"Oh, how nice, Mandie. Now you can actually see each other from the road. Nice. That was very creative thinking on his part. I must say, I'm impressed."

This really meant a lot to Mandie. From the way her Moma had always talked about Mitch, she thought that she'd never come around. She was so happy to find that her Mom was pleased.

At that moment, Shane and Derek joined the family for breakfast. "Good mornin' all," Derek saluted.

"Good morning," replied the party.

"Shane, you're mighty quiet today," remarked Mrs. Margie.

"Yes, ma'am." Suddenly, his attentions turned to Mandie and her package. "Whatcha got in the box?"

"It's a webcam that Mitch sent to me. Now we can Skype," she said.

It was like night and day-the change that occurred on Shane's face. "Will you please let me use it? Gwen asked me if I had one, and of course I don't; but she does! Mandie please can I use it?"

"Oh! Now you want to be all nice to me! When I have something you want, you can be all nice," teased Mandie.

"Now, Mandie, that ain't right. Don't do that to your brother!" admonished Derek. "Can't you see he's tormented!" he continued.

"I sure can see that! Why do you think it's so fun! You reap what you sow, dear brother!" she answered with a devilish smile.

Mrs. Margie looked at her daughter with raised eyebrows.

"So, of course I'll be letting you use it-sometimes-just until you can get your own!" she emphasized.

The smile radiated from his face like the morning sun. "Thank you! Thank you so much!" said Shane.

"Mandie, did you bring your laptop down, this morning? I'd be glad to hook it up for you," offered Derek.

"No, actually, I didn't want to spill anything on it."

Mrs. Margie suddenly realized, "Ooh! I left my medicine upstairs. Give me your key card, and I'll pick it up for you when I come back."

"Thanks, Moma. I appreciate it," said Mandie as she stood to get her a quick plate of breakfast.

Shane quickly began the questions once Mandie had left the table. "Do you think it's too early to text her? It's seven-thirty. Surely she's up by now."

"Son, seven-thirty is too early in the morning to be calling anyone. I wouldn't call until at least after nine o'clock in the morning," answered Mr. McCormick.

"Yeah, Daddy, but we're talking about texting. It's a little bit different," Shane argued.

"It's still not polite, son. It's too early," Mr. McCormick said as he shook his head.

"How soon do you want to leave today, Mr. Brian?" asked Derek as he took a bite of his waffle.

"Around nine, maybe by nine-thirty or so. That will get us to Louisville just in time to take the stage for our dress rehearsal," replied Mr. Brian as he pulled out the chair for his returning wife.

"Here you are, Mandie," she said as she passed the briefcase containing the laptop to her daughter. "I suggest perhaps, moving to another table, without any food or drink?"

"Um," Mandie agreed as she swallowed her Cranberry Blend. "Good idea."

"I'll throw the trash away and help you," said Derek as he stood and cleared their area. He walked to her table after disposing of the breakfast plates, and sat down to install the webcam for her. As Derek tinkered with the PC, Mandie sent a text to Mitch for him to be ready-that they were gonna give it a test run over the hotel WiFi.

Shane stayed at the table with his parents. "Look at 'em. Can't you see 'em turnin?" he asked.

Mrs. Margie took the bait. "See what turnin'?"

"The Wheels," Shane replied in his usual fashion.

"What wheels?" asked Mrs. Margie.

"The Wheels of Love," answered Mr. McCormick, much to Shane's surprise.

"How'd you know?" Shane asked.

"The same way you knew, Shane; the way he looks at her; the way he picks at her all the time; and he's got it bad, too. Any man who will sit there and fix up some contraption so that the woman he loves can talk to another man is either lovesick or crazy. He'd do anything to see her happy," said Mr. McCormick.

Mandie clapped her hands in delight-Mitch had popped up on her screen. Derek moved out of the chair, and let Mandie sit in front of the webcam, and quickly showed her how to use it.

"See-he's got it bad. And the real shame is that her Wheels aren't spinning back," Mr. Brian lamented.

🚌 🚌 🚌 🚌 🚌

Derek was right on time for Mr. McCormick as he had the Family Tour Bus leaving the hotel parking lot at nine-thirty on the nose. The clan was bound for Louisville, Kentucky for their part of a Gospel Music Celebration sponsored by several area churches. The family would be sharing the stage for three days with two other performing groups, The Griffin Family and an 'a cappella' quartet who called themselves, 'One Accord.'

The four and half hour drive to the Louisville Memorial Auditorium was uneventful, as the family ran over their line-up for the concert that night in the upper lounge. Derek took advantage of the opportunity of solitude.

While he drove alone, he was busy thinking and praying. He saw how Mandie's face just lit up whenever the Skype started working. *'She must really care about him; Lord, I pray that Your will be done; whether she be with me, or him, or someone else. I only want to do what's right. I pray that You'll keep taking care of my family back home, and my new family here. Please guide Shane in the right way to go Lord, as he certainly seems to be in love. Thank you for placing me here. I thought that it would be harder for me to leave Tennessee this morning, but I really feel at home here with this family, and I thank you for that, Lord. Thank you for this new friendship with Mandie. Even if it never develops into anything else, Lord, I thank You for it.'*

The night's concert was a success, and something happened that night that had never happened before. Shane wanted to skip autograph session. He wanted to get back to the bus so that he could call Gwen! Mrs. Margie remarked to herself, *'Now whose Wheels of Love are spinning!'*

The next day, the McCormick's decided to tour the town, and the unanimous vote was for the Louisville Slugger Museum and Factory. The family had a wonderful time touring the museum and factory. They were able to see Babe Ruth's Louisville Slugger that he used to hit twenty-one home runs-they could even see the notches that Ruth carved in the top of the bat himself! At the end of the factory tour, they all received miniature souvenir Sluggers! The tour was interesting, but Shane, Derek, and even Mandie couldn't wait to hit the batting cages! They were able to test out the latest line of aluminum baseball and softball bats! Shane was the first to step in the cage and went twelve for twelve! The family couldn't believe it, and neither could Shane. Derek did well, eight for twelve, but when it came around to Mandie, it was a different story.

"Mandie, really, how could you miss all of them? Just put the stick out there and catch one!" blurted Shane.

"I guess I'm just really out of practice. I want another round; Derek, slip another token in there; no one's waiting," she begged.

Derek did better than that. He grabbed a helmet, stepped in the cage, and then dropped the next token. He walked up behind Mandie, who was waiting for the machine to start shooting out softballs again. She still had the helmet on, and didn't hear him walk up behind her-he almost scared her to death.

"Ooh! What are you doing?!" she screamed.

"Just hold the bat like this..." Derek began as he placed his arms around her, grabbing the bat along with her. "Now, just keep it level, you need a level cut."

Mandie held on to the bat and waited for the pitch. When the time was right, she felt Derek's arm pulling back slightly, which she did also, finally swinging. The ball went sailing up towards the nets. Still, Derek stood there, hanging on.

'He can let go any time now,' Mandie thought to herself. The second pitch came, and he helped her again. Again, she hit the ball. "I got it, now, Derek; you can let go," Mandie yelled.

"Are you sure?" he replied. "Let's try one more!"

Mandie began to get angry. *'Boy, a couple of days of friendship, and he thinks that he can move right in for the kill!'* she thought to herself as she sprung around, and pushed Derek back. "Thanks, but I got it!" she yelled as she quickly turned back around to catch the next pitch. WHAP! Mandie sent that one sailing!

"See! All you needed was a little pep in your step!" Derek said as he stepped back towards the back of the cage.

The McCormick's just stood back and laughed-and Shane led the choir! The more they laughed, the harder Mandie swung; and through her rage, she improved her batting average!

The next day, the family was able to get a last minute booking on the *Belle of Louisville* riverboat. There was a cancellation an hour before the departure for the lunch cruise, and the McCormick's were happy to take the tickets! After an exciting morning of traveling up the Ohio River, the family returned to the Auditorium's dressing for some rest before afternoon dress rehearsal. Mandie took a minute to get in touch with Mitch via Skype. They chatted for a moment, until Mitch had to ask.

"Baby, you look like something's bothering you. Is there anything you want to tell me?"

"Well, it's just that I thought that things were okay with Derek, but yesterday he helped me out in the batting cage, and at first I didn't think much about it, but, then it got a little weird," she answered.

"What do you mean?" Mitch asked.

"Well, he put his arms around me to help me hold the bat more level, which helped; but then it made me feel uncomfortable. I know he was just trying to help..." she explained.

"Look, I told you the other day, I don't care if he called a 'truce' or not, he's after you. We, uh, 'had words' back on Jekyll Island before I left, and I'm telling you that he's after you."

"You never told me that y'all got into an argument. I'm gonna talk to him! He can't do that!" she said angrily.

"No! Don't let him know that I told you! It could make matters worse! Just stay away from him!" Mitch warned.

"Well, I tried today; he followed me around the riverboat like a lost puppy! Maybe it's not all that I'm thinking it is. Shane did spend a great amount of time on the phone with Gwen today, perhaps he just felt left out, that's all. Yes; that has to be what it is. Please just ignore me. I'm just imagining things."

"I don't like it. I just can't stand him being there with you when I can't be! You let me know if he tries anything again," Mitch commanded.

"But, that's just it, Mitch. He didn't 'try' anything! I'm sorry that I mentioned it. There's nothing to worry about. Please just forget about it," Mandie begged, as she began to worry about the stew that Mitch was getting in. He had really turned out to be the jealous type-extremely possessive. "I need to go. We are having an afternoon rehearsal, and I've got to get ready."

"Ok, Doll. I'm serious now, if I need to know anything else, tell me. I can't have that hillbilly harassing my lady!"

Mandie laughed. "Okay. Talk to you later."

"Goodbye, dear. I love you," Mitch closed.

"Me too," replied Mandie as she clicked the window closed. *'Well, I guess I know what I half to do. I can't let him get too close. It's just not fair to him.'*

"Therefore all things whatsoever ye would that men should do to you, do ye even so to them: for this is the law and the prophets."

Matthew 7:12

Chapter Sixteen

After Louisville, the bus rolled another two hours or so up to Lebanon, Ohio for a week-long camp meeting. The sponsoring church had facilities that allowed the bus to be parked on the church property, which was very helpful to the McCormick's. The week was filled with fantastic preaching, and music from other Southern Gospel families and groups from all over the country. On Thursday morning, Shane had made his way to the foyer of the sanctuary to talk to some of the new friends he had made. In mid-sentence, he felt someone quickly step up behind him and place their hands over his eyes.

"Guess who?" the delicate voice asked.

"No way!" exclaimed Shane as he spun around to see his beautiful lady. "Gwen! How in the world?!..."

"Well, I knew that you'd be here, and my Daddy has always wanted to come up to this Camp Meeting, so I..." explained Gwen as Shane interrupted.

"So you begged, and whined until you got your way?" he asked.

Gwen looked playfully shocked at first, but then she innocently smiled and nodded.

"Good girl!" remarked Shane as he reached his arm lightly around to guide her through the crowded foyer to the sanctuary.

While walking towards their seats, Gwen saw an old friend. "Stephanie!"

"Gwen! When did you get here?" her friend replied as she ran to her for a hug.

"Just now! Daddy and Mama are parking the car and coming in any minute!" Gwen replied. "Stephanie, you know Shane McCormick, don't you?"

"Well, we've not been formally introduced, even though we've been enjoying his family's music all week!" she answered as she reached for his hand.

"It's nice to formally meet you Miss Stephanie Patterson," said Shane as she shook her hand. Turning his attention to Gwen, "We've shared the stage with the

Patterson family before at other meetings. I didn't know you two were friends!"

"Oh, yes! We meet two years ago on the 'Singing At Sea" Cruise. We try to keep in touch with Facebook and email..."

"But sometimes it's difficult!" Stephanie filled in. "Will you be sitting with Shane?"

"Of course she will!" Shane added as Gwen giggled.

"Okay, I'll bring my Bible and purse back here; that is, if that's okay with Shane?"

Shane rolled his eyes in jest; "Okay-if you must!" he said and then finished by laughing. He motioned for Gwen to have a seat. "I'm so glad you're here! I really missed you, and I didn't think that I'd get to see you before we came home for Christmas break!"

"Well, to tell you the truth, I just couldn't wait. I must confess to you-I did tell Stephanie that I was coming, but she didn't know about 'us'."

"Wow. I really like the way you said that just now, 'US'!" Shane reflected aloud.

Gwen blushed. "Well, she's been wanting to meet someone here all week."

"Oh, really? Anyone I know?" asked Shane.

"Uh-hum. It's Derek. She said that she'd seen him here all week, and that she really loves the 'whole cowboy' thing that he has going when the guys are outside after the services."

"No kidding!"

"But, I wasn't sure what to tell her, because I thought maybe he and Mandie were talking," Gwen suggested.

Shane laughed. "Oh, my. You couldn't be any more wrong. Mandie absolutely detests him."

"But they got along so well that day at the park! I was sure that they were a couple. The way that they looked at each other..."

"Each other? Now, I can understand Derek, but Mandie?" Shane asked.

"Well yes. I caught a few glances, and a lady knows," Gwen explained.

"I see," Shane remarked as he filed that thought for future reference. Just then, Stephanie approached their pew. "Stephanie, Gwen has enlightened me to your little problem."

Stephanie looked at Gwen aghast! "Gwen! You told?"

"I'm sorry. I had to keep Shane in the loop. He can introduce you, right?"

"I'd be glad to, after the service this morning. Derek was on the phone with his Mom, when I left the bus. He hasn't seen her in well over a month now, and sometimes it's hard to cut the conversation short. He'll be here any minute now. In fact, let's move down a little, and I'll save this seat for him here on the end, so that he can slip in." Shane suggested, as Stephanie's face radiated with delight.

As predicted, Derek did swoop in at the last minute for the morning service. As he sat down, he noticed Gwen and Stephanie sitting beside Shane, and he cast a surprised, but glad and smiling 'hello' to Gwen. He leaned over to Shane's ear, "The Lord gives us wonderful surprise blessings, doesn't He?"

"He sure does," answered Shane, as he thought about how he would introduce his friend to the lovely lady on Gwen's right-hand side.

After the service, the young people stood up to gather their items and make their way to the fellowship hall for lunch. Shane was never one to beat around the bush, so he jumped right to it.

"Derek, there is a young lady whom I would like you to meet. Miss Stephanie Patterson, please meet Mr. Derek Jensen," he said as he directed their attentions to each other.

"Ma'am, it's nice to meet you," Derek said as he gave his customary nod.

"Same here," replied Stephanie as she smiled incessantly.

"Derek here is our Minister of Transportation," continued Shane as the group chuckled.

"Wow, Minister of Transportation. That, um, has a pretty good ring to it!" Derek sported.

"Well, now that we all know each other, Shall we go to lunch?" Shane asked in his false British accent as he extended his arm to Gwen for escort.

Gwen giggled and accepted his arm, "Oh, yes, let's!" she said as she played along. Shane escorted Gwen towards the door.

Derek turned and motioned to Stephanie, "After you, Ma'am!" as he presented the way.

"Thank you," she replied as she turned to follow Shane and her friend.

🚌 🚌 🚌 🚌 🚌

After the service had dismissed, the congregation separated for lunch. Mandie raced to the fellowship hall, grabbing her plate to go, and raced back to the bus so that she could try to Skype Mitch for a lunch date. They had kept this lunch date daily during the work week, and she had really come to look forward to it.

"So, I've got some good news," she began.

"Oh, really? Well, spill," he answered.

"Well, I don't think you'll have Derek to worry about any more."

"And how do you figure that? I happen to know first-hand that he doesn't give up easily." Mitch replied remembering the encounter with Derek as he left Jekyll Island over a month ago.

"Well, I saw him and Shane, along with Shane's girl, and her friend, and I think that Shane's trying to set him up with her. He looked like he was having a good time, so, at the very least now he'll be distracted," Mandie explained.

"Well, I wouldn't count on it. Like I said before, for the few days that I spent with him, I found him to be extremely determined."

"Well, don't you worry about a thing. When I'm done with him, he'll wish that he'd never even thought about me. I can't wait until he gets on the bus tonight. Now that I have something to hold over him, it'll be a lot easier to put some distance between us."

The evening service went well, and the McCormick's finally made their way to the bus for the night. Much to their surprise, Mr. Brian was waiting at the door for everyone, directing them all to the upper lounge for a 'family meeting'. Those words: 'family meeting' seemed to ring terror in the hearts of Mandie, Shane, and even Derek!

As the three made their way upstairs, Shane spoke up, "Why do I feel like I've been sent to the principal's office?"

"Those were my thoughts, exactly," Derek echoed.

"Oh, you're having thoughts now?" asked Mandie as she began to poke him.

"From time to time," he answered in an attempt to simply absorb it.

Mrs. McCormick walked right in and took a seat.

"Mom! What's going on? We haven't had a family meeting in like, forever!" Mandie remarked.

"I'm not sure. I'm just as surprised as you are," she confessed.

Just about then, Mr. McCormick entered the lounge. You could have heard a pin drop. "Well, good. We're all here. Now we can get started."

"Dad, whatever I did, I'm really sorry," Shane began, as the group began to laugh; even Mr. Brian.

"Son, it's nothing like that-not this time any ways," he said with a smile, picking on his son.

"Well, I've got some terrific news, some bad news, and some good news-but it's all kind of mixed up so-I've just start at the beginning. We've been invited to sing at the 'West Coast Gospel Jubilee' at the Greek Theater in Los Angeles in January."

The group gasped! No one could believe it! Mrs. McCormick spoke first, "California? Brian, we've never been west before!"

"I know, and I'm working really hard re-arranging some of the schedule to accommodate the trip. Most of the pastors have been very helpful. We only had a few shows on the docket for after New Year's anyways. The Lord is really opening some doors for us."

"So, what's the bad news?" Shane asked.

"Well, the bad news is that we won't be able to spend New Year's at home. I had planned to be at home for the Watch Night Service at the Lighthouse with Pastor Creighton, but instead we will be spending it at Pastor Bledsoe's church in Augusta," he explained.

Mandie's face could have illuminated the entire town! "Oh, Daddy that's wonderful news! I'll get to see Mitch at Christmas and at New Year's!"

"Nope, I think he had it right the first time-bad news!" taunted Shane.

For the first time, Derek spoke up. "I'm a little confused. You said there was some terrific news, some bad news, and some good news. So what's left? L.A. sounds pretty terrific to me, and getting on the road a little earlier than expected is really not that bad, so, what's the good news?"

"Well, actually, the good news was about the Greek Theater. Are you ready for the terrific news?" teased Mr. Brian. The group was sitting on the edge of their seats. "I met one of the representatives from Templeton Tours today, and after we make our way back from the West coast, we will have to make our way down to Jacksonville, Florida to catch the 'Singing At Sea Cruise'!"

The entire group exploded in applause and cheering, and laughter-all except for Derek. "Excuse me, sir!" he managed to get out before running down the stairs to the restroom. He had already broken out in a cold sweat, and he barely made it to the restroom before he started heaving.

"What in the world?" asked Mr. McCormick.

"Do you think he's coming down with something?" asked Mrs. Margie.

"Guys: I think that Derek has a problem with water. I noticed back down in Georgia, when we rode over to St. Simon's Island that Derek didn't hardly breathe when we were on that bridge-and he mentioned something about 'all that water'. I thought something was up, but we were just getting to know him, so I didn't really ask him about it," Shane confessed.

At first, Mandie thought she'd hit the gold mine. *'A brave cowboy, afraid of water? Oh, this will be too easy'* but then, the Lord smote her thoughts, and she realized that there was something more there, and that this was not something that she should use against him.

The group turned quiet as they heard Derek's boots clomping up the stairwell. As he walked back into the upper lounge, the family tried not to stare at him, but he looked absolutely green!

"Derek, honey, are you okay? You don't look so good," asked Mrs. Margie.

"Yes, Ma'am. I'm gonna be okay," he answered.

Mr. McCormick treaded lightly, and asked, "Son, are you gonna be able to handle this? I was actually able to secure a ticket for your Mother and your Uncle Joe. You've been such a blessing to us that I wanted to be able to give you something in return! A family reunion would be in order, or at least I thought so," Mr. Brian explained.

"Oh, thank you, sir. That's wonderful. I don't deserve such a blessing. Everything will be fine, and I will be able to go, sir. Thank you again," he replied as he took his handkerchief and wiped the returning sweat from his brow. "Everything will be alright."

"*Many waters cannot quench love, neither can the floods drown it:*"

Song of Solomon 8:7a

Chapter Seventeen

The Camp Meeting ended with a bang as several souls were saved, and the Lord seemed to do a mighty work. The McCormick's saddled up and said their goodbyes. As the crew headed towards Zanesville, Ohio for a three-day concert, Mandie, Shane and their parents retreated to their cabins for a little rest-it was only a two hour drive, and there was no need to drag out the instruments for practice. There would be plenty of time to rehearse once they reached the Auditorium.

Shane spent his morning emailing Gwen. After he had finished his love letter, he hollered up the aisle for Derek. "Hey, Derek; I'm done with the computer, you want me to email Stephanie for you while I've got it up?"

Mandie's ears perked up. "Shane! I'm surprised at you! You wouldn't want to dictate your love letter to Gwen for someone else to type up, would you?"

Derek jumped right in. "Who said anything about a 'love letter'? Stephanie is a nice young lady, and that's all. She gave me her email address, and I'll send her a line or two to be polite, but that's all."

Mandie just couldn't let it go. "Oh, now, don't try to hide it there, Tex. You know you've found your little lady. Now, I'm trying to help you out with Shane. You need your privacy just like everyone else. Shane, he can't dictate a letter through you like that. A man can't say everything he needs to if someone else is listening!"

"I never do have any problem speaking my mind, Miss Mandie. You ought to know that by now," he argued. "Shane, come up here, and take down this letter for me!" Derek ordered.

Mandie simply shook her head. "Men. Y'all are simply ignorant in the ways."

"Says you!" Shane said in defense as he walked up to the driver's cab with the laptop. "Okay, Derek. Now, what do you want to say?"

"I don't care. Just give a generic 'It was nice meeting you letter'. That will be fine," he whispered so that Mandie couldn't hear.

"Are you using this girl to make Mandie jealous?" Shane asked with a greedy smile on his face.

"Well, now I wouldn't call it that-I am being polite in that I'm responding to her request to write, but I won't be emailing her daily. She's just not the one for me. Don't worry. I'm not one to string anyone along. You can write that I enjoyed meeting her, but that I'm involved with someone right now."

"Involved?" Shane asked with a curious look. "Is that what you call this? She hates your guts."

"I know. But, that's where I'm at-involved," Derek answered in all depressing honesty. "I can't very well be out looking for someone to start a relationship with, when I don't have a heart to give away. It's not mine to give. Someone else already has it. I can't help what she does with it," he stated with a forlorn look on his face.

Shane looked down at the ground in sympathy for his friend. He wished that the Wheels of Love would spin back for him, like they had with Gwen. His thoughts were broken as Derek spoke again.

"But-Mandie doesn't have to know what my letter says, or when I go to check my email every day, she doesn't have to know if I'm reading a letter from Stephanie, or if I'm reading spam!"

"I see. Do you really think that she'll be jealous?" Shane asked.

"I don't know. But, it's worth a shot! It gives me something to look forward to!"

"Why do you torture yourself, Bro? Maybe you should try talking to this girl for a while. You never know!" Shane suggested.

"Well, I wouldn't want to lead her on. That wouldn't be fair."

"Well, it's also not fair to you to spend your life pining for someone who doesn't love you," Shane answered bluntly, but honestly, for his friend's own good.

"I see your point. Okay. I'll give it a while, and we'll see how it goes. That's all I can promise."

"That's all I ask!" Shane said as he began to set up the email. "So, what do you want me to type?"

"I'm not sure now. I'll email her tonight, when I've had more time to think about it."

"Fair enough," Shane answered as he made his way back to his bunk with the laptop. As he passed Mandie's bunk, he couldn't resist. "Um, Um! That was some juicy letter!"

"Juicy? Please! They only just met a couple of days ago!" she retorted.

"Sometimes, that's all it takes! Don't you believe in *love at first sight*?" Shane said in his falsetto as he batted his eyelashes. "You know *I do!*"

"Maybe for you and Gwen, but not for ole' Tex, there."

"How do you know?" Shane teased.

"I know he doesn't love her." Mandie said as she continued flipping through her Bridal Magazine, turning down pages.

"Why-because Derek couldn't possibly love anyone but you?" Shane rubbed in.

"He doesn't love me. He only thinks he does. He's in love with an illusion of me. He doesn't know the real me to love!"

"Mandie, he knows more about the real you from living with this family on this bus than ole' Mr. Wonderful knows about you. To tell you the truth, I think he's the one in love with the illusion. You'd better be careful with that," Shane answered as he pulled his divider closed for a quick nap.

His words rang in her heart and mind, and she became afraid. *'What if Shane is right? What if Mitch is in love with an illusion? Does he really know the real me? And, what's worse is, am I in love with an illusion? Do I know the real Mitchell Collins?'*

🚌 🚌 🚌 🚌 🚌

The family spent that night and the next two days in Zanesville in concert. The first two days, the family spent on the bus, resting from the Camp Meeting the week before; but on the last morning, they ventured out to try and tour something of the locality, as they always did. That was part of what made their life so great. Not only did they get to serve the Lord through music, which they loved, but, they got to see so many of the wonderful places that God allowed to grow in America.

There in Zanesville, they were able to tour the P.U.R.E. Center: The Putnam Underground Railroad Education Center. This was a museum devoted to educating the public about the Underground Railroad. It contained many artifacts from Africa and the Civil War Era.

Mrs. McCormick was so moved by the museum, that she asked Mr. Brian if they could change their line-up for the evening to include the song, "Thank God I'm Free". That night on stage, she remarked how it was really something how some of the slaves made it to freedom through the help of God's people putting themselves in harm's way to help folks that they didn't even know. Through tears, she compared it witnessing for Jesus. "You know, folks, as we approach the Thanksgiving holiday next week, I think about things that I am thankful for. I am thankful for my being saved, first of all, and I am thankful for my freedom. Today, at the P.U.R.E. Center, I thought about some things. We often lack the courage to tell others about Christ, because we are worried that they will be rejecting Him by rejecting us. They are not hurting us; they are hurting themselves, and grieving the heart of Jesus. Those brave souls on the Underground Railroad risked their lives to help those slaves make it to freedom. And yet, we are so afraid to help show others the way to spiritual freedom-and it doesn't cost us anything! All I can say is that if we are truly thankful to be free, let's share that message with others so that they can be free, too!"

The crowd rallied as the family sang the chorus again, *Thank God I am free, free, free from this world of sin; Washed in the blood of Jesus, I've been born again!"* The entire audience was moved with her testimony, as the family ended the concert with that song, and a standing ovation.

🚌 🚌 🚌 🚌 🚌

The next morning, Derek drove the family an hour west on interstate seventy to Wheeling, West Virginia where they would begin their trek towards home. The family spent their Thanksgiving there performing at the Oglebay Park Winter Festival of Lights. The family had one concert to sing in a local auditorium in celebration of the upcoming holidays, so the McCormick's added some Christmas music to their line-up.

The rest of the week was spent at the Oglebay Park Spa as part of a couples' retreat being held there, sponsored by a local church. The family enjoyed staying in one of the beautiful cottages on the property. There was so much to do there, even in the winter months. The six-mile display of lights was just the first activity that Shane, Mandie and Derek wanted to experience. The resort was able to rent Mr. McCormick a van so that the family could view the total lights display without freezing!

After the ride was over though, the family split up to do some quick touring before turning in at the cottage. Shane, Mandie and Derek took the red-brick walking path from Christmas Tree Garden to the Greenhouse to catch some fresh, crisp, winter air. Shane took the opportunity to call up Gwen, and spread some Christmas Cheer a little early. As usual, this left Mandie and Derek alone-which Mandie hated.

"So, Mandie, did Mitch have a good Thanksgiving?" Derek asked, trying to begin a conversation.

"Did Stephanie?" she asked.

"I'm sure that she did, I, uh, really haven't checked my email lately to see." Derek answered truthfully.

"Why do you even care? It's not like you're really interested." Mandie complained.

"I'm only talking to you, Mandie. I do care about what happens in your life."

129

'I know; and that's the problem,' she thought to herself. "Well, he had a good day, missing me, of course," she answered.

"Of course. You know, I thought about going up to the Planetarium and watching the stars, but I really do prefer to look at them out here. It's so clear tonight," Derek began as he stopped to look up at the sky.

"Is that why it's so cold, too?" she asked.

"Yep. It would get like this back on the farm; only it was much easier to see the stars, because there were no other lights to distract you. The sky would be a dark navy blue, depending on how full the moon was, and every star would shine bright, and a couple of them would even twinkle," he reminisced.

"I'll bet it was the most beautiful thing that you'd ever seen, right?" Mandie said almost sarcastically with a little laugh.

Derek turned from his star-gazing and looked at Mandie with an honest, loving look and answered, "Nope; not even close."

Mandie looked down at the ground. She knew exactly what he meant. "Why? Why, Derek? Why do you do that?" she asked in frustration.

"Do what?" he asked, as if he didn't know where Mandie was going with this.

"Why do you say things like that? You know that I'm with Mitch. You know that I'm never gonna be with you," she said quickly.

Derek got that crushed look again. "I say those things, because they are the truth. I say those things, because you deserve to hear them. I say those things because you deserve to be walking through this Winter Wonderland with a real man who loves you, and sees you for the beautiful person that you are inside and out-and not as a possession to be fought over. That's why I say them; but don't worry. You won't have to hear them anymore," Derek said sadly as he walked away. "See ya back at the cottage," he called back over his shoulder to Shane and Mandie as he rounded the corner that led back there.

Mandie felt like dirt. *'Why does defending my relationship with Mitch have to hurt him so badly? And why does hurting him hurt me so badly?'* she thought to herself as she jogged up to Shane to finish their walk to the cottage.

"Let not mercy and truth forsake thee: bind them about thy neck; write them upon the table of thine heart:"

Proverbs 3:3

Chapter Eighteen

After the retreat in Wheeling, the family was due in Martinsburg, West Virginia for a three day concert series there, and then there would be a one-day concert in Danville, Virginia before the weary travelers made their way home to Campbell's Grove for Christmas. The entire group was longing for the familiar sights, sounds and smells of home-especially at Christmas. Mandie wanted nothing more than to slip into her family's kitchen and begin baking with her mother. She really wanted to take special note this year of the kitchen appliances and gadgets that she used the most so that she would know how to fill out their Wedding Registry when the time came.

After a successful first show at the Historic Apollo Civic Theater, the family took their usual tour of the town, and that Tuesday night, Shane found a place that made him feel right at home. At the train station down town, Martinsburg held their weekly Bluegrass Music Jam. It was open to the public, and anyone who wanted to 'pick along' could join!

As soon as Shane read the brochure, he began packing up his instruments-the mandolin, the acoustic, the banjo and the resonating guitar. "Derek, you know I'm pretty good, but I only have two hands, so I guess you're gonna have to come along and help me carry all of these."

"What am I? Your burro?" Derek said with a laugh. "Just kidding! I'll be there. You know, I know that you don't have a lot of time, but I would really like to learn how to play the bass."

"Really? All you had to do was ask! I've heard you singing in the congregation during some of the church services, and really, you could be a true asset to the family's vocals!" Shane suggested.

"Whoa, brother! Whoa! One thing at a time! I just wanna learn how to play, that's all," protested Derek.

"Well, just think about it-and over the Christmas break, I'll come over and we'll work on the bass lessons in peace and quiet. Mandie will be having Mitch up from

Augusta, I'm sure, and I don't think that I'll wanna be around the house."

"That sounds like a plan."

"Now, of course, my nights will be taken, Skyping, with Mandie's webcam, of course."

"Of Course," Derek repeated sarcastically.

"...and maybe, I might get to ride over to Sunset and see her. Man, I tell ya', she sure is something!" Shane said as he loaded his instruments into the small rental car that he and Derek split.

"Yeah, she really seems to be a great girl. I guess that 'free man' stuff's all over and done with, huh?"

"I do believe so, my friend. Other girls pale in comparison."

"I have noticed that our trips to the fast food joints just aren't the same," Derek said with a laugh. "You're so young to be so sure so fast!"

"Hey, when you know, you just know, right?" Shane declared.

"Yeah, I know," Derek answered sadly as his mind wandered to her again, like it always did. "You know, she's barely said two words to me, since Wheeling; and the words that she does give me are not too nice."

"Yeah, what happened there? I knew that you two had a little 'tiff', but it didn't look all that hostile. I couldn't tell, I was on the phone, and I was trying not to mind your business," Shane said with a sly look.

"Sure you were," Derek said with a smile. "Anyways, let's just say that I complimented her, and she didn't take it well, so I told her that I wouldn't do it anymore; which you think would make her happy, since it upset her so in the first place. But now, everything is short and snippy. I don't know how to please her; it's a wonder that that sniveling excuse for a boyfriend keeps her happy either. What does he have that I don't? What makes him so much better than me?"

"Well, he doesn't have a Cowboy hat, boots, or a belt buckle larger than Texas!" Shane replied.

"Do you really think that's it? My style? It's a part of who I am. I just can't see changing who I am just to please her, though. If she doesn't love me the way that I am..."

"Then that's just it, isn't it?" Shane asked solemnly.
"I guess so, Shane; I guess so."

The concert series seemed to fly by, as did the series in Danville, until finally the McCormick's were on their way home for Christmas. The whole family cheered when Derek pulled that big bus onto the long dirt driveway that led to the McCormick Homestead. When Grandpa George heard the bus turn onto the driveway, he ran onto the porch. Staying home guarding the property was very restful, but was also very boring, and he couldn't wait to see his family!

Derek saw his uncle's jeep via the side-view mirrors, pulling into the driveway behind them. Uncle Joe had come to pick Derek up and take him home for Christmas. Derek drove the bus into the McCormick's yard and parked it behind the house, where it would sit for the next two weeks. The family quickly gathered their things to take into the house where they would enjoy the holidays together.

After watching Mr. and Mrs. McCormick and Shane step off of the bus, Derek grabbed his duffle bag. Taking one last look at his "home" away from home, he turned and stepped down the stairs to find Shane waiting on him. Shane extended his hand to his friend. While Derek accepted it, Shane pulled him into a big bear hug. "Merry Christmas, brother."

"Merry Christmas, to you too. I'll see you at church this Sunday," replied Derek. Shane turned and headed toward the house with his own duffle bag thrown across his back, leaving Derek there standing at the steps of the bus alone.

As always, Mandie was the last to step off of the bus. She tried to blow right by Derek, but then she stopped. Mandie fidgeted with her bag, twisting it around in small circles by the straps. For some reason now, she felt awkward telling him good-bye. She thought that this would be the happiest moment since 'Tex' had first set foot on their bus. She knew that her mother still secretly hoped that they

135

would be together, but there was no way that Mandie would let that happen-not with this goober. *'Why do I feel so weird about not seeing him for the next two weeks? This should be a welcomed vacation!'* Mandie thought to herself. *'I suppose that I must say something, after all it is Christmas,'* she determined, just to be civil. "Merry Christmas, Derek. We'll see you at church on Sunday," said Mandie as she turned around and headed towards her family's home. She felt his eyes watching her strides, and she thought to herself, *'Please don't call me. Please don't call my name.'*

"Mandie," called Derek.

'I knew it. I almost made it inside,' she said to herself as she stopped dead in her tracks. She squinted her eyes in preparation for what smart comment lay ahead. She turned and faced him, begrudingly.

"Well, Good-bye, Mandie." Derek said, and then he paused, as if he were searching for the right words to say, "I hope you get *everything* you want for Christmas," he said as he turned and headed towards his uncle's jeep, and on to his mother's house, leaving her standing there, speechless, in her own backyard.

'That was it? That was all he had to say? What does that mean?' Mandie reasoned as she turned and walked into the back door of her long-lost home, ready to begin the Christmas holidays with some baking-first up: fudge.

🚌 🚌 🚌 🚌 🚌

Uncle Joe's jeep had no more than entered the driveway when Derek jumped out to snatch up and hug his Mama, Sophia. She had been waiting on that porch for at least half an hour, and the McCormick's only lived ten minutes away! It had been too long since she had seen her son, and he couldn't get there soon enough!

"Son, it sure is good to see you, but if you don't let go soon, I'm gonna pass out!" she said as she gasped for air.

"Sorry, Mama. It's just good to be home!" Derek confessed.

"What's the matter, they ain't treatin' ya good on that big ole' tour bus?" teased Uncle Joe.

"Oh, no! They're the best, really! But even though it sounds silly, there really ain't no place like home!" Derek said with a laugh.

The three of them went inside and quickly made themselves ready for a hot, home-cooked meal that Sophia had waiting on the stove. All through the meal, Derek kept his family in stitches with tales of the escapades of him and Shane. However, Sophia couldn't help but wonder why she never heard mention of one name. She chose not to ask about that name until Uncle Joe ran out to the store for some more staple items.

"You know, son, that fella' Shane sounds like a real character," she began.

"He is Ma. He's like the brother that I never had."

"Well, I noticed that you haven't said a word about a certain person," she continued.

"Hum," laughed Derek silently. "I was wondering when you were gonna get around to that."

"You know, son, I've never been one to play match-maker, but I won't lie to ya'; I've have been praying that if the Lord wanted to supply you a wife through this new assignment, that he would; whether it be Mandie, or someone else. I've been praying for you; but from the way you've been avoiding talking about her, I sense that you've had a time," his mother confided.

"Wow! Well, I'll just say it this way : I sure wouldn't have wanted to experience Mandie McCormick if you hadn't been praying for me!"

"Son, what happened?" asked a hurt and confused mother.

"I guess, I'm just not her type," he said as he began to open up as he never had before. "Ma, I haven't felt this way about anyone since..." he stopped. He couldn't bring himself to say her name without tears.

"Allison?" Sophia gasped.

Derek couldn't answer her; he only nodded through his silent tears, as he slumped down on the couch. "She, um..." he tried to continue, but he just couldn't.

"Son, I'm sorry. I had no idea that it had gotten that far for you. So she's..."

"She gets under skin-she irritates you so bad, but then, you just can't make yourself stay mad at her," Derek said as he wiped the tears away from his face, laughing at the memorizes and thoughts of her. "You know, I can tell when she really gets mad at me; her nostrils flare out! That's when I know that she's just about had enough! And all I can do I push those buttons again! I love it! I love...I love her. I love everything about her. I love watching her work. Mama, she's so talented. And she sings with such passion; and you should see it when the Lord speaks to her and inspires her to write songs! She's amazing!"

"Keep talking, son. It's good for the soul," Sophia coaxed.

"Yeah, but, there's really nothing more to say. She's not interested in me. She's with some clown with money, and she thinks she loves him, but she doesn't. I know she doesn't. She puts up this whole façade when they're together. He doesn't even know who she is-not like I do," Derek reasoned. "I told Shane once that you can't run from life. So, I'm not running anymore; but I tried to walk in a different direction, I guess. I've been emailing this nice young lady that sings with another group, and she's really nice; and pretty; it's been strictly friendly; and even though my mind would like it to be more, my heart won't let me do it. I've got to cut her loose. It's not fair to her."

"That's very wise, son," Sophia answered.

"I was reading my devotions this morning before we left, and I read Philippians 4:11, '...*for I have learned, in whatsoever state I am, therewith to be content.*' So, that's what I'm getting for Christmas, Ma. I'm asking the Lord for a boxful of contentment."

"Oh, Christmas! Well, I happen to know that you've got a little more under my tree than boxes of 'contentment'," his mother said with a smile in an attempt to cheer him up.

Derek laughed! "Boxes...boxes. That gives me an idea. Thanks." Derek said as his mind drifted off for a moment. "Speaking of gifts, Mr. McCormick has a gift for you and Uncle Joe."

"Really? He didn't have to do anything!"

"And guess what it is? It's something you've always wanted to do. The McCormick's have been booked on the 'Singing at Sea' Cruise, and you and Uncle Joe have free tickets."

Sophia stopped smiling at the statement made. "Son, are you going?"

"Yes, ma'am; I will be there," Derek said sternly.

"How? I don't see how!" she objected.

"God's grace is sufficient, Ma. It'll be okay," he answered solemnly, as the issue had been decided.

"And he said unto me, My grace is sufficient for thee: for my strength is made perfect in weakness."

II Corinthians 12:9a

Chapter Nineteen

The aroma of fresh baked cookies filled the kitchen as Mandie and Mrs. Margie continued to find old family recipes in the "box" that had been passed down from generation to generation. Mrs. Margie always knew that the family gained more weight when they were home because she couldn't keep herself out of the kitchen! She loved the space of the kitchen, the larger oven and refrigerator.

"Moma, how often do you use this food processor?" Mandie began.

"Goodness, Mandie, I don't remember the last time that I used that thing! It's probably been under the counter for at least a year or two. Why?" Mrs. Margie asked.

"Can I have it?"

"Why on earth do you need a food processor? What are you going to do with it?" her mother asked.

"Oh, I don't know. I just thought that I'd start a...collection," she said as her voice trailed off.

"Um hum," Mrs. Margie said with that tone that only a mother could produce. "This wouldn't happen to be an item for your hope chest, would it?"

"Yes, Ma'am, it is," she confessed.

"How soon do you plan on filling that chest? Are you in a hurry?" Mrs. Margie probed.

"Maybe."

"Do you need to tell me something?"

"No Ma'am. I just have a feeling that I will get something special for Christmas," Mandie revealed.

"Really? What gives you that impression?"

"Well, things are just falling in line. Mitch has his job, and now he has an apartment, and he tells me how much he misses me, and he can't wait for me to get home, so he can come up and visit. When can he come up, Mama?" she asked.

"Well, I suppose he could come up at any time; we're here; we're not going anywhere."

"Oh! Good! I'll text him right now," Mandie squealed as she whipped out her cell and got right on it.

"Mandie; Are you sure that you're not rushing things? Is your relationship with Mitch really as serious as you think it is?" asked her mother. She had her doubts. There was nothing about the couple that screamed 'impending engagement'.

"Yes, Moma; I'm just sure that he is going to propose at Christmas. I've seen all the signs! I can hear it in his voice! Can't you be happy for me?" she begged.

"Well, if he does plan on asking you to marry him, then he'd better talk to your Daddy first," her mother warned.

"Moma, this isn't the Medieval Age. I am over eighteen. I don't need his permission," proclaimed a defensive Mandie.

Margie wanted to 'tear her out the frame' for that comment. She remembered just a few months ago when her daughter had a heart to heart with her about wanting someone special; and how sincere and forlorn she was about it. She and Mr. McCormick had been praying that God would send the right man for her. They were both happy that Mandie was having a good time, but even though they had no problem with Mitch, they just didn't see them in a marital light. She realized that she needed to choose her words carefully.

"Well, technically, that's right. You don't need your Daddy's permission to marry anyone. How would you feel, though, if your Daddy didn't approve of him, and I'm not saying that he doesn't by any means, and you went ahead and married, against his wishes?"

Mandie stopped and thought about it. "I see what you mean. There would always be this wedge between us," she realized. "I'm sorry; I really didn't mean that. I hope that Mitch would want to talk to Daddy first..." she began.

"But, you don't know if he would? You don't know him well enough to know if he was the type of man who would want to ask for your hand?" she asked as she provoked a very sobering thought. "I am so happy that you are happy right now, and I know that you're excited, but, things are happening awfully fast; marriage is once and forever; you must pray. You must seek God's face on this."

Mandie stood there silently for a moment. "I will, Moma. I will."

🚌 🚌 🚌 🚌 🚌

Christmas Eve came quicker than ants to a picnic; and with it came Derek's Bass lesson.

"Hello, Shane! Come on in!" Sophia welcomed.

"Hello, Mrs. Jensen; it's good to see you again," Shane said as he walked into the living room.

"Derek's out back in the shop. He's been out there for days now working on something special for Mandie for Christmas," Sophia explained. She stopped for a moment, and decided that this would be the right opportunity to share. "Shane, before you go back, do you mind if I speak with you a minute?"

"Oh, no Ma'am; I don't mind at all!"

"Thank you; just have a seat here," she said, offering the loveseat to Shane.

"First, let me start by saying 'Thank you' to you and your family for giving Derek this opportunity to work with you. He has been thoroughly enjoying it! Second, please relay my thanks to your father for securing tickets for me and Joe to go on the cruise with you all! I don't even know what to say!"

"Aw, shucks, Mrs. Sophia! The card you sent was plenty of thanks!" Shane responded.

"Well, anyways, here's my real issue. I think that you probably know by now, from your travels, that Derek is uncomfortable when it comes to water," she began.

"Yes, Ma'am. When Daddy first told us about the cruise, he barely made it to the bathroom!"

"Well, I'm not surprised. No one in Campbell's Grove, except Joe, Pastor Creighton and I know Derek's entire past." She paused for moment, but then realizing that it for his own good, she continued. "When Derek was eighteen, he was in love with a beautiful young lady named Allison. She was the sweetest thing-polite, a good Christian girl, and she loved the Lord. Everyone just knew that they would end up married, serving the Lord, with lots of children."

Shane just smiled as he listened on to her account.

"Well, one evening in the summer after graduation we held a barbecue. We had to cut it short-you know how those summertime thunder storms just pop up outta nowhere!" she said with a smile. "Well, Allison stayed behind to help me in the kitchen, being the sweetheart that she was. It was well after dark when Derek bid her farewell; the only problem was, she never made it home."

Shane's smile faded as he listened.

"The roads were still very wet, and evidently she lost control of her little car and went hydroplaning off of the Mirror Lake Bridge."

Shane's face grew somber, and he felt tears welling up for his brother. *'No wonder he can't stand the thought of going on the cruise.'*

"Well, you know how it is in the country-everything's so spread out. By the time someone noticed the torn grass on the shoulder and the busted guardrail, the car had already sank to the bottom. The EMS and fire department worked together to hoist it out with the wench, but of course, it was too late for poor Allison. Derek was devastated. He couldn't eat or sleep. We didn't know what to do except to pray. The Lord really helped him then. He got back up on his feet. He had decided that the Lord would have him start his own trucking business. I felt like he just needed the time alone with the Lord-riding those highways, just trying to make sense of it all."

Shane brushed the tears from his eyes. Derek had always presented himself as strong; it was then that Shane realized that Derek had only been a mirror, reflecting the strength of his Saviour.

Mrs. Sophia continued. "Then his Daddy died a year later. It almost killed him," she said with tears welling in her eyes at the recollection of her beloved, gone home to be with the Lord.

"Then, that crazy wonderful son of mine, took his life's savings-against my orders, mind 'ya,..." she said as Shane laughed. He knew Derek. "...and helped me out with the farm so that we could move down here with my brother, Joe. He wanted to run the roads with those big rigs-I think mainly to out run all of the heartbreak from Allison's death; but his Daddy's passing and our poor planning ruined that. He had really started seekin' the Lord when he thought he was supposed to go into the Army-and I thought that he turned it down because he was afraid of losing me, too. But then the Lord sent you and your family..." she said as she began to weep. "...and I've haven't heard him happier on the phone since her. I just think that this cruise might set him back. I know that he loves your family, and I also know that..."

"He's in love with my sister," Shane answered for her.

"Yes; and from what I understand, she doesn't care for him?" she asked.

"No, Ma'am. She's pretty much and idiot," Shane said with a sarcastic smile.

"Now, now!" Mrs. Sophia said with a laugh as she again wiped her tears. I know that's just brotherly love talkin' but..."

Sophia continued talking to Shane, and didn't hear Derek as he came in from the shop. He rounded the corner to find a tear-stained Shane listening as his mother begged him to convince Mr. McCormick to let Derek pass on the cruise.

Shane looked up and, seeing Derek, quickly wiped his face. Derek knew from Shane's look what his mother had done. "Well, I guess you know all about me, now," he said in a playful but sarcastic voice-trying to lighten the mood. "Mama, I've already told you, I'm going to be fine. I've been out there in that shop all week, working and talking to the Lord. It's time to stop living in the past. It's time for me to be truly content where I am and with what I have."

Shane remembered their 'man-to-man' talk during their very first night drive. "A wise man once told me that you can't hide from life," he said with a smile.

Derek remembered all too well. "That's right, and I figure that since God has blessed me with another family to be a part of, that I might as well be not only content, but thankful!" He turned and looked at his mother. "I'll be fine Mama, just fine."

🚌 🚌 🚌 🚌 🚌

Christmas day came and went, and three days later, Derek met the McCormick's to head out to Augusta for the trip to Mitch's church. As the family boarded the bus, Derek passed out his Christmas gifts to the family. To Shane, Derek gave a new V-neck 'Man-Sweater' that Shane had admired at the Underground in Atlanta. Derek fully denied that such a thing as a 'Man-Sweater' existed, but since Shane had admired it, he acquired it!

Derek gave Mr. & Mrs. McCormick a nice plaque with the poem, "Footprints" inscribed on it. As Mandie drew nearer to the bus, she noticed that Derek was handing out gifts, and that he had received a new brown cowhide vest from her parents. *'Man, they couldn't have gotten him a present that was any more 'him',' she thought to herself.

When she reached the steps to the bus, she stopped and looked at Derek, expecting a gift. "Hello, Derek. Did you have a nice Christmas?" she asked.

"Hello, Miss Mandie. Yes; my Christmas was very nice, thank you. Now, hurry up and load up, so that we can get on the road," Derek said as he reached down to pick up her suitcase. "And how did your vacation go?" he asked, as he had already inspected her left hand, and noticed that it wore no diamond ring.

"It went fine, thanks," she answered as she boarded the bus and headed towards her bunk, assuming that Derek had nothing for her. *'After all, why should he give me anything? I've treated him like dirt for the past month!' she reckoned with herself.

Derek led her down the hall to her bunk with her bag. As he neared her bunk, he decided to let her in on his surprise. "Oh, by the way, I have a little something for you," he said as he directed her attention to the wooden box wrapped with only a red velvet bow, sitting on her bed.

146

Mandie's jaw dropped as she gently set her bag down on the bed and began to untie the bow. It revealed the beautiful, handmade wooden box. There were scrolling designs in the corners, framing the wood burning on the lid-Mandie's name. She stared in awe of the craftsmanship as she ran her fingers over the letters. Underneath her name was the portion of the verse from Proverbs 31:10, '...her price is far above rubies.' Tears began to well up in her eyes. "Derek...you made this?"

"Yeah, you know, besides Shane coming over to teach me how to play the bass, it was little boring. Life on the road is hard, and tiring; but I've found that staying at home all day, and watching TV is just plain torture. So, I spent a little time in the workshop behind the house."

She looked down again, staring at the verse he had burned into the wood. 'her price is far above rubies,'. She knew that she didn't deserve those words. She had not shown her herself to be worthy of anything from Derek. She opened the box to find that it was lined with red velvet. She ran her fingers over its sleek texture, as she felt the warmth of the tear falling down her cheek.

"What's wrong?" he asked in confusion, "don't you like it?"

She set the box on the bed and did something that Derek did not expect. She wrapped her arms around him in a warm embrace. In the shock of the moment, Derek froze.

"It's beautiful. I don't deserve it," she confessed. She pulled back and released him. "Derek, I've been..."

He stopped her. "It's okay, Mandie. We're good," he said as they stood there.

She looked up at him with her eyes full of remorse, wishing that there was something that she could do to make it right.

"We're good; now, I've gotta get this machine movin'!" he said as he walked towards the captain's chair.

"Hatred stirreth up strifes: but love covereth all sins."

Proverbs 10:12

Chapter Twenty

Derek drove the family with no problems to Augusta. It was a long haul, but he was surprised to find that he missed 'being in the saddle'! The trip seemed like days for Mandie. Her Christmas gift from Mitch was not a diamond ring, but a Dooney & Bourke purse. She loved the bag, but was a little disappointed. However, she thought that perhaps, with New Year's approaching, just maybe, Mitch would pop the question then. She rode that bus to Augusta on pins and needles!

Pastor Bledsoe met the McCormick's at the hotel that the church was providing for them. He wanted to give them a good night's sleep before the family headed West on their California Adventure tour! He explained that he would be at the church on the next day so that they could get in a good rehearsal before the Watch Night Service that evening. Mr. McCormick was delighted, and planned on checking out of the hotel before going to the church; that way they could all grab some sleep on the bus and leave early in the morning.

Mitch picked Mandie up for a nice dinner that evening, and she came back to the hotel a little gloomy. As she laid herself down on the hotel bed, she went over the events of the evening again and again. She wondered why Mitch had not been more excited about tomorrow's service. She entertained the thought that Mitch would not propose to her at all. In fact, he seemed almost nonchalant about everything during their dinner. The conversation was really about nothing at all, and he didn't really seem excited that she was there. The entire situation was very perplexing. Usually everything he did for her seemed to be larger than life. And then it hit her: *'he's trying to throw me off by pretending that nothing special will happen tomorrow! He wants it to be a total surprise! So I will be a good girlfriend, and be totally surprised tomorrow when Mitch wants to talk me, privately. Or perhaps he will choose to do it publically! Oh! I'm so excited!'* she thought to herself as she sprang up and began to dress for bed.

🚌 🚌 🚌 🚌 🚌

Derek and Shane had turned in for the night, but Derek couldn't sleep. After about an hour of tossing and turning, Shane couldn't stand it anymore.

"Man, are you ever gonna get to sleep tonight?" he asked in exasperation.

"Shane, I'm sorry. I've just got a lot on my mind," he confessed.

"What do you mean? I thought you had the whole ocean voyage thing under control?"

"Oh, yes. We're past that now. It's something else," Derek said as he tried to avoid the subject.

"You mean someone else, don't you," Shane revealed. He knew that Derek hadn't escaped thoughts of her over Christmas break, and he probably never would.

"I'm sorry man. Did you hear her talking to your Mom earlier this evening? She really thinks that it's serious between them. She's gonna get hurt; it's comin'. I don't know when or how, but he is gonna break her heart, and then I'm gonna break his face," Derek threatened.

"How do you know? Do you know something that we don't?" Shane asked.

"Not really-I just know that he doesn't love her; she's ready to take the vows, and he's an idiot. In all of his 'plastic chivalry' over Christmas break, like at church-the opening of doors, all of the 'ladies first' charade-none of that was from his heart, if he even has one."

"Dude! How do you know? I even agree that he's a goober, but he looked pretty sincere to me, even at the house."

"I'm just telling you. She's nothing more than a possession to him. He's all about money. He either thinks that your family is loaded, or that Mandie will progress him in his career or something, because, he doesn't treat her like someone in love; and that I do know," said Derek as he made his case against Mitch.

"Well, I know that she was mighty disappointed to get that stupid bag for Christmas. Really! Who spends that kind of money on a bag? And with someone else's name on it, to boot! He could've at least gotten her a gift with her name on it!"

Derek laughed under his breath at the remembrance of Mandie when he gave her the box with her name engraved on it. Maybe Shane really did know a little bit about his sister. Derek knew that Mandie loved his gift to her as well as he knew his own name, even though Shane obviously didn't know anything about it.

"Well, either way, I have a feeling that tomorrow will tell the tale," Derek began.

"How so?"

"Well, tomorrow night is New Year's Eve. It's the beginning of a New Year-and something's gotta give. After tomorrow night, we'll be leaving for the West Coast. She'll want some sort of resolution before we travel. She's looking for the long haul, while he's looking for the three-hour tour-I can tell. I can feel my joints aching; tomorrow's forecast is rain."

As promised, Pastor Bledsoe met the McCormick's at the church around two o'clock in the afternoon. Of course, Mandie had sent a text to Mitch, letting him know that they would be at the church early to rehearse. No sooner than the bus had pulled into the parking lot, Mitch rolled up behind them. Derek couldn't open the doors to the bus fast enough for Mandie.

"Mitch!" she cried as she ran to his car.

"Hey, Beautiful! Mitch answered as he stepped out of his car and caught her in a hug. "How are you?"

"Better, now that I've gotten to see you!" she replied.

Mr. McCormick stepped off of the bus to 'round up' his troops. "Alright! I need all of mine in the church for setup!"

Mandie turned and looked and Mitch. "I've gotta go. Are you staying for a while?"

"I've got something that I've gotta take care of; but I will be back to take you to a nice supper," he promised.

"Sounds great! Bye," she said as she turned around with a taunting smile that left Derek breathless as he watched on from the steps of the bus.

Mitch slipped back into his car and drove off. As Mandie walked in to the church, Derek peered on. "Whatcha lookin' at, Tex?" she asked, without even looking at him.

"Not much in that direction," he said as he nodded towards the end of the parking lot where Mitch had driven off.

"Hum. You've always got jokes, don'tcha?" she said with a smile and a confident shake of the head as she never broke her stride.

"I can usually find a few clever things to say," Derek said as he left the bus steps, locking the door and joining her in her walk to the church.

Remembering his heart-felt gift, she just couldn't make herself go to war just then; so instead, she stopped in her tracks at the church doors, as Derek grabbed the handle. And with the most solemn look she replied, "And that's what makes you..." and then she broke a smile, "...*a most worthy adversary.*"

Derek laughed out loud, this time, opening the door for her majesty.

🚌 🚌 🚌 🚌 🚌

Mitch returned to pick up Mandie for their nice supper together. He drove her to Luigi's, a small bistro about five blocks from the church. Just the sheer romantic atmosphere poured fuel on Mandie's fire of anticipations. And then, as the waiter seated them, came the icing on the cake. Mandie was seated first, and as the waiter walked towards Mitch's chair and presented it to him, Mandie noticed the box. There was a small box-shaped protrusion from Mitch's pants pocket.

As the meal progressed, Mandie participated in the small talk, but she was floating in a cloud. She knew what was coming. She knew that Mitch was going to propose tonight. *'On New Year's Eve! How wonderful!'* she thought to herself as she caught herself daydreaming at the table! "Mandie? Mandie, dear? Are you okay?" Mitch asked.

"Hum? Oh, yes! Yes, I'm just fine. What were you saying?" she asked as she genuinely tried to come back down to earth.

"I was asking if you would mind if I spoke with you privately about something this evening-something very important."

"Well," she began nervously, "...there's no time like the present!"

"Well, I don't think we should talk here; maybe later, like between the services, or even better-right after midnight tonight?" he offered.

Mandie was a little disappointed, but she rationalized that he must have his reasons for not asking there in the restaurant. "Okay. That will be fine. Remind me, okay?" she playfully suggested as she took another sip of tea. As if she would forget!

"What time is it, Shane?" Derek asked.

"Time for you to get a watch!" he answered with a laugh.

"I forgot-you don't know how to tell time!" Derek shot back. Shane stopped smiling. Derek reached around and pulled his cell phone from his belt clip to see that it was seven-thirty; the service began at eight. "Church will start in about thirty minutes. I'll just go ahead and set this to 'Silent' now, just in case," he decided.

"Oh, who'd call you tonight?" Shane asked sarcastically.

Derek stretched his eyes open in mysterious jest, *"You never know!"* he remarked, teasing him. "Well, everything is set up and tested; I'm gonna take a quick break before the folks start rollin' in. You'd better take one too," he advised.

"Yeah, I wanted to call Gwen before their service gets going good. Man I wish I could be there with her tonight," he whined.

"I know; but really, it would just make tomorrow even harder. The West Coast tour is right at a month. That's a while..."

"Don't remind me. Thank the Lord for Skype!" Shane proclaimed.

"Yeah. She might forget what you look like!" Derek said with a laugh; but he laughed alone, as Shane now slipped into worry-mode.

"You think so?" he asked in fear.

Derek looked at him with the *'Oh, please; what do think,'* look. "No!" he answered as he walked towards the Men's room in the back of the church.

Derek had no sooner entered a stall in the restroom, when the door burst open loudly as a boisterous group entered, laughing and carrying on. He remained silent, as he recognized one of the voices-Mitch. From the nature of the laughter of the others with him, it sounded sinister. As he listened on, he stealthily took his cell phone from his belt clip, and pressed the button to make a voice recording, and then stood perfectly still, so as to capture every word.

One voice began, "So, Mitch. This is the big night. I can't believe that you're gonna ask that girl to marry you."

Another joined in, "Ole, Mitch is taking himself off the market. Hearts will break all around the world tonight," his friend said in jest.

Then Mitch took the opportunity to make a speech to his cronies. "Yeah, fellas, when Diane hears my proposal-and sees how serious I am about choosing her over the *'Great Mandie McCormick, because I am seriously in love with her...'*

"And her Daddy's money," another one of his cronies chimed in.

"...she will gladly accept, and I will be in," he boasted proudly.

"Well, when will you cut Mandie loose?" another asked.

154

"Well, that's the beauty of it all, gents. Ever since Diane and Murray broke up again, I've been feeding Diane stories about how Mandie has been chasing me-trying to woo me into a relationship; and how I've been talking with her because I've been feeling sorry for her. She's very sympathetic, you know," he said with a devilish grin. "She has no idea how I've been stringing Mandie along all these months. So, I'll ask Diane first, and then if all doesn't go like I plan, I'll just propose to Mandie instead. Having a star on my arm won't go as far as Dr. Livingston's Medical Contacts, but it will definitely get us into the Country Club, and it's all up from there! I can't lose!" he said laughing as he and his crew made their way back towards the sanctuary.

Derek forgot all about taking a break, and took great pains to leave the restroom unnoticed by its former occupants. He quickly made his way to Shane.

"Man, you've gotta come with me to the bus, right now," he said as he grabbed his arm.

"Dude, I'm on the phone with Gwen, and..."

Derek grabbed the phone from Shane. "Gwen? Hi! I'm sorry, Darlin', Shane's gonna have to call you back," he said as he pressed 'end' and shoved the phone back into Shane's hand.

"DUDE! I can't believe that you just did that!" he yelled as Derek drug him to the bus that was parked behind the church. They climbed aboard, and Derek locked the door behind them. He carefully and quickly walked on towards the galley, where there were no windows. He called and made sure that they were alone before he shared the terrible news.

He began cueing up his cell phone as he explained. "Okay; remember last night when I couldn't sleep? And I told you that I thought something was comin' down?"

"Yeah, rain, achy joints, I got it," Shane recalled.

"Well, even I wasn't looking for this..." Derek said as he played the recording for Shane.

The more that played, the angrier the both of them became. "I'm gonna kill him!" Shane shouted as he turned and began to run off of the bus in a rage driven stupor.

Derek caught him by the arm. "Stop! You can't just go off beating up people! First, you gotta tell Mandie before she walks right into his trap!"

"Me tell her? Why me?" Shane rebutted.

"Well, she surely won't take the news from me-her Nemesis!" Derek screamed.

"Yeah, you're right about that. But, Why me?" again he protested. And then the light bulbs came on for the both of them as Shane read Derek's mind: "It's time to call in Mom!"

The young men raced back to the sanctuary to find Mrs. Margie, but the service had already started. They slipped into their pew, but only for a second; Pastor Bledsoe had just called the family to the front to sing a song or two before the first preacher. It was too late to talk with her then, but Derek had an idea. He scrambled for a sheet of paper, and wrote a note for Mrs. McCormick to meet him in the counseling room in the foyer as soon as possible-that it was VERY important. Then he also left a note for Shane to join them, a minute or two after watching his mom leave, so that Mitch wouldn't notice that they were all three gone. Then Derek made his way immediately to the small room just off of the church's foyer.

As he slipped into the little room, decorated comfortably, he took full advantage of the purpose of the room-to cry out to the Lord. "Lord, please, through all of this chaos and deceit, please help us put our hurt and anger aside and do what's best for Mandie. Lord, I know that this is going to break her heart. Please help her," he prayed as just then Mrs. McCormick knocked on the door.

"Derek, honey? Are you in here?" she asked.

Derek arose and opened the door. "Please, come in quickly."

"Goodness! What's going on?" she asked.

"Did anyone see you leave?" he asked.

"I'm sure that someone did. What's all this about?" she asked, as just then, Shane knocked at the door.

Derek opened the door, and Shane jumped in. "Does she know yet?"

156

"Do I know what? Come on boys, this is getting' old. We need to get back in there!" she protested.

"Mom, please this is really important. Just listen!" Shane insisted as Derek began to play the recording.

As she listened her eyes grew bigger by the minute. "That cur! Derek, how did you get this?"

"I was in the restroom already when he and his goons came in. I could tell by the laughter that the conversation was no good, so I just followed the 'nudge' that I had to record it."

"Well, you did the right thing in coming to me, boys. Derek, let me keep this; you press this button?"

"Yes, Ma'am"

"Okay. Now you two get back out there. We need to stay in the service as long as possible. Shane, when we break for refreshments, you go get your sister and tell her that I need her help in here-right away. You two make sure that she makes it here first-before that scoundrel manages to corner her or try to take her anywhere again. I'll talk to her; and boys-pray for her," she said with a somber resolve as she knew what she had to do-and she took no pleasure in it.

The young men did as they were asked, and in their absence her Mother's heart broke wide in two. '*Lord, please give me strength.*'

🚌 🚌 🚌 🚌 🚌

Pastor Bledsoe blessed the food from the pulpit and then dismissed the congregation for refreshments and fellowship. Derek had never seen Shane move as fast as he did that night.

"Hey, sis! Mom needs your help right away. She's in the counseling room."

Mandie immediately became concerned. "Is she okay? Excuse me, Mitch," she said as she followed Shane to the room. He opened the door to find his mother sitting there on the loveseat, waiting for them.

He ushered his sister in, and then with a look from his mom, he silently backed out of the room. Mandie was almost in tears in fear. "Moma, what's going on? What's all of this about?"

"Sit down, honey. There's something that you've gotta hear," she said as she took the cell phone from her purse. "Honey, I know that you've been very excited about the possibilities between you and Mitch..."

Mandie's mood remained confused and now solemn. "He said that he had to talk to me privately about something later tonight, but what is this?" she asked as her mother pressed the playback button.

Mandie sat there, listening to the conversation that Derek had recorded. Her face was set in stone as the cold reality set in. She had been played. Her mother stopped the recording when it had finished; and still yet Mandie sat there, with no expression-only one single tear ran down her cheek.

"Mandie, honey; I'm so sorry," Mrs. Margie said. And still yet, Mandie sat there motionless and speechless. "Honey, say something, please!" her mother begged.

"What's there to say?" Mandie replied as she wiped the tear-stained trail from her face. "I know what I have to do," she said with resolution as she stood from the loveseat and turned towards the door.

Margie sensed the 'tough' coming out in her daughter, and at that moment, she was mighty proud.

Mandie suddenly turned to her mother, "How's my makeup?"

"Not even a smudge-good girl!"

Mandie managed to force a smile while clutching her purse. She took a moment to take in one deep breath before placing her hand on the doorknob. Then it occurred to her. She looked at the phone that still rested in her mother's hands. "That's Derek's phone, isn't it?" she asked cooly.
Mrs. Margie nodded silently.

"Hm. He always does look out for me, doesn't he, Mama?" she asked with a faint smile on her face.

"Yes; he does," her mother replied without a hint of any 'I told you so' tone.

Mandie laughed softly in sarcastic recollection. "Poor fool," she mumbled under her breath.

"Derek, or you?" Mrs. Margie asked.

Mandie once again smiled at the irony of her own question. "I haven't decided yet," she said as she put on her game face and walked back to the cad waiting for her.

"Be strong and of a good courage, fear not, nor be afraid of them: for the LORD thy God, he it is that doth go with thee;"

Deuteronomy
31:6ab

Chapter Twenty-One

She found him waiting in the hallway that led to the fellowship hall-surrounded by his buddies. She wasted no time. "Mitch? Mitch, dear?" she called to him, laying it on thick, just for his friends' benefit.

"Mandie! How is your mother? Is everything okay?" he asked.

Mandie smiled as if she knew nothing. "Oh, yes. Shane over exaggerates everything so! Listen, you asked me to remind you-you needed to talk to me about something? And dear, the truth is, I've really been needing to talk to you about something, too!"

Mitch's friends began to snicker, throwing Mitch off guard, but giving Mandie the upper hand.

"In fact, Mitch, I wanted to wait until tonight to tell you, but, it's just not fair to keep leading you on this way, and I may not have another chance to talk to you. I know that you thought our relationship would just go on forever, but, we're leaving for the West Coast in the morning, and I realized that, I really need to keep my options open! So, thank you so much for the fun we've had. I really did enjoy it,"

Mitch stood there in complete confusion. *'Where did I go wrong?'* he thought to himself. He could do nothing but stand there with the proverbial egg on his face and endure some more.

"My parents want us to turn in right after the last 'amen' tonight so that we can pull outta here first thing in the morning, and I was afraid that I wouldn't have enough time to talk to you after the service. You understand, don't you, dear? Fellas, maybe y'all can help him find someone to keep him company while I'm gone, huh? I've gotta run now-I need to meet with Mama and Shane to check up on the next set of songs for the last service. Goodbye, Mitch," she said as she gently touched his hand, bidding him 'farewell' in the most elegant performance of her life.

She walked down the hallway of darkened Sunday School rooms, unknowingly passing her hidden guardians, Shane and Derek, who had heard every word she so eloquently delivered. As the aroma of her perfume floated into the room with her passing glides, Shane could hold back no longer. "And the Oscar goes to..." he said to Derek with a laugh.

Derek stood there, leaning with his back to wall in the dark, smiling through the hurt he felt for her. *'You go, Mandie...'* he thought to himself as he motioned for Shane to follow him out. He had never been prouder, but at the same time he knew what was coming.

Shane followed behind him, "I'll bet you a million dollars that I know where she's headed right now."

"Where do you think I'm going?" Derek said as he picked up his stride.

🚌 🚌 🚌 🚌 🚌

Tears. Tears. That's all there were-tears. That was the scene that Derek and Shane walked in on when they entered the bus. Mandie and her mother, sitting on her bunk as Mandie fell apart. The warm droplets fell down her face until their salt began to sting the tender skin of her cheeks. Then the tears coupled themselves with the rage that began to sweep over her body as she shook with incessant sobs. They overtook her while the words from the device rang through her memory, over and over again screaming, "...*choosing her over the 'Great Mandie McCormick...'*" Mitch's voice pierced the rose colored dreams that had paraded in Mandie's heart and mind, as early as just this morning. She thought that he was 'the one' and he had mocked her in every possible fashion. *'My final hope of ever marrying and having a family is gone,'* she thought to herself.

How could she have been so wrong? Mandie became lightheaded as she pondered that last few months. Everything had been a lie. Every outing, every kiss, everything was merely a ploy to build a relationship that was for "sale to the highest bidder". *'The girl with the bigger, better deal would go home with today's fabulous prize!'* she thought to herself. *'How could I have fallen in love with a man who would treat someone this way?'* she thought to herself, only to fall back into the trap of emotions that engulfed her, falling victim to his flawless features and charms once again.

Margie reached out for Mandie to hold her in a mother's embrace, only to have Mandie fight her away, as she did not want to be consoled. But as always, Mama knew better. Margie caught her hand and pulled her in quickly and held her tightly until she fought no more. She continued to rattle with grief.

Stunned at the scene that unfolded before them, Shane and Derek were paralyzed. Neither man had moved a muscle during the saddening spectacle. This sight was in such contrast to the cool and confident woman who had only just sent this rogue down the river like an aristocrat. And now...this pitiful scene had blown Derek and Shane away.

Derek slumped down into the captain's chair. As he sat there in the driver's seat, he had hung his head to give her some privacy, and to hide his own fury that was building inside. His heart ached because of the anguish that consumed her, and at the same time he wanted to rip Mitch's head off and feed it to his dog back home.

Suddenly, realizing that the boys were there, Mandie quickly sat up and attempted to wipe away some of the tears and smeared mascara that streaked her face. She looked at Derek, who was still staring at the floor in respect. "I'm sure you've got something just dandy to say about all of this, don't you, Tex!" she attacked in her grief.

Derek lifted his head and turned to her, "Not this time, Mandie...not this time." With that he steadied his Stetson, and opened the door to the bus, bolting out, with Shane following on his heels.

Derek walked down the alley separating the church and the bookstore next door and stopped at a dumpster, kicking with all of his might. "How could he do this to her? I knew he was a rat from the first time he started coming around, but this is...I mean to lead her on like he did..."

"I'm just thanking the Lord that you were in the right place at the right time and found out about it, before it went any farther than it did. She already had her heart set on a

163

wedding-you've seen all of her magazines and junk," Shane replied. "But apart from kickin' his butt, what else can we really do about it?"

Derek stood there, leaning against the brick wall of the church, wiping over his face in frustration, when a thought occurred to him. "Hey, do you know this girl, this 'Diane Livingston'?" he asked.

"Yeah, her daddy's the richest guy in this town-a doctor, or surgeon, or so I've heard. We've been coming here since we first started singing on the road, and all of the guys that I've met from here have made a big deal about her, and how much money her family has."

"I think that, under the circumstances, she won't mind us paying her a visit," said Derek as he started back towards the street where there was a phone booth. He entered quickly and grabbed the book, flipping through to the 'L' 's. "Here's the address. How far is this place from here?"

"Only about four blocks, we can walk from here." Shane answered.

"Well, then-are you coming?" Derek asked as he closed the door to the phone booth.

"Do we get to kick his butt?" asked Shane in greedy anticipation.

"Shane... really?" Derek looked at him as if to say, *'now you know better'*. "I wanna kill him just as bad as you do-maybe even more; but we've gotta protect our testimonies. That's all we have! If we lose that, we may never get it back! There'll be no 'butt-kickin' tonight, no matter how bad we want it! But, if we hurry we might beat him there, and then we can watch *her* take care of *him*! There's no need in two girls gettin' hurt. Come on, let's go."

🚌 🚌 🚌 🚌 🚌

"Mandie, why don't you go wash your face and get ready for bed. I'll explain to Pastor Bledsoe that you're not feeling well, and you can't finish the service tonight," her mother offered.

164

"No, Moma. I can't do that. I can't let everyone down!" she protested.

"Now, is that pride talking? You don't want Mitch to think that he's won, is that it?" Mrs. Margie asked as she brought Mandie a cool, wet washcloth for her red, swollen face.

"I'll admit, I'm not crazy about standing up there now with everyone looking at me, especially him; but, the Lord didn't have to save me from messing up my life. I need to sing for Him, in thankfulness for his mercy to me-a stupid, lovesick moron. If Derek hadn't been there..." she began as her voice trailed off.

"But, he was there, just like you said earlier. And he had enough sense about him, that he knew something wasn't right. God put him in the right place at the right time. It was no coincidence. I know that you've always thought that I was trying to play match maker between you and Derek, but the truth is that God may have brought him here for you, honey. I know that you're upset, and I know you don't want to hear anything about anybody, especially not about men, but I'm just gonna give you one piece of advice."

"What's that Moma?"

"Don't be afraid to take that second look."

Mandie rolled her eyes. "Mama, no matter how many times I look at him, I see the same old thing-a country hick who's stuck on me, and who loves to pick on me all the time. I think he actually picks on me more than Shane does! He's more aggravating than a brother any day of the week! He's a friend-and that's all we'll ever be is friends!"

"Mandie, do you remember the story of the Elijah and the widow of Zarephath?" Mrs. Margie asked.

"The widow of Zarephath? What does that story have to do with this situation?" asked Mandie as she thought that her mother had finally fallen off the deep end.

"Well, it seems to me that this is an account of another brave woman, just like you. Oh, at first she didn't seem brave. When she met Elijah she was gathering sticks to build a fire to cook a last meal for her and her son. Can you imagine: knowing that you were cooking the very last meal that you would ever be able to provide for your child-knowing that there was nothing else that you could do for him-knowing that he would die?"

Mrs. Margie began as her heart melted within heart, thinking of her own two children. "Well, in my book, that took an awful lot of courage to pull it together and determine to do every last thing that she could for her boy. But then, she met Elijah, God's man; and he wanted her to make him a cake first. Can you imagine how mad she probably was, knowing, that she only had enough to feed her child one last time, ever, and this stranger asked for her child's food? I think that if it were you or me, we probably would have spit in his face! But not her-she was a woman of compassion and faith. When Elijah first asked her for a vessel of water, she didn't hesitate. She brought it to him right away, without question, because it was within her power to do it."

Mandie listened on, not sure where her mother was going with this, but she knew that she had her best interests in mind.

"But, this woman was broken. God had prepared her to meet Elijah-remember? God told Elijah to go there and that He had commanded a widow woman to take care of him. The Bible doesn't say how God had made this preparation for her to take care of Elijah. Perhaps it was the desperation. Perhaps it was the fact that she had already given up and she knew that she had no power within herself to take care of her child, and she was looking anywhere and everywhere to see how the Lord would provide. She knew the circumstances. She knew that there was only so much meal and oil to make a cake of bread. Common sense and logic reminded her of this. But, Elijah told her that if she obeyed, then the meal and the oil would not fail."

"Yes, ma'am. I know the story. But what is this second look you are talking about?" Mandie asked as she was desperately seeking the application.

"Well, it's simply this. The widow woman obeyed. She made Elijah the cake first, and then one for her and her son. But, on the next day, what would have happened if she had never gone back to the barrel and taken a second look?"

Mandie sat there in silence. "What do you mean?"

"What if the widow never again looked in that barrel of meal? She *knew* that she had used all of the meal. She *knew* that she had used the last drop of oil. So what if she had never had enough faith to go back to the barrel to see if there was actually something there?" her mother said.

"She would have died; her and her son," Mandie answered.

"That's right. You can be obedient all day long; but if you don't have enough faith to step out there and take God at His Word..." Margie began.

"...then it's impossible to please Him," Mandie answered, remembering the scripture.

"Yes. And look at the blessing she would have missed: her life and the life of her son!" confirmed Margie.

"So..." started Mandie was she was still struggling.

"So, reading your Bible, and praying is the right thing to do. It's obedience. But now, Mandie, you've gotta go back to the barrel."

"Huh?"

"Before you wither and die from this, Mandie; before you give up your heart's desire - finding a husband and having a family, you need to take a second look. You've gotta believe that the Lord will honor his promise that if you delight yourself in Him, He will give you the desire of your heart. Look again in that barrel. Even though you *know* he's not right for you; even though you *know* he's not your type; you've gotta have enough courage and faith to go back and look in that barrel again-you just might find something in there that you haven't seen before," she finished as she patted her daughter's leg, and stood up to stretch.

"I'm gonna go talk to Pastor Bledsoe and tell him that you're not feeling well, okay? You need some rest," she suggested again, as this time Mandie nodded quietly, and laid back on her bunk, pondering the jewels of truth shared with her that night.

"But without faith it is impossible to please him:"

Hebrews 11:6a

Chapter Twenty-Two

The laughter startled Mandie as the family entered the bus. She couldn't believe that she had been sleeping for over an hour. At first the voices meshed together with laughter, but then, as they walked past her bunk, and up the stairs to the lounge, she became more alert and caught on to their conversation.

"Boys, I can't believe that you went over to that girl's house!" exclaimed Mrs. Margie. "And, you, Brian-I can't believe that you went with them!"

"Well, they filled me in on the way; I wanted to string the boy up by his toes-I still do-but, going to visit the girl's father was the responsible thing to do; the Bible does teach us that if we know to do good, and then we don't do it-we have committed sin. From what I learned tonight, Mr. Livingston doesn't go to church with his daughter-but he was impressed that strangers cared about the integrity of his daughter. I tried to get a witness in through the situation, and I think that he may actually start attending services with the young lady. That's my prayer, anyways."

Mandie walked up the steps to get the full story. Upon seeing his sister, Shane exploded. "Oh, Mandie! You missed it, girl!"

"Missed what?" she replied with her eyes opening slowly, still laden with sleep.

"We got Mitch good!" Shane began. "Me, Dad and Derek all went over to Diane's house..."

"Daddy? You went over to her house?" Mandie said as she felt a tinge of betrayal.

"Yes, honey. It was the right thing to do. She didn't know the whole story, just like you!" explained Mr. Brian. "We went in and met with her father; and then he called her down. Derek played the recording for her, too. She was just as angry. No one likes to be made a fool of."

"And then the best part," Shane started, "was when Mitch showed up!"

"Mitch went there?" Mrs. Margie asked.

"Yeah! He had no idea that we had gone over to her house. I guess when you broke it off with him, he knew that

169

he'd have to try and lie his way out of his own mess before word got to Diane that you had dumped him!"

Mandie stood there beside her mother listening to Shane's exciting rendition of the encounter. Derek had still not said a word since the group came into the bus.

"Ole' Mitch thought he was gonna be something! You should've seen the look on his face when Mr. Livingston opened the door wide enough so that he could see us sitting in his den! Then he threw him out! It was great!" Shane cheered. "And you'd think that he'd get the idea-and leave, but oh, no-not Mr. Wonderful! He just couldn't leave it alone."

"How do you mean?" Mrs. Margie asked.

"He waited outside for us-well, not for all of us," Mr. Brian began as he directed his attention towards Derek.

Mandie looked at Derek with concern. "He was waiting for you?"

Before Derek could speak, Shane jumped in again. "Mandie, you should've seen it!"

"Seen what, Shane? Spit it out!" Mandie yelled.

"Yeah, ole' Mr. Wonderful was hiding in the bushes at the end of the driveway. As soon as Mr. Livingston closed that big wooden front door behind us, he jumped out at Derek. He grabbed him by the collar and *tried* to throw a punch at him!"

Derek hung his head in embarrassment as the story continued.

"Emphasis on the word *'tried'*," said a smiling Mr. McCormick who had decided to chime in. "Derek caught Mitch's fist as he swung at him, and wrapped his arm behind his back, pinning him to his own car!"

Shane was holding his sides, he was laughing so hard. Even Mrs. Margie had begun to snicker under her breath at the story. As soon as he regained his composure, Shane continued, "And that ain't even the best part! When Derek slammed him into the car, he... busted... Mitch's lip!" Shane reported as he lost himself in laughter again.

And this time he was not alone! Mr. & Mrs. McCormick were both in stitches! Mrs. Margie then stopped herself! "Oh! We shouldn't be laughing and carrying on!

This is really terrible! We're supposed to pray for our enemies!"

Mr. McCormick came to Derek's defense. "Margie, I was right there. The boy was only defending himself, and your daughter's honor. He did exactly what he was supposed to do. Trust me; he could have really put a hurtin' on that boy, but he didn't."

Derek still sat there, looking at the ground, until Shane went to speak again.

"And Mitch knew it too!" Shane said.

Mandie stood straight-faced, still taking it all in-until she finally directed her attention to Derek. "Well, what do you have to say for yourself?"

Derek looked up at Mandie, surprised that he should have to explain himself! "He shouldn't have put his hands on me!" he said without remorse.

"That's one mistake Mitch will never make again, I can promise you that! You shoulda seen his face when he told him..."

"Shane!" Derek said in an attempt to cut him off.

"What? She needs to know!"

"Ugh!" Derek said as he rolled his eyes, and looked back at the floor again.

Mandie again directed her question straight to Derek, "What did you tell him, Derek?"

Derek sat there like a knot on a log-silent; there was no need for him to speak. Shane was simply busting at the seams!

"Ole' Mitch was hollerin' at Derek about how this was his fault-and that he knew Derek had planned to steal you away from the beginning! And Derek said..."

Mr. Brian decided to take over before Shane forgot the important parts, "...and he told him that you had been faithful to him; that you had never betrayed his trust, like the way he had betrayed you. He defended your honor, first of all."

"And then he told him that he had better not ever, EVER, see his ugly mug around you again. And that he had better not call, or text, or contact you in any way-or he'd have him to deal with," Shane said as his smile quickly changed.

"And then, *to my dismay*, he had grabbed your webcam that Mitch had given you, and threw it at his feet, telling him to take his junk and to get outta there," he concluded as he looked at Derek, "Dude, I really needed that webcam!"

Derek looked at Shane "I'll buy you a new one! There were bigger issues at hand!"

Mandie couldn't believe what she was hearing. "You really told him that?"

Again, Mr. McCormick rushed to Derek's defense before he could speak. "And if he hadn't told him so quickly, I would've done it myself! I am very proud of you Derek, and also very grateful," he said before extending his hand to Derek for a shake of appreciation. "Goodnight, son."

"So am I," responded Mrs. Margie, as she giggled, thinking about the rumble again. "You really made him bleed?"

Derek rolled his eyes in dismay. He hadn't intended to be so rough. "Yes, Ma'am. I didn't mean to..."

Mrs. Margie patted him on the shoulder. "I know," and as she giggled again, "He sure did deserve it though! Goodnight," she said as she followed her husband to their Master bunk.

"Whew! Well, it sure was some kind of New Year! You sure **RANG** it in! Ha ha!" Shane said. "You've got a busy day tomorrow. We'd all better turn in," he suggested. "Good night, y'all"

"Good night," Derek replied as he nodded to Shane.

"Good night," Mandie answered as she stood there, staring off into space, thinking about all of it.

As soon as Shane had cleared the stairwell, Derek began, shaking his head, "Mandie I'm..."

"Sorry?" she said as she cut him off. "Don't be." For the first time, she showed a slight smile, "He **did** deserve it. I owe you, Tex-big time. Thank you-for everything," she said as she turned to take the stairwell down to her bunk.

Derek followed her down, as he was on the way to his lower level bunk to rest up for the long haul that they would begin in a couple of hours. When they reached the galley, it was time to part ways.

Mandie turned to Derek with a faint laugh, "In a way, I kinda wish you hadn't told him that I was faithful to him- and had never cheated. I would have like for him to feel *some* pain."

"No, Mandie. You know you're not like him. He needed to hear the truth. He needed to know what a treasure he was losing-someone pure and honorable. There's no way I was gonna let him accuse you of anything. You were only guilty of following your heart; and you can't really fault someone for following their heart, now can you?" he asked with a smile.

She returned his smile. "No, I guess not. Well...good night...and thank you again."

Derek still stood there and holding his Stetson in his hands. "Mandie, I really am sorry that things didn't turn out like you wanted them to tonight."

"Oh, yeah...well..." she started as her thoughts trailed off to what she had anticipated.

"Well, good night; Oh, and Mandie?" he called as she had turned to go to her bunk.

"Yes?" she answered.

"I'm praying for you," he said as he took the lower steps to his room.

🚌 🚌 🚌 🚌 🚌

The dawn broke through way too soon for Derek. The whirling events of the night before still drained all of the energy from his body. *'Duty calls...'* he thought to himself as he rolled out of his futon. He made it to the shower, but he wasn't alone...he had his thoughts-and plenty of them. He wondered what Mandie really thought about how he had handled Mitch. He knew that she was devastated, and that she probably wasn't processing everything that she heard last night. He just knew that it would only be a matter of time before 'Miss Sunshine' came out to harass 'Tex' again. But if that's what she wanted, he'd be glad to have it.

After slipping back to his room to finish up his morning routine, Derek heard Mr. McCormick stirring in the galley. He slipped up there for a quick bite of breakfast, and a travel plan. "Good morning, sir. Did you sleep well?"

"You might not believe it, but that's the best few hours of sleep that I've had in a long time," confessed Mr. McCormick.

Derek understood. "My conscience was eased, but my body can't agree! I think that all of this driving and riding, and lack of physical exercise has inspired me to find the fitness room at our next hotel!"

"Well, you certainly looked like you could handle yourself, and anyone else that gave you trouble."

Derek looked a little ashamed. "I hope that I didn't lose any ground with you sir. I'm usually not a physically aggressive man."

"Derek. Let me share something with you. A few months ago, my daughter was crying on my shoulder wishing...hoping...praying for a Godly man to share her life with. Actually she shared this with her mother, and then ended up on my shoulder in the hospital, when Grandpa had his heart attack; and she was rather embarrassed that I knew about her need, isn't that something?"

Derek smiled as he listened to Mandie's father. "I can see that about her, sir."

"Well, long story short, I told her that I was praying for her; that I was praying for the Lord to send her someone who loved Him, and wanted to serve Him; someone that loved her with all his heart. In fact, I told her that I wouldn't give her up to anyone else but a man like that; and I'll tell you this-you can have her," he said as a tear ran down the side of his face.

Derek sat there stunned and amazed at what he was hearing. "Well, sir..."

"I know, I know. Usually it's the other way around. Usually the man goes to the father and asks for her hand in marriage. But I don't know any other man alive that is more suited for her, or that loves her any more than you do; and I'd be proud to officially call you my son," Mr. McCormick said as he dried his eyes with his handkerchief.

Derek was overcome on so many levels. "Thank you so much, sir. That means more to me than you'll ever know.

The only problem is that she doesn't love me. I'm more like a brother to her; and I'm not sure that she'll ever see me as anything else."

"Well, son, we'll just pray about that now, won't we?" Mr. Brian answered as he pulled out his planner and mapping directions.

"My heart prays for it daily, but I've come to accept that it may not God's will; and I have learned to be content with what the Lord sees fit to me have," he confessed.

Derek looked down at his hands and thought about that. The fact that Mandie's parents loved him so much that they hoped and prayed that Mandie would love him was just about more than he could handle; but he continued to be content and thankful for everyday that the Lord gave him, just being able to be near her and her wonderful family.

"Well, Derek, I have been able to pick up several meetings on the way to and from the West Coast Gospel Jubilee in L.A. This is going to be one of the most challenging hauls, and I need for you to be well rested. There will be days that I'll need for you to drive seven or eight hours straight." Mr. McCormick explained.

Derek smiled. "The Lord will give me strength. I know that everything will work out well, sir. So where are we going?"

"Are you ready for this? We need to head seven hours west for Quitman, Mississippi for a stop there for a new church in that town-this will be a one-night stop during their revival. Then from there we need to head straight for Dallas, Texas for a one-night spot in the 'Homecoming on the Range' Gospel Festival. As soon as we can leave there, we're off to Carlsbad, New Mexico, where we'll get one day to rest a bit. After that we're heading to Los Angeles to set up and rehearse for the West Coast Gospel Jubilee at the Greek Theater. It will be a little different for us because it is an open-air amphitheater."

"I Googled it. The view is amazing!" Derek agreed.

"Well, here's where we need to start praying. We've got a week in between the Jubilee and the next show in El Paso, Texas, when we begin our trek back home; but I know that the Lord will provide."

"I'll be praying about that, sir," Derek promised.

"After El Paso, we'll go to Mobile, Alabama for a three day Festival, and we'll just make it in time to Jacksonville, Florida to meet up with your mom, your uncle, and Grandpa on the ship. Are you sure you're alright with going on the cruise? Shane told me about your anxiety concerning the water. I'm so sorry for your loss."

"Thank you. Yes sir, I'll be fine. God has helped me immensely. Things will be fine."

"That's great; now, son, let's get this heap a'movin'!" teased Mr. Brian.

"I'm on it!" said Derek as he slipped on his Stetson and saddled up for a long, seven hour drive.

Chapter Twenty-Three

The ride to Quitman, Mississippi was one of the hardest that Derek had ever made. His body was so tired, and the interstate was so straight, that he begged God in his heart to keep him awake. The Lord brought them safely there to meet with Pastor Chip Averman at the Back to Bethel Community Church. They had arrived just in time for the church's picnic supper on the grounds. The weather there had been strangely and unseasonably warm for January, and Pastor Averman had decided to take advantage of the beautiful conditions, knowing that there would be other dinners in the fellowship hall. The entire congregation and the guest evangelist, Kevin Hutchinson, were gathered in the back yard of the church with a swarm of grills, coolers, steaks, burgers and hot dogs.

The McCormick's were thrilled to join in the fun and festivities. The church's youth director had set up several games for the children, and the whole church seemed to be having a wonderful time.

While Shane and Derek were all too willing to jump in and join the fun, Mandie was still, understandably, a bit reserved. She was sitting at a picnic table alone with a Diet Soda when her mother approached her.

"Mandie, why don't you go out there with Shane and Derek and have some fun? It'll do you no good just to sit here at this table and mope!"

"No thanks, Moma. I'm too old for that stuff!" she answered as she sipped some more of her drink.

"Derek's older than you, and he's enjoying every bit of the fresh air and exercise. I know he'd rather be in the bed right now, as long as he's been up and driving, but he's not letting life pass him by."

"Well, that because he's...Derek! I'm not going out there to make a fool of myself!"

"Well, did you get anything to eat? There's plenty on the buffet spread." Mrs. Margie offered.

"No, Ma'am. I'm not hungry," Mandie answered as she kept sipping on her drink. "I just don't feel like eating."

"Well, okay for this time. But you've gotta eat something sooner or later. You've gotta take care of yourself," she admonished.

"Okay, Moma. Dad's over there motioning for you. You'd better go," Mandie began.

Margie got the gist of what Mandie was saying, and she quickly sat down at the table with Mandie, and sidled up close so that she could hear her whispers. "Your Daddy can wait just a minute. His hands aren't broken-he can get that drink or dessert for himself-I know that's what he wants; and I also know one thing, girl, now you listen to me: you are not gonna shut me out, do you understand? You are my daughter. I am extremely proud of you. You are strong, because of the One who lives in you, but you will not try to get rid of me so that you can wallow in self-pity. Now, go get yourself a hot dog and a cookie or something. Life goes on; and I will be back to check on you," she said as she kissed her daughter's temple, and proceeded to her husband who was having issues cutting the coconut cake.

Mandie sat there for a few moments and watched Derek and Shane from her table. Several of the smaller boys and girls had started a game of kickball, with Derek being captain of one team, and Shane the other. As she watched them, she noticed how Derek was having a wonderful time. He was playing first base, with one man on. As the ball was kicked, he wrapped his arms around the boy trying to run to second, holding him back while yelling, 'Run, run! He's coming!' The little boy was just laughing and trying to get away. It was evident that he loved children. *I'll bet Mitch didn't even like kids,'* she thought to herself as she sipped her drink again.

"Hum, hum," Mandie heard from the direction of the buffet line. It was Mrs. Margie reminding her that she had not eaten yet.

Mandie mouthed the words, 'Okay', to her mom as she finally picked herself up from the table and went to the end of the buffet line, picking up a plate.

She was almost bull-dozed by Shane as he ran up to the table. "Mandie? Would you fix me something to drink? I sure am thirsty," her brother asked.

178

"What's wrong with you? You've got two hands, just like everyone else here. I'm not your slave, you know!" she replied.

"Oh, come on! I've gotta get back to the game! It'll be my turn to kick in just a minute!" he cried.

"Fine. What do ya want?"

"A bottle of water would be great, thanks!" Shane said as he quickly ran back to the game.

'Really! The things I do for him,' she thought as she made her way to the large cooler over by the fence. *'I'll bet that Derek needs one, too. I might as well pick up two, so that I won't have to make another trip.'*

Mandie carried the two bottles over to the green where the young men rallied their troops in a wonderful game of kickball, which would soon have to come to an end, as the McCormick's needed to set up their sound equipment for the service that evening. Mandie waited for Derek to call the game as officially over. Oh, how the children wailed and cried for them to continue. Several of the little boys latched on to Shane's and Derek's legs, forbidding them to leave!

Pastor Averman walked up and explained that the family had to go work on their songs, so that everyone could enjoy their music later on that night. After many, 'Aw's' from the young crowd, Shane and Derek were finally released. Mandie took that opportunity to refresh them.

"Here you go," she said as she practically threw the bottle at Shane.

"Well, thank you, Miss High and Mighty," Shane responded.

"And here's one for you too," she continued as she handed the bottle to Derek, hardly looking at him.

"Thanks! You didn't have to bother getting me anything!" he said as he wiped the cool bottle to his forehead. "But it sure was nice of you!" he said with a smile.

"Yeah, well, I just didn't wanna have to make another trip back there, Tex!" she said as she walked away, back towards the bus.

"Hey, wait up!" shouted Derek as he ran behind her. She stopped for him. "Did you wanna get a bite of something sweet? I got swept up in a game before grabbing dessert.

I'm gonna get one of those cupcakes with the sprinkles-they look good; then I'm gonna help with equipment and crash. I've gotta catch up on my sleep!"

"No, thank you; I'm really not hungry. I'll see if I can help Shane with the equipment though, if you wanna turn in early," she offered.

"No way! You can't lift some of those huge crates!" Derek objected.

"I can lift some of them, sir; and looking back, since you've joined us, I don't really think that I've been pulling my weight in that department. I'd been sorta 'pre-occupied'."

Derek smiled. "Well, that's alright. You don't have to help if don't want to; but I won't stop you."

Mandie smiled back. "Like you could!" she teased.

"Oh, I could, now!" he said with an even bigger smile as he watched her walk away towards the storage compartment where Shane had begun to unload a few boxes.

'I guess I'll get that cupcake to go!' he thought silently as he watched Mandie begin to pick up milk crates filled with microphone cords.

Watching from the table beside her husband, Mrs. Margie noticed that Mandie never did fill that Styrofoam plate with anything to eat.

🚌 🚌 🚌 🚌 🚌

The revival meeting in Quitman went wonderfully! The preaching was moving and there were four precious souls saved that night. After the tear down of the equipment late that night, Derek promised Mr. McCormick that he'd give him an early start in the morning, as eight hours driving time alone to Dallas would be a full day.

And a full day it was! Derek drove all day, only stopping twice for the rest areas. The family ate and rehearsed on the bus so that they could drop out of the bus and almost directly onto the stage when Derek stopped it!

That was the fastest that they'd ever gone into a show! Mr. McCormick met with the show's promoter afterwards, thanking him for the opportunity, and thereby secured a two-night spot in that same show for the next year!

The family all fell into their bunks after the show. Mr. and Mrs. McCormick were the very first to turn in. Shane made his way to his bunk to put in a call to Gwen before calling it a night, but not before having to wake Derek up from the small breakfast nook in the galley to point him in the right direction of his lower level bunk.

At about three o'clock that next morning, Derek felt that awful rumbling in his stomach that only Chocolate Puffs could fill. Grabbing his tee shirt, he trudged up the small stairwell to the galley to grab a quick bowl before turning back in. As he rounded the final turn, he noticed a small light, moving around in the room. Mandie almost jumped out of her skin when he walked in.

"What in the world are you doing up at this time of the night?" he asked.

"Well, I suppose that I could ask you the same thing!" she said as she continued rummaging through the galley cabinets.

"Mandie, why don't you just cut on the lights?" he said he as he switched the small light over the sink.

Mandie quickly closed her eyes, squeezing them shut. "Please, please..." she begged as she waved one hand over her eyes, and the other at Derek, motioning for him to cut the light back off.

"Oh, I'm sorry," Derek whispered. "Do you have a headache?"

"Um, hum. I've carried it pretty much all day. I sang through it, though," she said as she grabbed her head, rubbing it, hoping that the throbbing would stop."

"Here," he said, as he took the small Mag-lite from her hand. He guided her to the breakfast nook table, and sat her down. "I'll find it for you."

"Thank you," she whispered, holding her head with her elbows propped up on the table.

Derek searched through the cabinet until he found the Headache Relief bottle. Bringing her two caplets to the table, he stopped on the way to grab a cookie to go with the medicine. He brought her a drink, and gently placed the caplets in her hand.

"Thank you," she whispered. "Is this Diet?" she asked.

"No; I can get you some though..." he began.

Mandie shook her head. "No, it's okay. It's only a little sip to take this," she said as she downed the caplets, taking some of the drink behind it.

"You should eat that cookie, too. Those pills could be rough on your stomach, if you don't," Derek offered.

"No, it's okay. I've taken them without anything to eat many times; but thanks for thinking of me. I'm gonna go lay down now," she said as she trudged back to her bunk.

"I'll take my cereal downstairs to eat it," Derek said as he sprang up to fix his bowl. "Goodnight," he whispered to her as she pulled back her divider just enough to step in. She waved one hand 'Goodnight' to Derek, as she avoided having to speak through her migraine.

Derek did eat his bowl of cereal, and then couldn't go back to sleep. So, by four-thirty a.m. he had the family tour bus on the road, beginning his seven hour drive; this time to Carlsbad, New Mexico. The family had no show there, but Mr. McCormick had always wanted to see the famous Carlsbad Caverns. It was another fourteen and a half hours from there to Los Angeles, and even though Derek said he could handle it, Mr. McCormick knew that they would have to break it up a little.

Derek and the family arrived there around eleven-thirty a.m.; just in time for lunch, according to Shane. Mandie spent her time "sleeping-in" and didn't join the family for lunch. She told her mother that she'd pick up a banana on their way out to the caverns.

The family decided to take a self-guided tour, starting with the Natural Entrance Route. Just looking at the open mouth to the cave, Mr. Brian and Mrs. Margie looked at each other. They were thinking the exact same thing-how much it reminded them of what Jesus' tomb may have looked like. As they entered the wondrous cavern, Shane began reading the map, noting the highlights of the tour.

182

"It says here, that they have, a lake in here called 'The Devil's Spring'; and then there's 'The Witch's Finger' which is a giant stalagmite coming up from the floor; then we wind down to "The Devil's Den';"

The family's faces just kept contorting as Shane read on all of the horrible names for such beautiful sights!

"Let me see that," Mr. Brian said as he took the map from Shane's hands. "Well, here's one called 'The Rock of Ages'-now that's more like it!" he said with a smile.

"Yeah, but..." began Shane as he snatched the map back from his dad, "...but that's on the Big Room Route. We've taken the wrong route, Dad! Look right here in the brochure it says that everyone should tour the Big Room tour, because this one, the Natural Entrance Tour is impressive but very steep!"

"Oh, well! Let's just enjoy the sights and not worry about what they're called! We'll make it through and then catch that route next!"

So the group continued their tour winding down further into the caverns. As they neared the exit, Mandie found that the climb was very steep indeed. She used the handrails, but about half-way up she collapsed.

"Mandie!" said Mrs. Margie as she ran to her side, followed closely by Derek.

"Moma! I'm so sorry. I don't know what's wrong. My legs just started trembling, and they gave way."

"Did you eat that banana this morning?" Mrs. Margie asked.

"No, Ma'am. I just had something to drink. I just wasn't hungry," Mandie confessed.

"That's what's wrong with you! You need to eat something!"

"Moma, I don't think that I can make it back up there. I'm too weak."

"You don't have too. I've gotcha. Come on, now. Can you wrap your arms around my neck?" Derek asked.

"I'll try," Mandie replied as she reached up and pulled against his shoulders to aid in his lifting. Almost as soon as he stood up with her, her arms fell. "I'm so sorry. I just can't hold on."

"It's ok. Just rest, Mandie. Just rest on me," Derek said as he carried her up the hill.

🚌 🚌 🚌 🚌 🚌

The family went back to the bus for their lunch. Derek carried Mandie onto the bus, and straight past her bunk to the breakfast nook in the galley. There, her mother made sure that she ate a peanut butter and jelly sandwich. After lunch Mr. McCormick helped Mandie to her bunk, for a mandated nap.

After Mandie woke up from her nap, she was feeling much better, and promised her Dad that she could make it on the second tour. The family did catch the other route, and took a look at the other sights. Mandie's favorite was 'The Dolls Theater' which looked just like a theater curtain with magnificent stalactites creating a beautiful illusion.

She thought about the next show at the Greek Theatre. She had looked over Derek's shoulder when he researched the place. It was the most beautiful performance stage that she had ever seen. She couldn't wait to get there.

Since Derek had also taken a good nap after lunch, the family was set for a long night drive. Derek promised Mr. McCormick that he would pull over at a rest area when he needed to rest. So, at sundown, Derek embarked on the longest drive of his short career with fourteen and half hours staring him in the face.

At around one o'clock the next morning, Derek did have to pull over and spend the next three hours sleeping. At around four-thirty, he roused up to get a quick bite of breakfast before hitting the road again. At five o'clock sharp, Derek pulled that bus back onto the interstate.

Shane got up and at 'em around eight o'clock- riding shotgun with Derek, taking in the sights of the cross-country drive. They both wondered why Mandie had not awakened to take her place in the upper lounge as she usually does.

"I'll bet she's just tired from all the climbing and walking we did yesterday at the caverns. She's a little out of shape, you know," Shane said with his usual brotherly tone.

184

"She is not. She's just right; and that's not it. I've noticed that she's not been eating much at all here lately. I think that your Mom's been noticing it too," Derek revealed.

"Well, that's never been a problem before. She's never had a problem eating too little; she's always been eating too much! That's why she's out of shape!" Shane rebutted.

"Don't even go there. She is not out of shape! She's grieving! I know that she's hurt, but these are some pretty serious signs. There's more going on there than just Mitch. You'd better be praying for her," Derek said in a more serious tone.

With a couple of pit stops, Derek had the family pulling into the bus parking area of the Greek Theater at around one-thirty in the afternoon. Shane ran to the upstairs stairwell and yelled for his parents to come on down as Derek put on the parking brake. Shane stopped and ripped back Mandie's divider to drag her out of bed.

"Come on, Mandie! We're finally here! California! Come on, let's go!" he continued as he began to tap on her arm to rouse her up. She didn't move. "Mandie, wake up, girl. Quit playin'" Still she didn't move. Shane put his hand to her cheek. "MOM!" Shane yelled. "Come quick! Mandie's burnin' up with fever.

"Hope deferred maketh the heart sick: but when the desire cometh, it is a tree of life."

Proverbs 13:12

Chapter Twenty-Four

Mrs. Margie came running down the stairwell to check on her daughter. She felt Mandie's forehead, and she was indeed suffering from a high fever, and she couldn't wake up. Mrs. Margie called for her husband.

"Brian, I don't know what to do. We don't know where any hospitals are around here, and we don't know any doctors. She won't wake up!"

"Just calm down, Margie. Listen, I will call the promoter. He is more than likely here on the grounds; he can point us in the right direction. Just stop and think-how would you treat the fever if you were at home?"

"Well, a cold, washcloth soaked with alcohol, but she's never been unresponsive!" yelled Margie with tears in her eyes.

"Margie. Keep calm. Treat her that way, while I'm finding out what we can do. The Lord is in control. Rest in that," he said as he pulled his wife in for a brief hug. "Now get to...Hello! Mr. Patrick?" he said as he walked off to a more quiet area to explain the situation.

Mrs. Margie turned around to begin her search for the washcloth and alcohol, but she turned to find Shane standing right there with both items, waiting to help. Mrs. Margie doused the already cold cloth with the alcohol, and began to wipe down the sides of Mandie's face, that was wet with sweat.

Slowly, she began to awaken, and Derek began to breathe again. He had stood back watching in slow motion from the beginning of Shane's panicking call for his mother. He took a step closer to assess the situation.

As Mandie finally woke up, she opened her eyes very slowly. Her eyes were red and glassy from the fever. "Moma? I don't feel good," she managed to say before vomiting right there on her bed.

"Ugh! Mandie that is foul!" Shane said in repulsion.

"Oh! Okay. Don't move Mandie. I'll be right back," she said as she went to get another cold washcloth for her face.

187

"Shane, stay here while I go below and get some trash bags from the storage compartment," Derek said as he ran out of the front doors of the bus.

Mrs. Margie quickly returned with Mr. Brian on her heels. "Mr. Patrick has a personal physician on-call for these events. He and Dr. Belton are on the way to the bus right now."

Derek returned with the trash bags, passing them off to Mrs. Margie. "Thanks, Derek. That was quick thinking. Now, if you boys will step outside, I've gotta help her get changed before the doctor gets here."

"A doctor? Who's sending a doctor? Is this someone we can trust?" asked Derek in genuine concern.

"Yes. Mr. Patrick has his personal physician coming to look at Mandie," Mr. Brian assured him, "Everything will be alright. The Lord is in control; now come on, let's step outta here for a minute.

The men walked out of the bus while Mrs. Margie helped Mandie get out of her soiled pajamas, and then stripped her bed, while she sat slumped over against the wall.

Outside the bus, the men took a step back and looked at the now pressing issue at hand. "Men, more than likely, Mandie is fine. We've got to think about tonight's show. She's not going to be able to sing," Mr. McCormick concluded.

"Well, Mom can fill in for her on the vocals; that's no problem," Shane offered.

"Yes, but, Mandie doesn't need to stay alone. If she's sick, she's gonna need help, and your mother can't be in two places at once!" Mr. McCormick reasoned.

"Well, that leaves me. I'm the only one not on stage. I'll stay with Mandie and take care of her," said Derek.

"Derek, I can't ask you to do that. You could catch what she has, and then you'd be down, and not able to drive the bus..."

"Well, you said we've got a whole week after this show filled with absolutely nothing-the Lord had that open for a reason. And who knows? Maybe I won't get sick! We'll just take this one day at a time; but for right now, Mrs.

Margie can sing for Mandie, and I'll stay with her on the bus tonight during the show."

Dr. Belton came and examined Mandie, and made an initial determination of a simple virus. He drew two vials of blood to have tested just to be on the safe side. He sent them with his Medical Assistant, who ran them to the lab at his office immediately. In less than an hour, the Assistant called the doctor on this cell, reporting that the electrolytes were extremely low from the onset of dehydration.

Mrs. McCormick explained that she had not been eating properly. With that information, Dr. Belton concluded that she had indeed more than likely picked up the virus in her weakened condition, and that it could run its course in as quickly as twenty-four hours. He had the assistant fill a prescription for Phenergan tablets to aid with the nausea and recommended a rotation of Acetaminophen and Ibuprofen to control the fever. He really wanted to provide an Intro-venous fluid regimen, but opted to try ice chips and sips of Electrolyte solution to drink instead to rehydrate her.

Mandie had it rough the next few hours, getting sick three more times. By the time her mother had to leave for the show, she had calmed down, and the nausea had stopped. She had drifted off to sleep again-which gave her mother mixed emotions. "I know it's just a virus, Derek, but please watch out for her while she's sleeping. Sometimes that fever creeps back up when you're sleeping."

"I will take good care of her, Mrs. Margie. No worries!" Derek assured her.

"I know you will, Derek. Thank you," she said as she joined Shane and Mr. Brian in the wings to prepare for their first outdoor event.

Derek had taken preventative measures while the doctor was examining Mandie earlier in the day. The head janitor for the facility had loaded him down with Lysol, extra trash bags, and Sanitizing wipes. No sooner than Mrs.

Margie had left, Mandie began to awaken. "Mom?" she called.

"No, Mandie, it's just me. You're Mama's already gone to the show," said Derek apologetically.

"Oh! I can't believe that I've had to miss our first West Coast show. This is terrible! I feel so terrible," she said as she began to cry.

"Oh, honey! Please don't cry! That's not gonna help anything," Derek said as he passed her a tissue. "There's another show tomorrow night, and the doctor said this thing could be passed by then. You'll get your opportunity; but not if you don't get some rest. Now just lie back, and try to relax. I'm here if you need anything, and I'm gonna be listening out for you. If you need anything I'll be right here, lickety split," he said as he stood up to go.

"Where are you going?" she asked in concern.

"Well, I'm a man on a mission," he said as he placed his Stetson on his head. He then turned to the side to reveal that he was wearing a double gun holster, and each side was filled with a can of Lysol. He pressed the playback button on his cell phone which bellowed out the all too familiar sounds of, 'The Good, The Bad, and The Ugly'.

Mandie began to laugh, weakly.

Derek stood at attention to draw, and draw he did; spinning the can of Lysol in his hand, "This bus will be sanitized!"

With that, Mandie burst into laughter, only to suddenly wince in pain, as her sides were so sore from heaving all afternoon.

"Oh, honey! I'm so sorry! I shouldn't have made you laugh. I didn't think about you being sore! I was just trying to make you feel better," he said with sympathy.

"It's okay-you are making me feel better-just by being here," she said as she laid herself back, and closed her eyes, just as she was told to.

Derek waited until he was sure that she was asleep again, and then he continued on his mission. He sprayed every compartment on that bus, and wiped down every light switch and handle that could have possibly been exposed. When he was finally done, he jumped in the shower to kill any germs that decided they wanted to hitch a ride on him. He bagged up his clothes to be washed later.

Just as he had finished cleaning up, he heard Mandie scream. He raced upstairs to her side to find her brow again, wet with sweat, and burning up from fever.

"Spiders! The Spiders! They're everywhere!" she screamed.

"Mandie! Mandie! Wake up, honey! It's just a bad dream!" Derek said as he tried to wake her up with the cold washcloth doused once more with alcohol.

Mandie did open her eyes, suddenly, as the cold cloth gently touched her skin. "I'm sorry," she started.

Derek continued to bathe her face with the alcohol, until she could sit up and take over for herself. "Why are you sorry? I'm sorry you're sick!"

"I'm sorry that you're stuck here with me like this, when you could be out there enjoying the show."

"I'd rather be here, helping you," he said honestly.

"Well, I still feel bad," she said as she propped herself up and tried to pick up the small cup of ice chips. Her hand shook in weakness as she attempted to lift the tumbler.

"Here. Let me help you," Derek said as he took the cup from her hand, and slowly lifted the spoon of ice chips to her lips.

She took them graciously. "You know, you might as well go on out there. I'm gonna end up all alone one day, and I'll have to take care of myself anyways," she pouted.

"You are not gonna be alone, Mandie. You're not alone now!" Derek said as he took the opportunity to give Mandie some advice. "This is just a trial. Life is full of them. Usually, when we go through trials, we are only thinking about ourselves; you know, the little pity parties with only one person on the guest list-you! The key to making it through a trial is not looking at ourselves, but looking at Jesus. He is the Strength that you need to make it through. He knows what you can handle and what you can't. He knows every move and every thought that enters our minds before we make it. We are not alone. If we focus on Him, and what he went through on Calvary for us, our problems don't seem so bad. Do you want some more?"

"Ice chips or lecture?" she asked as she smiled weakly.

"Both!" Derek replied.

"Okay. I'm too tired to fight," she answered as she opened her mouth for the spoonful of ice chips that was rapidly approaching.

"You're not alone now, and you never will be. You've got your wonderful family here for you right now-and they'll always be there for you. And you've got these..." he said began as he pulled up a plastic grocery bag full of her Bridal Magazines. "I retrieved these from your trashcan earlier in the week, when I was trying to pick up around the bus. I can't believe that you threw these out."

"Well, I don't need them anymore. I lost my chance. I'm just about past the age of marrying," she complained.

"Please! How old are you now, Grannie?"

"I'll be twenty-one next month," she said as tears began to fill her eyes.

"Well, I guess that puts me with one foot in the grave and the other on a banana peel! Goodness, I'm only two years older than you, and I've got my whole life in front of me!"

"Well, you've got your e-mail girl from the Camp Meeting, what's her name, Gwen's friend?"

"Stephanie?"

"Yeah-you've got Stephanie; and I've got no body."

Derek never told anyone but this mother that he had bid Stephanie 'farewell' via e-mail; and now didn't seem the appropriate time to open up about that. He picked up the magazines and laid them on her bed. "Don't give up on your dreams. The Bible says that if you delight yourself in the Lord, he will give you the desires of your heart. You've got your family-and one day you will marry some very blessed man; and you will be a wonderful wife to him," he began. He looked away, mustering the courage to continue. "But, even if God didn't have anyone out there for you, there is still Someone Who cares for you-and that's Jesus. Jesus cares for you; and He's enough. He satisfies the soul; at least, that's what I've come to learn," he finished as they both heard the front door to the bus open.

"It smells like a lemon farm up in here!" Shane shouted as he wandered on the bus.

🚌 🚌 🚌 🚌 🚌

The morning provided a healthier and happier Mandie. Her fever had finally broken in the night, and she was well on her way to being on the stage for that night's performance. The virus had indeed run its course.

The prior night's show had gone well, and the promoter was extremely pleased, even with Mandie not taking the stage. He was so impressed, that he not only booked the family to return to this event the next year, but he also booked them for the first ever Canadian Gospel Jubilee set for the end of April in British Columbia.

Derek had spent the morning resting, after such an eventful day before, and was surprised at the visitor that darkened his door that mid-morning.

"Derek, dear, may I come in?" asked Mrs. McCormick.

Derek sat up quickly and grabbed his tee shirt. "Yes, Ma'am. Come on in."

"How are you feeling today?" she asked.

"Oh, I'm fine! I was just catching up on some rest before we hit the trail for parts unknown tomorrow morning," he said as Mr. McCormick's plans were still unsure for after the end of the Jubilee that night. "Please, tell me-how is Mandie today?"

"She is much better, praise the Lord. I'm extremely glad to see that you are not sick. I was concerned that you would catch it from her. I must say, I was impressed with the way you cleaned this bus; and in record time, too!"

"I thought it would be best for everyone," he replied humbly.

"It was a good idea, but..." she paused as she searched for the right words to say. "...evidently Shane did not escape. He started getting sick about three o'clock this morning," she reported.

"Oh, no! What are y'all gonna do about the show tonight?" Derek asked.

"Well, dear, that's why I'm here. We can't cancel tonight, and as you know, Shane is a key part of the performance. Mandie is well enough, she assures us, that she will be back on stage. So we are selecting some songs that she will play on the piano; but we still need a bass player."

"Surely, you're not here to ask me?" Derek said in sheer terror.

"Shane says you're ready-that you know several of our songs by heart!" she pleaded.

"Oh, Mrs. Margie! I don't know! This is a big show for the family! I'd feel awful if I messed it up!"

"You won't mess it up. Brian's got everything wrapped up for next year anyways! I need to stay in the bus with Shane to help him get better. We only have Mandie and Brian left. Please Derek-we can't go on tonight unless you help us! It's time for you to go from 'Minister of Transportation' to Bass Player, and I need you to change hats fast!"

Derek couldn't let the family down-not after everything that they had done for him. "Alright. I'll get up and meet Mandie and Mr. Brian in fifteen minutes."

Mrs. Margie quickly hugged Derek's neck. "Thank you, Derek. Thank you so much!"

🚌 🚌 🚌 🚌 🚌

While waiting to go on, Mr. McCormick had a word of prayer with Mandie and Derek before taking the stage. He prayed specifically for the Lord to calm Derek's nerves, and for the Lord just to take over his fingers as he played the bass.

"So, are you ready for this, Tex?" Mandie asked in an attempt to encourage him.

"I'm as ready as I'll ever be!"

"You can do it. If you can handle my whining and complaining, this ought to be a piece of cake!" she said with a smile. "Thank you for taking care of me last night."

"You're welcome," he said with a peaceful, relaxed smile.

Mandie turned and faced the stage; but just before she stepped on, when she spoke to him over her shoulder, "You're gonna make some lady a great husband one day."

Derek took to the stage behind her and played the bass flawlessly that night, because he didn't think about anything; his mind was on Mandie's compliment. He knew the music backwards and forwards, and it came natural to him, just like Shane said it would. When the show was finished, he marveled at how God had allowed him to come from the bus driver to the back-up bass player! He became keenly aware of a ray of hope: *With God, all things are possible,* he thought to himself.

Mr. McCormick met Mandie and Derek back at the bus to find Shane, faring much better than Mandie had at that point in time the night before.

"Well, troops-this concert certainly turned out a mite different than we thought it would, but the Lord has blessed us indeed. We've got bookings for next year-big ones; and I shared our 'empty week' with Mr. Patrick to see if he had any suggestions."

"What did we get, Dad-another big show close by?" Shane asked weakly.

"Nope! Mr. Patrick was so pleased by the way we 'bounced back' through adversity, that he thought we deserved this next week off, so, he's offered us his cabin at Big Bear Lake-free of charge."

"Oh, Brian! I've always wanted to go there!" Mrs. Margie exclaimed.

"Rest and relaxation, here we come!" said Mr. Brian as he sat down in the breakfast nook with a sigh of relief!

"And he said unto them, Come ye yourselves apart into a desert place, and rest a while:"

Mark 6:31a

Derek transported the family to the cabin in record time that very night. The family deserted the bus quickly, and found their rooms almost immediately. Shane was already gaining strength and vowed that he and Derek would be fishing at sunrise, so he and his parents turned in early.

The cabin was perfect. The deck faced the beautiful lake, lined with pines and other evergreens. The deck also came complete with white rocking chairs. Derek thought that it had to be the closest place next to Heaven, except his Home back in Tennessee.

He was so tired-so spent-but yet he couldn't quite turn in yet. Even though it was only a two hour drive from Los Angeles to Big Bear Lake, he was played out just from the exhilaration of performing on stage for the very first time. *'I honestly don't know how they do it all the time,'* he thought to himself. He was over-tired. His legs felt like they weighed ten tons a piece, but he knew that they'd carry him a few steps further-to the rocking chair. As he slid into the seat and leaned back for that first rock, he closed his eyes. He took a ride back in time to his old house at the farm. The night air was so cool and moist; only this place was better than home- there were no mosquitoes! He opened his eyes and lifted them up toward the heavens, to find a silvery moon casting its lonesome shadow over the lake-lending its light to dance across the waters. The country night was so quiet he could hear the calm waves lapping against the shoreline, and he heard Mandie's stealthy approach just the same. "Good evenin', Mandie," he spoke without turning his head.

His voice startled her, and she stopped in her tracks. She stood there until she found her voice. "Hey, Derek. I'm sorry, am I disturbing you?" she asked sheepishly.

"No, not at all; please; come and join me," he replied without ever turning his glance towards her. He couldn't. The scene was too right. It couldn't be more perfect. Mandie walked to the rocking chair next to him and took her place. She laid her head back and began to rock. She could see how

Derek was so lost. The mountain lake view was intoxicating. Soon she was just as entranced as he was.

"You know," Derek began, "I'm pretty sure that there will be rocking chairs in Heaven."

Mandie let out a tired giggle. "What makes you say that?"

"Because Heaven is full of perfection," he answered.

"And a rocking chair is perfect?"

"Well, maybe not the chair itself; but it's the duty it performs. It upholds the person sitting in it; it comforts them, as they rock back and forth; it soothes the aching muscles of the weary, and the souls of the troubled. It offers safety and security, like a mother to a baby."

"Well, that's...pretty deep, Tex," she replied. "Are you gonna whip out a guitar now and burst into song like a cowboy 'round the campfire on the cattle drive?"

Derek slowly turned his head and looked at her. "You just don't get it;" She looked puzzled. It was like bearing his soul to her about contentment last night was of no help at all. She was right back to 'Me-Me-Me' mode. He thought that maybe he'd broken through to her. He turned back and looked at the lake with the most forlorn expression. "Maybe you never will."

In the midst of paradise, Mandie gave in to her frustration. She had recovered from her sickness, but she still couldn't see the light at the end of the tunnel. It was as if their conversation from the night before had gone in one ear and out of the other. "I know I don't get it. I know I don't." She jumped up out of her rocker and strolled toward the deck railing, overlooking the lawn that led down to the bank. "I've prayed and prayed for something to happen. I've done right by people. I've read my Bible. Why hasn't the Lord answered my prayer?"

He had only just reminded her how Jesus cared for her; and about how she would never be alone. How could she still be so oblivious? Once again, she had gotten under his skin in the way that only she could. Derek, closed his eyes, and mustered the courage to stand. "Mandie, do you know why you don't understand the rocking chair?" he asked as he began to slowly step up beside her.

"I'm talking about important stuff here, Tex, and you're back to the chair again! Aren't you listening?"

"Are you?" he retorted. "The reason, your grace, that you don't understand the rocking chair is because you don't understand the concept of slooooowwwww," he replied as he emphatically drug out the word.

"I understand that some of you farm hands don't always get to go to school, but even in the Carolina's, there is *some* education," she said as she allowed her sarcasm to get the best of her.

"No, Mandie; it's about slowing down-and resting-and waiting. That's something you just don't understand-waiting. I tried to explain it to you last night; about being content and waiting on the Lord."

"I've been waiting! I'm tired of waiting! I want a husband and a family!" she spoke loudly as she turned to Derek in exasperation.

Derek responded in kind, but with hushed tones, stepping towards her, so as not to wake anyone in the cabin. "I guess I should have thrown those magazines out like you wanted to. Maybe you'd be easier to get along with! Do you really even know what you want? You think you want a husband; but you don't want a husband. You just want to get married-so bad, in fact, that you don't even care who the groom is!" *'And she told me that I'd make someone a good husband! I thought she was making some headway!'* he thought to himself as she rambled on.

Her loudest whispers returned, "That is not true! I didn't try to jump at the first thing that came along! I felt at peace about him! I thought he was Mr. Right. Now, I'm so confused! You're right. I know I should be content. But, I don't even trust myself! I thought he was right, but he was oh, so wrong! And I didn't know it! How do you know when something's right?"

"You know, Mandie, you just know. I was at peace about joining the army. I got as far as to even put my hand on the door, but the Lord wouldn't let me pull it. I never told anyone but my Mama about that day. I didn't want others to know my struggle. There are so many things that I've been through, that you just wouldn't understand; things that

199

make your little episode with Mitch seem like dandelions floatin' on the breeze! I battled there with the Lord in the parking lot of the recruiter's office that day, but He wouldn't let me do it."

As Derek continued to bear his soul to her, for her good, the rest of his emotions rose to the surface as well. The tension drew them closer to one another and he could fight his passions no longer. He tried to calm himself, and once again he tried to reach out to her and help her to understand. As she stepped towards him, he placed his hand over hers that was resting on the railing of the deck. "When the Lord speaks to you, Mandie, you know it right here," he said as he pointed to his heart.

"Right here?" she asked, as she reached out and covered his hand with hers beside his heart, moving in closer.

Her surprising boldness was welcomed, as he reached out and caressed her face, drawing her to him, "And I know when it's right..." he whispered as he pulled her lips to his in the lightest most ginger kiss that she had ever known. She became lightheaded and faint, and let out a whimper. Derek responded by securing her at the small of her back.

After a moment, Mandie pulled back. "No, No; this is wrong. You're not the right one...I don't..."

Derek interrupted her by pulling her back to him. "Don't fight this, Mandie. We both know that we're right for each other..." he said as he leaned toward her again. Again, she willingly pressed her lips to his, giving in. When she became completely breathless, she again pulled away, this time stepping back. A panting Derek lost his grip. "Mandie...please..."

"I'm sorry, Derek...I'm so sorry..." she whispered as she ran from the deck, and back into the cabin.

Derek turned towards the lake and leaned on the railing. *'Why? You idiot! Why did I rush things?! I was trying to tell her not to rush things, and I was the one who rushed in! Ugh! I was content! I was happy to be alone, without her! But, then I thought she knew...I thought she finally knew what I've known for months. What do I do now? She'll hate me forever! How can I make her see?*

Lord, please show me-what do I do now?' he prayed as he slouched his way back to the rocking chair, slowly slid himself into the seat, closed his eyes and began rocking.

🚌 🚌 🚌 🚌 🚌

The alarm clock went off way too early for Derek; then he remembered-he promised Shane they'd go fishing this morning. He was so tired; but he had promised, so he sat up and swung his legs over the side of the bed, and just sat there for one more minute, resting. He had spent most of his night rocking in the chair on the porch praying and asking the Lord to forgive him for his actions. He had tried to restrain himself, but he had given in to his flesh. His mistake had thrown a rock in his and Mandie's friendship. It would never be the same, no matter what. He knew that he was going to have deal with the situation, and worse-he was going to have to tell Shane.

As soon as he thought about him, there was a knock at the door. And of course, it was Shane. "Hey brother, are you ready?"

"Naw. Gimme a minute and let me find my jeans, and I'll meet you on the pier."

"Alright. I've already got your gear," he whispered as he stepped quietly down the stairs so as not to wake the household.

Shane opened the blinds and let the moonlight shine through until he found his pants. *'This is going to be so hard,'* he thought to himself as he dressed for the trip. He slipped on his boots, and grabbed his faithful companion, his Stetson, and headed for the pier.

Shane looked up as he heard the planking of Derek's footsteps coming up the pier. "Alright! Let's go!"

"Are you feeling better this morning? We're not gonna get out there on the lake and then have to cut the trip short are we?" he asked in an attempt to get out of going.

"Naw-Don't worry about it! I'm 100% better, now let's go!"

"You've got me a life jacket in there?" Derek asked.

201

"Yes. We're good to go, now come on! The object is to get on the water before the sun comes up," replied an impatient Shane.

"Alright," he answered as he moped on into the boat.

Shane and Derek paddled out a ways, and then Shane pressed the pedal on the trolling motor. The two young men got the rods, reels and tackle prepared and starting casting out their lines. Then the silence ensued. After about fifteen minutes of not one word being spoken, Shane couldn't stand it anymore. "Alright, what's the deal?"

"What do you mean?"

"What's going on with you? You've been way too quiet the whole morning. Something's up and I wanna know what it is," he demanded.

"I'm really tired," Derek replied. He thought that his short, succinct answer would satisfy Shane's curiosity.

"Uh-Uh. I've known you for a while now Derek Jensen, and I know it's more than that. You're my brother, and I know when you're hiding something from me. *How could you?*" he said in his female falsetto to break the tension.

Derek laughed. "Okay. You're right. I've gotta tell you anyways," he paused as he searched for the right words to begin. "I... I messed up last night."

"What are you talking about? What do you mean you messed up? Daddy said that your performance was perfect!"

"With Mandie. I messed up," Derek answered with as little information as possible.

Shane's countenance suddenly changed. It went from quizzical, to careful interrogation mode. "Care to share?"

"Well, I went out to the porch after unpacking, to rock in the rocking chair and really rest, you know. The night driving is so tiresome," he paused, in effort to change the subject.

"Go on," Shane prodded.

"Well, Mandie tried to sneak up on me, but I heard her coming a mile away." Again, he paused.

"Yes..."

"Well, she sat down in the rocking chair next to me, and we started talking a little, and then she went totally bezerk, complaining in her usual way."

"And..."

"And, well, she stood up...and I tried not to... but I did...and then I walked over there to where she was standing... and I was trying to make her see that she had no patience... and then she walked closer to me... and well..."

"Oh, don't stop now. Please go on..." Shane said with a stonewall face.

"Oh, come on, Shane, you know what happened. Don't be like that," Derek retorted in shame.

"No, I wanna hear you say it," Shane demanded.

"I kissed her, okay. I kissed her," Derek answered as he hung his head in dismay.

Shane sat there for a moment, and looked at the bottom of the boat. Then he turned and looked at Derek, expressionless, but only for a moment. The corners of his mouth began to turn up, just ever so slightly. "Well...alright!" he cheered loudly. "It's about time! What happened? What'd she do? I always knew you were gonna be my brother FOR REAL!"

A shocked Derek quickly put on the brakes. "Whoa, Whoa! Did you not hear me say that I messed up?"

"How did you mess up? Everyone knows that you're in love with her! We just figured she didn't love you back," he explained excitedly.

"Well, that's just the thing. Everything happened kinda fast. We were really fussing at each other. I was sharing some...things...and anyways, basically I was fussing at her about..." He stopped as he laughed at himself in irony, "...about not having patience. And then here I go kissing her."

"So what's the problem?!" Shane said in frustration. "Isn't that what you wanted?"

"Yes; but evidently it's not what she wanted," he answered.

Shane's smile began to fade. "I don't understand, what are you trying to tell me? Did she want you to kiss her?"

"Well, yes, I thought so...she reached out to me, and I couldn't stop myself. But she did try to pull away, and I stopped her. But then she did eventually run away."

Shane stopped smiling as he realized the seriousness of the situation.

"You see, now, you see? I've messed it all up! I thought that she had finally come around, but then, get this, she says, 'I'm not the right one, and that she's sorry,' and then she just runs away."

"Oh, man. I'm so sorry-for you and for her," Shane said remorsefully.

"It's all my fault. I'm the man. I should have never left the safety of the rocking chair. It's always safe in the rocking chair! I should have taken charge of the situation, and bid her goodnight shortly after she arrived on the porch. But, once again, I transformed into 'Droolie-Man' and lost it all. She don't love me no more than the Man in the Moon, and now she probably hates my guts-and I have no one to blame but myself," he lamented.

"What are you going to do about it?" Shane asked.

"I'm gonna Man-up."

Chapter Twenty-Six

The morning sun warmed the lake as Shane and Derek headed back to the pier. The early fishing trip had been very productive, even though they hadn't caught one fish. As Shane steered the boat back towards the pier, Derek's heart sank into his stomach-Mandie was sitting on the end of the pier waiting on him.

Shane hollered up at Derek, as he began to slow the boat down. "So, I'm guessing we're going with Plan A, then?"

Derek turned back to look at Shane, and nodded-affirmative. As Shane slowed the boat, Derek stood up at the bow of the boat to brace for the impact. The only problem was that Mandie still stood dangerously close to the edge of the pier where the boat was headed. "Mandie, move back!" Derek yelled, as he waved his hand.

She took a few steps back. Derek continued to wave her back, and she continued to step back. She realized that she needed to get out of the way. Derek took his eyes off of her just in time to catch the pier, but they hit it a little harder than he wanted to. Derek pressed his strong hands against the pier to stop the boat. As soon as he looked up, he saw Mandie teetering on the edge-she had kept on backing up, just as Derek had told her. "Mandie! Hold on!" Derek yelled as he watched her fall backwards, with arms flapping desperately to grasp anything to help her remain on the planks-but it was too late. Down she went, hitting her head on the tip of the pontoon floater of the cruiser tied to the other side of the pier. The sound that it rang out was unmistakable.

"Mandie!" both Shane and Derek yelled. Shane struggled to turn the boat parallel to the pier and rope it off, but Derek had flipped into panic mode. He immediately leapt from the boat, tossing his Stetson to the side, and dove in the water after her. He felt around frantically in the murky waters to find what his eyes couldn't see. His right hand found an ankle, which he followed to hoist her up speedily to the surface.

As his head broke through to the surface, he shook the water from his eyes, and screamed for Shane. "We're here! Help me!" he cried to him while dragging her towards the pier, where Shane reached down and barely pulled Mandie onto the pier. She was unconscious.

"So much for Plan A!" Shane said as he reached down to get ready for CPR. Shane quickly went through the checklist of steps in his head. '*A: Assess the situation-my sister's not breathing-no good. Okay. B: Breaths-awkward, but necessary.*'

Derek pulled himself upon the planks and crawled towards her limp, lifeless body, laying there with horrific memories sweeping over him like early morning fog rolling across the fields being chased by the sunrise. '*God please-leave her with me just a little longer,*' he prayed as he looked to Shane with beseeching eyes.

Just as Shane tilted her head to open the airway, she began to cough and sputter out the dirty water that had trickled half-way into her lungs. He responded quickly, and rolled her onto her side, to help her expel the liquid.

"Thank you, Lord!" Shane screamed as Mandie tried to sit up. He lent his hands to help her. She latched onto Shane's neck, hugging him in sincere thankfulness; and he held onto her just as tightly.

"Man, am I glad that you're okay. I really wasn't looking forward to kissing my sister; as if I needed any more mental scarring," Shane said in an effort to lighten the mood.

Derek sat with his head between his knees, regaining his own breath now that the adrenaline rush had subsided. He looked over at Mandie and Shane. "Check her head. Is it bleeding?"

Shane ran his hands around her head, and she winced as he found the goose egg left by the large pontoon floater. "OW!" she yelled as she pulled away in pain. Shane pulled his hand away and checked it. Thankfully, there was no blood on it.

As soon as Derek saw that she was out of danger, he picked himself up and made his way to the white rocking chair on the porch and slid right in. He began rocking slowly.

Shane helped Mandie up and walked her up to the porch. He seated her in the other white rocker, where she had begun her teasing tirade the night before.

Shane headed over to the small storage shed where he had found all of the fishing tackle and life jackets the night before in preparation for the trip. He grabbed three beach towels, handing one to Mandie first, then to Derek on his way to the glass sliding door that led to the cabin's family room. "Now...Plan A," Shane said as he began to dry his hair and walked in through the sliding glass door, closing it and then leaning on it, standing guard for Derek.

Mandie wrapped the towel around her shoulders for warmth, and began to rock in the chair as well. She was too tired to speak. As she sat there, reflecting on her life, and how close she came to losing it, she found the comfort in the chair. Suddenly, her mad need to rush her life to the next level didn't seem so important anymore. She looked over at Derek, slowly. How could she ever thank him for risking his life to save hers?

Derek rocked on in his chair, thanking the Lord for not taking her as he did Allison. *'Lord, I am so sorry for what I've done,'* he prayed silently there. *'I have been such a fool. I didn't let you have complete control of my life, and you reminded me today how helpless and weak that we all are. Please strengthen me, and help me to keep You first in my life. You are enough for me, Lord. I can be content without her, Lord. I know that I can.'*

"Mandie..." he called to her, "...we need to talk."
Mandie turned her head towards him. "Yes, we do..." she said as she stood and paced herself towards the long walk to the pier. "Would you like to talk a walk with me?"

"No. Haven't you had enough water today? Besides, it's safer in the chair. I'm not leaving this rocking chair. Have a seat."

Instead of returning to her white rocker, Mandie chose to pull up the wicker ottoman closer to him, but he stopped her before she got too close.

"Please, don't come any closer;" he said as he held his hand up in signal. "I've gotta talk, and you've gotta listen- not just hear me, but listen to me,"

"Derek, I want to thank you for saving my life..." she started.

"The Lord saved your life, not me. I just happened to be there at the right time," he responded. "But, now, we've gotta talk about last night. Here it is, plain and simple: I'm the one to blame. You were tired from being ill; you were frustrated and confused. You were vulnerable-and I took advantage of you in your time of weakness."

"No-I..." she tried to cut in.

"No. None of what happened last night was your fault. I take full responsibility. I apologize..." he continued as a tear ran down the side of his cheek, "...from the bottom of my heart. I...I was trying to help you to be strong, and instead I gave in to my own weakness. I only hope that you will forgive me. I know that our friendship will never be the same; I know that you don't love me. I should have never kissed you the way that I did. I only wanted to show you how loved you are and that you are safe."

Mandie looked down at the ground in humility. She was actually speechless.

"There is a man out there for you; and I won't stand in the way of anyone else who comes to call on you, or seeks you out. I promise that I will never take advantage of you again."

"No, Derek. You're wrong. I am the one who took advantage of you. I knew how you felt about me. I'm not sure why I did what I did. I was just in so much pain, that I reached out because you were there," she confessed.

"I know; you reached out to your friend, and I tried to give you something more, even though you didn't want it- even though you never will. Please forgive me. I betrayed your trust and I promise that I will never do that again."

"I will forgive you, only if you forgive me; I betrayed your trust just as badly," she said as she reached out her hand to him; but he would not take it.

"I do forgive you. But, I also promise to keep you safe. I've seen enough accidents for a lifetime; and the Lord has shown me today the price..." he said as he was interrupted by Shane's signal knock on the glass.

"What are you talking about? What price?" asked a very confused and now equally hurt Mandie.

"I just mean to say, that we're good. Everything between us is fine, and you won't have to worry about any more trouble from me," he said as he retreated from the safety of his rocking chair to the cabin.

The rest of week seemed to fly by as Mandie stuck close to her mother, swimming and enjoying the lake. Derek and Shane spent almost every moment on the lake, fishing, but these trips brought plenty of fish to the supper table. Mr. McCormick realized the horror that Derek must have experienced through Mandie's accident; and he could see the toll that it was taking on him. He seemed very withdrawn and sullen. Shane did everything that a friend could do to pull him out of it-starting with prayer. By the end of the week, Derek seemed to be coming back around to his usual clowning around with Shane; and only with Shane.

The ten and a half hour trip to El Paso came all too soon as the family left the beautiful cabin and the extraordinary week of vacation that none of them would soon forget. Derek would take them all the way there, driving with only the minimum amount of stops.

As she always did, Mrs. Margie fixed sandwiches for lunch while traveling long distances. And as usual, Mandie was chosen to usher the lunch to Derek who was at the wheel. Only this time, there were no clever words, only a faint smile and a polite 'thank you'.

"Oh, I'm sorry. I forgot your chips," Mandie said as she realized that she left them on the counter.

"That's okay, I really don't need any," he replied.

"I'll go get them. Would you like me to crush them for you?" she said smiling, in an effort to make Derek smile.

"No, really. You don't have to bother. Thank you for the sandwich," he said as he nodded to her to 'dismiss' her.

Mrs. Margie didn't miss the attitude that Mandie caught as she marched right past their bunks. She helped her mother in the kitchen, and then took her place in the upper loft, where she loved to watch the road. When Mrs. Margie climbed the stairwell on the way to her room, Mandie tried to catch her.

"Moma, can I talk to you, please?" Mandie begged.

"Sure," Mrs. Margie said as she made her way towards the cushioned nook in the upper level lounge.

"It's been a week since...well, I should really start from the beginning," she said as she began to tell her mother about the night that they had first arrived at the cabin, and about how she had run away from Derek.

"Oh, Mandie. Honey, why did you run? After all that you've been though, do you still think that he is so wrong for you? You know, Mandie, life is not a dress rehearsal. We only get one shot at this. We've gotta do it right the first time!"

"Hum!" she laughed. "It's funny that you would choose that word, 'honey'. When I was sick, and he was taking care of me, he called me that. I was so out of it at the time, that I didn't even pick up on it. You know I used to find him so repellent; so revolting. But even though I had been so hateful to him for so long, he didn't even think twice about staying to help me, when he could've gotten sick himself."

Mrs. Margie just sat there and let Mandie do all of the talking. She knew that she was heading in the right direction.

"That night, I had fever so bad, that I had the most awful nightmares. I dreamed that I was crawling with spiders-and I know that I woke up screaming but he was right there, dousing my face with alcohol. I can look back now, and I can see his face," she said as she closed her eyes. "He doesn't look like a hick anymore. All that I can see in my memory of that night is love and kindness." Tears came to her eyes. "How could he have continued to reach out to me in love, when I was so ugly to him, all the time?"

Mrs. Margie knew that she was taking her second look. "Honey, it's because he loves you. He loves you so much that he put your health above his own. That's what a husband does. He has to put his wife's and family's needs above his own."

"He treated me with such compassion," she said as she began to downright sob. "I ran away. I've hurt him so badly that now, when I look at him, all that I see is pain-pain that I caused."

"I've noticed a difference in him these last few days as well, but I couldn't put my finger on it. Now it all makes sense," Mrs. Margie realized.

"Moma, when he picked me up in the caverns and carried me out, he told me just to 'Rest on him'. This hit me hard this morning when I read my devotions. My daily reading for the Old Testament fell on the Twenty-third Psalm. I envisioned that Shepherd carrying his sheep when they were hurt, and the Lord kept bringing Derek back to my mind. And then, my New Testament Reading was in Matthew chapter eleven, when Jesus tells us that He will give us rest. That's what Derek kept saying to me: 'Rest on me'," she explained.

"I have seen the love of Jesus in Derek since the first day that he joined our family, Mandie. Derek is a good man," her mother said with confidence.

"And then in the midst of my sickness, while he sat there..." and then she giggled as she remembered the holsters of Lysol, "...trying to make me laugh, and cheer me up, he tried to encourage me by sharing what God was doing for him,"

"He'll make you a wonderful husband-in sickness and in health," Mrs. Margie said as she handed her daughter a tissue to dry her face that was soaked with tears.

"But the bad thing was that even when he took care of me, he said that he was content having no one. He had already moved on. Then I approached him like I did, and I took advantage of the feelings that he had for me. And he thinks that it was his fault; but it was mine! And now..." she cried, "...now my greatest fear is that he has shut me out. He'll never love me the way I..." and she stopped, as Margie looked square at her. The look on her face said it all as she realized what had happened. "...the way that I love him. I love him. Moma, he is the one that I want-I need him. I thought that I needed someone suave and sophisticated; but I really need someone that loves me, and will take care of me and make me feel safe."

Tears began to fill Mrs. Margie's eyes as her daughter finally understood. God had shown her the true desires of her heart.

"I ran away because I was afraid. I was afraid because of my own pride to admit that I had fallen in love with him; and now, it's too late Mama. He doesn't want me anymore-I've hurt him so badly, that he'll never take me now," she said as she faced the possibility that she may have lost him forever.

Mrs. Margie put her arm around her to console her. "I don't believe that for one minute! He loves you with a true, Godly love. Think about this. When Jesus was on His way to the Cross, the people beat him; they spat on him; they plucked the beard from his face-and these were the people that He loved and came to save; and the Bible said that he didn't open His mouth to rebuke them, or to even call upon the angels of Heaven to come down and destroy them all-and why? Because He loved them; He gave His life to save them from their sins, and His Arms are still out-stretched today to those who spit his face daily; they are still open to those who mock His name. He still loves them, Mandie. That's why we do what we do. We proclaim the Gospel through song, in hopes that someone will see Him still standing there, waiting for them to run to Him. I know that Derek still loves you. He's hurt, and you did violate his trust by running away, but I can't believe that he wouldn't accept you if you ran to him!"

Mandie hugged her mother. "Thank you for telling me to take that second look. I never would have realized the truth if you hadn't. Please tell me how I can make this right? How can I show him that I really do love him? How will he ever believe me after what I've done?"

"Just think about it, and pray about it. You'll figure it out," her mother said as she gave her one last hug. "Just reach out to him-I know he won't turn you away."

Chapter Twenty-Seven

The show in El Paso went off without a hitch. For Mandie, the days seemed longer and longer as she would try to strike up a conversation with Derek-and she would only get polite banter, either about the weather or about how good the show was. When Derek pulled the bus out, headed for Mobile, Mandie had just about given up. Shane rode shot-gun at the beginning of the trip, but around ten o'clock that Saturday morning, he decided that Gwen would be awake, and he couldn't wait to call her.

When Shane walked towards his bunk to grab his cell phone, Mandie stood at the foot of the stair-well, silently motioning for him to come over.

"Huh?" he yelled loudly.

She frowned at him, pantomiming for him to be quiet and to walk over to her. Finally he got the message and followed her to the upper lounge.

"What's all the whisperin' about? Whattya want? I've got to call Gwen. She and her family are going on the cruise next week, and we have things to talk about."

"What kind of things? Can it wait at all? I really need to talk to you," she begged.

"No; it can't wait. We have to coordinate apparel and accessorize," Shane said in an attempt to mock her.

"Come on! When have I ever really needed to talk to you about something serious?"

"You didn't say that it was serious-you only said that you needed to talk to me. Is it serious?" the teasing Shane asked.

"YES!" Mandie replied in exasperation.

"Then, I guess I can spare a few moments," Shane said nonchalantly.

"Good," she said as she grabbed his arm and pulled him over to the same place where she and her mother had spoken only the day before. "I need help."

Shane placed his hands over hers. "Admitting that you have a problem is the first step, Mandie."

"Grow up! I really need your help, Shane. This isn't funny."

"Alright, already. What can I do for you?"

Mandie struggled as she opened her heart to Shane. She knew that she was treading in dangerous territory. But she was desperate. She didn't know where else to turn. "Okay. Here's the thing. I'm in love with Derek." She closed her eyes, waiting for his response, as if she were waiting for a bomb to detonate. But instead, only silence ensued, which made her more afraid.

Shane sat there for a moment. "I missed the part where that's my problem."

"Shane, please! I need you to help me. I've really messed up," she cried.

"I'll say! You just don't go around deciding one day that you're in love with someone-especially after you've hurt them. Besides, I know too much already. I want out."

"Stop! What do you mean, you know too much? What do you know?" she asked as she pinned Shane down.

"Get off me!" he yelled.

"Not until you tell me what you know! I'm not playing around here; this is serious business!"

"Alright; just let me up! I'll talk," Shane said as Mandie finally released him.

"I know what happened between you two the first night at the cabin. I know that he's been in love with you since day one, and you treated him like the plague. The man's been trying to get over you since you made it quite clear that you disliked him. Then, when he was doing fine, and was just happy to be alive, you go and tempt him with your *feminine wiles'*..." Shane said sarcastically, "...and then you tell him it was a mistake and run away? If you hadn't been on the threshold of death when you fell off of that pier and hit your head, I was going to cut your hide myself!" said an angry Shane.

By this time, Mandie was in tears; being reminded of just how bad she had made it for Derek.

"And, I know that it almost killed him to dive into that water; he was scared to death. It was like Tennessee all over again," Shane said.

"What does that mean?" Mandie asked as she wiped her tears.

"Well, since you claim to love him, you might as well know. There was another love in his life before you-a wonderful girl named Allison. According to his mom, they would've been married soon, if she wouldn't have died."

Mandie sat there horrified. Her heart ached for Derek. "Shane, what happened?"

"She skidded off a bridge in a thunderstorm after leaving his house one night. Her car sank to the bottom of the lake before anyone knew what had happened."

Mandie felt sick to her stomach. Then she remembered. She remembered that Derek was about to tell her something before the knock at the window scared him away. "The price..." she whispered.

"What?" asked Shane.

Mandie turned and looked at him. "The price; right after my fall, when we were talking on the deck, he wouldn't even take my hand, Shane, when I offered it to him for a shake. And he said, 'he had seen enough accidents to last a lifetime, and that today the Lord had shown him *the price...*" and then you knocked and he cut the conversation short. From what you just told me, I understand about the accidents; I knew about his Dad being killed in the fields at his farm, but I had no idea about this. And now I know what he meant by 'the price'! Shane, he thinks that it's his fault! He thinks that Allison, his Dad, and my little fall were his fault. That's why he wouldn't take my hand. He said that 'he forgave me, but he also promised to protect me.' Derek thinks that he's being punished; or that he's cursed, or something!"

"He's been the brother that I never had, and he'd do anything for you, even at this very minute. I don't want to see him get hurt again, Mandie. I don't."

"I know; I know I don't deserve him," she cried. "But, please believe me Shane, I do love him. And as much as I love him, I also know that he had moved on. I know that he was contacting that Stephanie, girl, so, please let me know: is it serious with him and Stephanie? If so, I'll just be content to watch him be happy. He deserves to be happy."

"You'd give him up to another woman, if you knew that he was happy?" Shane asked sincerely.

215

Mandie answered without hesitation, "It would kill me, but yes. Yes, I would."

Shane took a breath and finally smiled. He knew that Mandie was genuinely in love. "Well, it's a good thing that he stopped emailing her about a month ago, or else you'd be a lonely girl!"

"So, do you think I have a chance? Can I win his heart back?" she asked.

"You never lost his heart, Mandie; you just broke it." Shane said.

"Well then, what can I do? What do I do to let him know that he means so much to me?"

"I don't know, Mandie. I tell you, I'm really uncomfortable being in the middle of all this now. It was fun at first, because I got to heckle you. But now, it's all so serious! I guess just let me talk to him. I'll tell him that you really love him."

"No! You just can't come out and tell him that! Not after what I did. I need something big; something unmistakable; a show-stopper!" she said. As soon as the words left her mouth, she knew how she could reach him. "I've got it! I know what to do!"

"Care to share?" asked a very curious Shane.

"No. It's a secret," she replied.

"Look here!" he said in amazement. "I thought we were bonding here!"

Mandie smiled in delight. "We are, Shane; we are! Oh, I love you! Thank you for all of your help," she said as she jumped on him and hugged him tightly.

"Stop! It burns! It burns!" he said in jest.

Mandie turned him loose. "Okay, okay! And remember-not a word to Derek. Do not tell him that I love him. That will just ruin everything!"

"So, let me make sure that I understand you-You called me up here for help. You need for Derek to know that you love him, but you won't let me tell him for you, and now everything's solved?"

"Yes, that's correct. I'm so glad you understand," said Mandie with a smile.

"Ok, I guess. Great! I'm off to call Gwen," Shane said as he made his way to the stairwell, headed towards his bunk.

"Great, because I've got work to do," she said as she began digging through the storage container underneath the cushions in the lounge area.

"See ya," Shane said as he descended the stairs and walked right past his bunk, back to the shot-gun seat next to Derek.

"Hey, Shane. What can I do you for?" Derek asked with a smile.

"Dude, we gotta talk."

"What about?"

"A lot of things; hold on; I need to make a list," Shane said as he jogged back to his bunk and grabbed a notebook.

"Really?" Derek asked in disbelief. "Man, what's going on with you?"

"Too much to explain really. Okay; first things' first. Even though I was not privy to the conversation on the porch between you and Mandie that morning..."

"Privy? That's a mighty sophisticated word for you, Shane," teased Derek

"I've been playing 'Words with Friends' with Gwen; now pay attention! I know that you think her little fall was somehow your fault. It wasn't. It was just an accident."

"You don't know what you're talking about. I didn't let the Lord have full control of my life. I had plans before He took Allison. Then I had plans before He took Daddy. Then I had plans to join the Army. The Lord put a stop to that, too. Then, I got this foggy notion that while serving Him by driving this bus, that I might win the heart of your darling sister. She made it evident, that that was not going to happen from day one. So, I sought the Lord. And I thought that I had a better handle on things. I was content to be single, forever, and serve the Lord as part of this ministry, giving my whole attention to Him. And then, we almost lost Mandie; and it was only because just for one night, for one moment, I thought that she loved me. I gave into my flesh for one moment, and the very next day the Lord sent me a wake-up call. I've asked her to forgive me, and she has, and now we'll just be friends, just like she wants; and I'll devote one hundred percent of my time and efforts to whatever God wants for my life."

Shane was blown away. Derek was ready to take a 'monk's life and be permanently single! "Okay. I'm searching for the right words here, gimme a minute-WAKE UP!!!!" he screamed at Derek while slapping him across the head. "You are so oblivious! Mandie's been trying to talk to you for over a week, and you haven't been giving her the time of day! I've been watching you, and at first I was rooting for you, because I thought she deserved it, but now..."

"'But now', what? I'm not going to put her in harm's way again. The Lord will take her out too, if I'm not careful."

"Derek. The Lord allowed those things to happen to you for a reason-but I'm sure that it was not because you were in love! Derek, you can serve the Lord whole-heartedly and still be married! Doesn't the Bible say that a bishop has to be the husband of one wife? Well, the last time I checked, you can't be a husband unless you're married! You've come too far to give up now. My parents are married and serving the Lord just fine!"

"I know, Shane. But what was the reason for her to get hurt? I think that He's just tried to tell me that it's not meant to be with Mandie and me."

"Derek, it was just a test! A test! Can't you see that? You overcame your fear of water in an instant to save a life! And it was her own stupid fault! She should've known not to be standing in the path of an incoming boat! Look, it all boils down to this: do you love her?" he asked, getting right in his face.

Derek stared straight at the road, afraid to answer.

"Answer me, boy!" Shane yelled.

Still he sat there, silently.

Shane read his thoughts, and went head to head with him; man to man with a boldness that he had never owned before. It was once and for all when he said, "For God hath not given us the spirit of fear; but of power, and of love, and of a sound mind. If you are afraid, it is not because of something that God has done. Fear is of the devil. Now, you said you were gonna Man-Up. It's time to put your money where your mouth is. Do you still love her?"

A tear ran down the side of Derek's face as God's Word sliced his heart like the two-edged sword that it is. He realized that the fears he had were of the devil-planted in his heart to rob him of joy, and possibly a wonderful wife to serve the Lord with. "Yes, Shane; you know that I do," he said quietly.

Shane dropped his head in relief. "Whew; good," he said as he slowly raised his head. "That's really good. Alright, now that we have that established, we've got a lot of work to do," he said as he opened the notebook and began to make a list.

"Shane, what are you doing?" asked a very confused Derek.

"Um, well, I...I can't tell you, but I've got a lot to do. I need to call Gwen," he said as he stood to retreat to his bunk.

"Whoa, brother! No, sir! You've done got me riled up now, don't leave me hangin'! We've got to come up with a plan, if I'm gonna win your sister's heart," Derek said with a new fire and a new zeal. He was ready and raring to go.

"But see, that's just it! You....Oh, man! Why do I open my big mouth!" Shane said as he caught himself. He almost broke his promise.

"Shane, what do you know?" he asked anxiously.

"I can't tell you-I promised..." he answered as he racked his brain for a way. 'How can I tell him, without 'telling him?' Shane thought to himself, as he searched his mind and heart; and then it occurred to him. "I got it! Listen to me, Derek; THE WHEELS ARE SPINNING BACK!" he said very deliberately.

"Huh?" he said as he tried to look at Shane and look at the road.

"Are you listening to me, Derek, I said, THE WHEELS ARE SPINNING BACK!"

"Shane, does that mean what I think it means?" he asked.

"Look, I'm limited on what I can say here-promises were made- but I'm tellin' ya this: THE WHEELS ARE SPINNING BACK!!"

"Are you sure? I cut it off, and she hasn't exactly been beatin' down my door..."

"Would you please quit talkin' and just get it through that thick head of yours! Why do think I came down here, for my health? I am wasting valuable 'Gwen-Time'!"

"Well, let's just say that, by some miracle you are right-then what's the list for?" Derek asked.

That's when Shane's face lit up. "I was hoping you'd ask..."

Chapter Twenty-Eight

Derek had never been to Mobile, Alabama before. He thought about that as he and Shane walked up to ramp as they boarded the "Singing At Sea" Cruise Ship in Jacksonville, Florida. The more he tried to remember the places that they toured, the more blurry they became and he just determined that he'd take a better look around next year when there was more time. Time, this past week, seemed to be in short supply-even though there are still twenty-four hours in everyday, just the same as it has always been.

His cell phone vibrated on his belt-clip. "Hold, up Shane. I've got a text. It's from Mama!"

Shane stopped, "Your Mom texts?"

"She does ever since I sent her a new smart phone. She says that Uncle Joe, and Grandpa George and her have all been checked in for about an hour; and that she's knows that we're busy, so they'll catch up with us before the concert tonight."

"So, she doesn't text-she writes books; Are you ready?" Shane said with a laugh.

"Yeah, everything's good, just in case. But, I still don't see it. This past week, she worked me harder than she ever has! There were times..." he started.

"She's Mandie. There will always be those times!" Shane said realistically.

"Yeah, I guess you're right."

"No, I know I'm right," answered Shane as they continued on towards the ship's purser.

🚌 🚌 🚌 🚌 🚌

"Moma, I'm so nervous!" Mandie said she primped at her hair and make-up for the twelfth time. "Do I look alright?"

"Yes, child. You look wonderful. Now, just say a little prayer. It will all be fine," Mrs. Margie answered.

"I've really tried to throw him off by being absolutely horrible to him all week long. I hope that it hasn't worked against me," explained a worried Mandie.

"He loves you, Mandie. Everything will be just fine," Mrs. Margie said with a smile.

"I just need him to be really caught off guard, you know? I want him to be surprised!"

"Oh; don't worry. He will be..." her mother said with a smile.

🚌 🚌 🚌 🚌 🚌

One of the best things about the Christian Tour was that all of the bars and casinos on the cruise were closed, and all of the entertainment was provided by the best in Southern Gospel entertainers. The cruise was not only a wonderful opportunity for the group, but a wonderful vacation and time of fellowship. Mr. Brian McCormick knew how blessed they were to be invited to this event.

Showtime for the McCormick's first concert was almost upon them-but first dinner! The families had been reunited in the Coconut Grove Grill for the special event. Even though Mandie was delighted to see Grandpa again, she couldn't keep her eyes off of Derek. He looked so dashing in his dark blue suit and tie, and she never thought it in a million years, but the Stetson was actually doing a little somethin' for her!

"Mandie? Mandie?" Grandpa George called.

The entire table's attention was directed at her, and snickers began to rise from Uncle Joe as it became evident that she was in a trance-and fixed on Derek. Even Derek himself caught her looking. Finally, Mrs. Margie shook her at the elbow to snap her out of it.

"Ma'am?" she answered as she came out of it.

"Honey, Grandpa's been talking to you for the last five minutes, and you've been on another planet!" she said with a contagious giggle. The whole table was cheesing it up!

Thankfully, at that moment, a lovely little blonde snuck up behind Shane, covering his eyes in her famous move. "Guess who?" she squeaked.

"Babycakes!" exclaimed Shane as he jumped up and grabbed her in a swinging hug. "It's been way too long!"

"I've missed you too," she whispered in his ear, as she was extremely bashful about displaying her affection for Shane. "Mama and Daddy are sitting across the dining hall, but, I was hoping that maybe I could sit with you tonight?"

Shane immediately transformed. "Of course! Waiter! Could we have another chair here, please?" Shane asked as he helped seat his date.

Derek watched them together. *'Oh, how I hope you are right, Shane.'*

The dinner was delicious, but neither Mandie nor Derek ate very much. They both just seemed to piddle over their plates. Forty-five minutes passed, and that was when Mr. Brian made the call. "Alright, troops! It's about thirty minutes 'til show time. It's time to fly."

Gwen promised that she'd be there on the front row with Mrs. Sophia, Grandpa and Uncle Joe in the reserved seats. The family made their way to the Promenade Deck towards the Palace Main Lounge where they would perform the first night. Derek and Shane found their way to the sound booth at the back of the auditorium and introduced themselves to the ship's audio man for their concert. Derek made himself at home, and got right to work on the best levels for each of the songs on the schedule for this evening. Shane noted the time, and stood up to join the rest of his family backstage for a final tune-up.

Derek grabbed him by the arm with his sweaty palms seeping through Shane's shirt, "Shane...are you absolutely positive about this?"

"You just keep listening out for those wheels..." he said with a smile, "Bye."

Now Derek was really confused. *'Shane and I never talked about 'listening' out for anything...'*

The Master of Ceremonies for the Cruise took to the stage and announced 'The McCormick's' with great pomp. The curtain rose and the family stood still, graciously thanking the crowd for their applause. Usually by this time, Shane had already started them off with the introduction to the first song, and the silence caught Derek by surprise.

"Thank you; Thank you, everyone," Mandie began with her microphone. "Tonight, dear friends, we'd like to start off with a brand new song. It's never been sung before; and you get to be our guinea pigs!" she said as the audience laughed. "No, but seriously, this is a very special song to me; I wrote it last week, inspired by one of the true loves of my life. I hope it will be a blessing to you," she concluded as Shane pressed the automatic playback button the stage's digital grand piano. Mandie's pre-recorded piano playing from earlier in the day bellowed through the speakers as she began to sing:

> In times of trial I often forget
> Everything but my sorrows
> And Heartaches, but yet...
> There is One who feels
> Every heartache with me
> He chose this road I'm walking
> And He knows just where it leads...
>
> He knows...
> Every move, every thought
> Every intent of my heart
> Every feeling that I've ever felt
> And that's just the start
> When I'm hurting and I think
> That no one's there,
> I just remember Who He is
> And that Jesus Cares.

Derek couldn't believe what he was hearing. He recognized and remembered every word that he spoke to her then, when she was sick. He was trying to encourage her not to give up on her heart's desires. He thought that she hadn't taken any of it to heart, judging from the way she acted that night at the cabin-but she had. She remembered. He stood to his feet, engrossed in her voice and song, and began walking towards the stage down the main aisle, stopping half way down, to enjoy the second verse.

Mandie, blinded by the stage lights, only then noticed a silhouette, approaching the stage. She knew that it was him in her heart, and she sang all the more.

> Remembering the Saviour
> Is the key
> He bore the cross of Calvary
> For you, and for me
> There is a purpose for the load
> Of burdens that we bear
> If we trust Him, He'll give us grace
> And His Story we can share,

By the second chorus, people in the crowd began to notice Derek standing there in the middle of the aisle. They started to look, and a few smiled and pointed, but he didn't see any of them. He only saw one beautiful woman singing just to him...

> He knows...
> Every move, every thought
> Every intent of my heart
> Every feeling that I've ever felt
> And that's just the start
> When I'm hurting and I think
> That no one's there,
> I just remember Who He is
> And that Jesus Cares.

By the end of the song, the crowd was on its feet shouting 'Hallelujah's and Amen's' to beat the band, and cheering as Derek had made it all the way to the stage. Mandie knelt down to meet him.

"That was...incredible. I'm so glad that I was able to help you by sharing what God had done for me. I know that it was a blessing to all of these people here," he said.

"I finally understood. He is enough. He knows me better than anyone; and I knew that I'd be alright. But, I must confess, even though God gave me the song, it wasn't only for Him today. *Today I did it for you...*" she said, as she was sure that he would know what she meant. And he did. She smiled and said, "Now, get outta here-I got a show to do!"

He laughed, shaking his head, "Yes Ma'am, Miss Mandie," and he tipped his imaginary hat to her.

When he turned to walk back up the aisle, he saw Shane, grinning from ear to ear behind her. Shane winked at Derek, and he nodded back-he heard 'em.

As the show ended, and the crowd once again stood to its feet, Derek began making his way to the stage, this time unnoticed, down the side aisle. He had heard the wheels that Shane told him to listen out for, and now he was stepping out on that limb.

Quickly, Derek stepped onto the stage, taking the microphone that Mr. Brian offered to him. Now, Mandie stood there confused, and in shock!

Derek spoke into the microphone as he approached Mandie in the spotlight. "Your show's over; now it's my turn," he said as he fell down on one knee. The crowd cheered and whooped and hollered.

Mandie began to shake.

With his trembling hand, Derek opened the box that he had just pulled from his pocket, offering to her a beautiful one carat Princess Cut diamond. The crowd cheered again, and then Shane got them quieted so that Derek could speak. "I've kinda been wantin' to ask you out on a date, so will you go out with me, everyday for the rest of our lives?"

226

Mandie threw her head back in laughter, as the crowd once again cheered. And then they quieted themselves as they all waited for her answer. "I will-in sickness and in health!"

The crowd might have thought it to be a strange 'yes', but they cheered anyways-and Derek understood. He slipped the ring onto her finger, and stood to his feet sweeping her into his arms. The ship's cheering stage crew then closed the curtain, to offer them some privacy. Mandie's parents and Shane also ran from the stage.

Derek simply couldn't believe it. Shane was right. He had to ask her, "So, Mandie, exactly when did you take the laser scope off of my head?"

"I only moved it-to your heart," she replied in her usually sarcastic wit. "When you took care of me, I realized you were what I wanted all along. I had never seen such compassion-such pure and true love; even when I had treated you so badly," she said as the tears of joy and remorse began to flow. "I knew that the only man that I could ever hope and pray to have as a husband was you."

Derek placed both hands on either side of her face, and wiped her tears away with his thumbs. "Mandie...I never thought that this would ever be real. I love you so much," he said as he pressed his forehead to hers.

"And I love you more," she replied.

"That's not possible," Derek said.

"Boy, don't get me started!" she said as they both laughed. "So, how does this work? Usually people date first!"

"Girl, I've been courtin' you since I stepped foot on that bus!" Derek said.

Mandie blushed.

"Aw. I *know* you didn't just blush!" he said as he tried to pull her close.

An embarrassed Mandie turned her head. "Stop-Derek, come on now," she begged as she tried to hide, it; but he only made it worse.

"So, when do you want to...get married?" She asked with squinting eyes, as if she was expecting to be let down. "I just want to make sure-that is what this means, right? I mean, you never did actually ask me to marry you?" she said.

"Okay, Miss Perfection. Have it your way; you always do! Miss Mandie McCormick-will you marry me..." he began as he looked at his watch, "...in two hours?"

Epilogue

Mandie's face fell. "Quit messin' around, Derek; that's not even funny..."

Derek looked into her eyes with deep sincerity. "Mandie, I couldn't be more serious."

"Derek, I don't have time to plan! I haven't got..."

"Woman, you've been planning your wedding for months! You just weren't planning on marrying me, that's all."

Mandie rolled her eyes.

"Shane lifted your Bridal magazines, and we teamed up with your Mama who is waiting for you right now in your stateroom even as we speak to help you dress."

Mandie gasped! "What? Derek! But I don't have a dress!"

"Yes, you do!" Derek said. "The princess dress from page forty-six of *Southern Bridal* Magazine is laying on your bed in your stateroom. Out of all of the pages that you had marked, that was the dress that I wanted to see you in, walking down the aisle to me."

Mandie was excitedly perplexed.

"And, that's not all: all of the floral arrangements that you had marked, we faxed to the ship's purser; they have been made and are waiting to be brought in and set up. We emailed Gwen the information on the bridesmaids' dress that you had picked out. She picked it up the day before yesterday on her way out of town; Shane said that you wouldn't mind having Gwen as an attendant," Derek said as Mandie was really beginning to look dizzily overwhelmed. "And last, but certainly not least, after you dress for our wedding, the ship's purser is having your bags moved to one of the Penthouse Suites on the Upper Deck. My things are already there. And on that King Sized bed is a special box, lying there just from me to you; and in it is that little pink item that you had bookmarked on page fifty-six."

Mandie's eyes got as big as golf balls, as she remembered exactly just what that little pink lacy item was!

"And we've gotta get moving! Your Daddy and I secured this time slot for this same auditorium with the ship's directors-in two hours," he explained to a very lightheaded and confused Mandie.

"Oh! Daddy! Did you ask my Daddy for my hand? I always thought that my fiance' would!"

"I didn't have to," Derek said with a look of humility.

"What do you mean?" she asked.

Derek shook his head at the miraculous realization that Mr. Brian had known how all of this would end, even back then. "He gave you to me the night that we went to the Livingston's home, to save Diane."

"What?!" Mandie cried.

"He said that there was only one type of man that he'd ever give you up for, and that I could have you. I tried to explain to him, that you didn't want me, but he..." Derek shook his head again in disbelief, "...he said he'd just pray about that."

Another tear ran down Mandie's cheek as she remembered that talk she had with her Dad that day at the hospital. She thanked the Lord for Godly parents right then and there.

Then it occurred to her, "But what about our families?"

"Honey, they're already here! My Mama, Uncle Joe, Grandpa, Gwen and her family! Who else is there?"

Mandie gave the expression of *'yes, I guess you're right.'*

"The only detail we weren't able to work out was Pastor Creighton. His wife went into labor yesterday!"

Mandie laughed. "Yeah, that's a pretty good reason to miss a cruise! Well, who's gonna marry us, the Captain?" she asked.

"Nope. We were able to get Pastor Bledsoe and his family on at the last minute. He was so relieved to hear that you weren't together with Mitch anymore! He had been watching him for some time! He was more than willing to marry us!" Derek explained.

"But Derek; How is all of this possible? How is this being paid for?" she asked.

"Well, actually, Shane brought this opportunity to my attention. He said that I'd be a fool to pass it up; he was right. As for the money, I've saved almost every penny that your Daddy has paid me since I started with y'all. It's my gift to you, my love."

Mandie simply couldn't believe what she was hearing. "Okay, Mr. Rocking Chair, why do this so fast? Didn't you fuss at me profusely for always being in too big of a hurry?"

"Well, now Mandie, I could say that it's because this is some girls' dream wedding and honeymoon package deal; but the real reason is that it's because I can't stand to be apart from you another minute."

Mandie blushed again.

"You know you're driving me crazy when you do that!" he said with a smile.

She rolled her eyes.

"Don't you love me?" he asked.

"Yes," she answered.

"Don't you want to marry me?"

"Yes!"

"Then, get going, Lambchop-and I'll see you in..." he stopped to check his watch, "one hour and forty-five minutes," he said as he kissed her on the cheek and ran away.

One hour and forty-five minutes later...

The processional played as Mr. Brian walked Mandie down the aisle to her handsome cowboy waiting for her at the altar. Even with all of her magazines and flowers and dresses, only one thing made this wedding perfect-and there he was, taking her hand from her father. He was dressed in a black tails tuxedo, with his faithful Dingos. Beside him stood his best man, his 'brother' and partner in crime, Shane, who was again smiling from ear to ear.

Pastor Bledsoe began, "Dearly beloved, we are gathered here today to join Mandie McCormick and Derek Jensen in holy matrimony,"

"Pastor Bledsoe, wait!" Mandie said suddenly.

Derek's heart sank. *'Oh, Lord, please don't let her be leaving me at the altar...'*

"Something's missing..." she said as she looked to her mother in the front row. Mrs. Margie smiled, as she stood up and brought Mandie Derek's Stetson.

Derek just laughed, along with the rest of the crowd!

Mandie set it on his head and he adjusted it to its proper place. "I figured that if I'm marrying you, then I'm marrying the Stetson, too."

🚌 🚌 🚌 🚌 🚌

After Pastor Bledsoe pronounced them 'Cowboy and Wife', as Mandie so lovingly requested, he dismissed the crowd to the reception in the one of the ship's conference rooms, just a few doors down.

Derek and Mandie led the way to the conference room that was decorated just as she had hoped her fellowship hall would be back in Campbell's Grove. The cake was from page twenty-two, and everything could not have been more perfect.

As Derek and Mandie entered the room, Shane, who had run ahead, grabbed the microphone and announced them personally, "Ladies and Gentleman, may I introduce the man who conquered the Wild Woman of Campbell's Grove, Derek Jensen, and his lovely bride, my sister, Mrs. Mandie Jensen!" As the crowd cheered he continued, "Sorry, Sis! I wanted to be the first one to say that new name of yours!"

Mandie rolled her eyes at her brother, but how could she be mad? She ran over to him, and hugged him like she never had before. With tears she told him, "I love you, Shane. Thank you for everything. You're absolutely wonderful."

"Thanks. I'll quote you on that!" he said in an effort to hide his own tears of joy for his sister. Then, he continued, "And Ladies and Gentlemen, I have another very brief announcement. Our 'Minister of Transportation', my new brother, has also inherited another title today. He has become the McCormick Family's new bass player. I will be coming off the road in July of this year to attend Atlantic

Coastal University to earn my degree." The crowd cheered as Shane took his last moment in the spotlight, for a while.

As Shane returned the guests to their merriment, Derek spied a private balcony, off of the conference room, and he took Mandie by the hand, slipping away unnoticed. He closed the door behind them, and then took her into his arms, for a long, passionate kiss.

After Mandie regained her composure, she asked him, "How did you know that I'd say, 'yes'?"

Derek smiled. "Shane said he saw 'em turnin'."

"He saw what turnin'?"

"The Wheels of Love!"

Mandie laughed at the thought of her brother. She looked through the window of the door, and saw him standing there, with his arm around Gwen; and she was so proud of the man that he had become. "That Shane and his wheels! He sure is something, ain't he?"

"Yep; he sure is," Derek answered with a smile. "But I really didn't come out here to talk about Shane..." he said as he moved in closer.

Mandie ran her hands along the lapels of his tuxedo. "Well, all I can say is, Thank you, Lord, for the Wheels of Love-because they carried me to you!" Mandie said as she wrapped her arms around her husband's neck.

"And I say..." Derek began as he dipped his squealing Mandie back, "Thank you, Lord, that she didn't have a flat!" and then he kissed her good- the way only a cowboy could.

Thank you again to my
"Super Models"
Mr. Gary Berry, Jr.
and his lovely wife
Mrs. Lacey Strong Berry!
I love you!

Full Words and Sheet Music for
'Mandie's Songs':

Jesus Cares
And
What God Had To Say

will be available on our website

www.vcpbooks.com

Stay Tuned!

Made in the USA
Charleston, SC
27 February 2012